THE NIGHT RAIDS

By Jim Kelly

a&b

THE NIGHT RAIDS

JIM KELLY

Allison & Busby Limited
11 Wardour Mews
London W1F 8AN
allisonandbusby.com

First published in Great Britain by Allison & Busby in 2020.

A CIP catalogue record for this book is available from
the British Library.

First Edition

ISBN 978-0-7490-2482-6

Typeset in 11/16 pt Adobe Garamond Pro by
Allison & Busby Ltd

The paper used for this Allison & Busby publication
has been produced from trees that have been legally sourced
from well-managed and credibly certified forests.

Printed and bound by
CPI Group (UK) Ltd, Croydon, CR0 4YY

For my mother Peggy Kelly
who survived the air raids alone, with my brother,
while my father fought in Italy

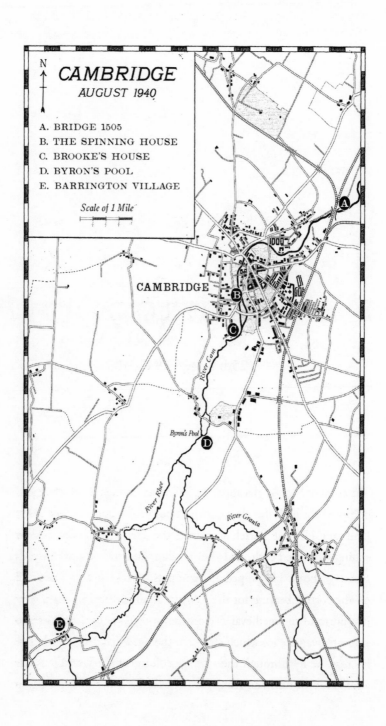

N

CAMBRIDGE
AUGUST 1940

A. BRIDGE 1505
B. THE SPINNING HOUSE
C. BROOKE'S HOUSE
D. BYRON'S POOL
E. BARRINGTON VILLAGE

Scale of 1 Mile

CAMBRIDGE

River Cam

Byron's Pool

River Rhee

River Granta

CHAPTER ONE

25th August 1940

The coast of East Anglia appeared below, a curving line of white surf glimpsed through the glass cockpit floor of the bomber. The pilot, Leutnant Helmut Bartel, imagined the Heinkel's moon shadow sliding over the beach, and the marshes, and then the wide fields that lay ahead. He tapped his compass, checking they were still on the correct bearing for their target, a railway bridge over a river just north of the medieval city of Cambridge. He used his glove to smooth away the ice which obscured the needle. Leaning back into his seat, he felt through the steering column the soft bump as the aircraft hit the warm air rising from the land below, slowly giving up to the darkness the heat it had absorbed during a long summer's day.

It had been a dazzling day in Berlin. He'd spent the morning with his family on the beach at the lake. His eldest daughter, bouncing on her toes in front of the ice-cream seller's bicycle, could never keep the cone upright. The baby had slept on a rug, in the shade of a parasol. His wife had worn a daring new swimsuit. Back at their flat, after a meal, his friend and co-pilot Walther Schmidt had picked him up for the drive to the airfield, and Bartel had waved through the rear window, watching his family diminish, standing against a backdrop of suburban trees.

'*Es is Zeit*,' he said, shattering the memory, his voice relayed to the crew, the radio signal almost obscured by static.

Schmidt, who was also the bombardier, unbuckled himself from the co-pilot's seat and wriggled expertly to the floor of the cockpit, where he landed softly on his knees. He spread his body out on the plastic flexi-glass, the line of his spine absolutely central, his feet pointing back across the North Sea, to the Frisian Islands and Berlin, his head set directly towards Cambridge. In this position he was able to rest his skull in the niche provided, and use his right eye to look down through the bombsight. His hand crept over the instruments set in the fuselage, his fingers finally resting on the bomb bay trigger, and beside it, the thumb-switch for the reconnaissance camera.

Bartel, staring into the night, noted the smell rising from the navigator: cold sweat and fear, mixed with the wax he used to sweep back his hair. Schmidt had been his best man, and the picture at home in the hallway showed off his confident smile as he threw an arm round the groom's shoulders. They'd been in uniform then, the promised war a glittering adventure, just beyond reach.

He checked the fuel gauge, a procedure he repeated at least once a minute. The electronic dial indicated that the Heinkel had enough to reach the target and return home. The thought of touchdown at the forest airfield at Waren, of walking to Schmidt's car after the debriefing, and simply being driven home, was so beguiling, so close, that Bartel felt his guts twist. He wondered, often, if this sudden unexpected urge to cry like a child marked him out as a potential coward.

He gripped the steering column and felt sweat trickle down his neck beneath his flying suit.

A burst of static rang in his headphones and he looked up to see the escort fighter tip its wings, and peel away to the north.

'*Allein,*' he told the crew. *We're on our own.*

He repeated himself twice, hoping to be heard above the roar of the twin exhausts, mounted just to the rear of the cockpit.

The night had been clear but now a great billowing ridge of cloud thudded against the aircraft, threatening to shake it out of the sky. They had been easy prey for British fighters, but now they were safe. Clouds had been forecast by Berlin, and clouds there were. The cheer from the crew was reedy but unmistakable. They had left the realm of the revealing moon.

Bartel took the aircraft above 18,000 feet to make sure they were firmly embedded in the high cumulus, but nevertheless there were intermittent glimpses of the land below, and so they saw towns twinkling faintly, despite the strictures of the blackout. Bartel smiled, because it meant there was a chance they were not expected, and that all attention had turned to the raids on the South Coast.

The Heinkel laboured onwards east. The crew was silent, but he knew they were all doing exactly the same thing: counting to themselves, recognising that as each mile went past they were, paradoxically, getting closer to home, or at least to a homecoming. All they had to do was destroy the bridge, then melt away, and fly back across what his father and grandfathers had all called the German Ocean.

This was not their first sortie. They had flown nuisance raids for a month, designed to harry the enemy and train the crew for the heroics to come. Morale had been poor because they felt themselves excluded from the great battles over the airfields of Kent and Sussex in which five hundred bombers, a thousand perhaps, rained destruction on the RAF below, clearing the path for an invasion by sea.

But Oberst Fritsch, the commander at Waren, had made it clear in his pre-flight briefing that this particular raid would write its own footnote in the history of this great war. Military intelligence had identified Bridge 1505 – a box-girder of steel – as a key link in the enemy's transport network. Destroy it, and the result would be chaos at a vital point in space and time. If the German landings came not on the South Coast but on the East Coast, the British would be unable to rush men and arms to repel the invaders.

'Five miles to the target,' said the navigator.

Bartel let the aircraft descend, and they quickly dropped below the clouds.

Even on such a dark night you could see below, strung across their path, a silver river. The old hands who'd flown in the Great War had said it was impossible to fly the bomber to its target without a clear sky and the moon. But Bartel and Schmidt had argued that the river would betray itself. And so it was.

Bartel noted the time. 'Walther?'

'Ready.' Schmidt pressed his face into the Plexiglas sight and began to take pictures.

The altimeter ticked down from 19,000 feet.

Behind the reinforced steel bulkhead at Bartel's back the bombs stood in two lines, cones upwards, held fast in place by iron clamps.

Bartel struggled with the controls: he felt sluggish, and when he tried to think, logical progressions escaped him.

He forced himself to concentrate on reading out their height.

At 10,000 feet he banked, turning the bomber south, so that they could track the shining water.

He braced himself against the pilot's seat and heaved up the bomb-door lever. The noise doubled. The urge to override Schmidt's trigger, and let the bombs fall now, so that they could turn home, was almost intolerable.

Bartel could see the river's mirror below, briefly holding in its surface a black silhouette of the Heinkel.

They'd expected anti-aircraft fire, but there was none.

'Five thousand feet,' said Bartel.

'Target in sight,' said Schmidt.

Bartel heard the bomb clamps spring and turning, saw the first shell slip away. The bombardiers at Waren had written in chalk on its side: *Erste Stoppe Cambridge!*

'She's gone,' said Schmidt.

Two more shells followed.

The river sped by below them, and then in an instant the target flashed past – a metal bridge, with its double line of tracks, then a series of narrow workers' streets, a gasometer and the rail yards.

Bartel checked the chronometer, which had been set to Greenwich Mean Time, and read 10 p.m.

The first of the falling shells had twisted in the air, the cone coming down, the fins taking control, reaching terminal velocity within a handful of seconds, which is when the screaming began.

CHAPTER TWO

Detective Inspector Eden Brooke sat at a trestle table in the public bar of the Wellington Arms, contemplating a pint of Ridley's Best Bitter. The pub lay in the maze of streets known as the Kite, a working-class district within a parallelogram of down-at-heel shop-lined roads, sandwiched between Parker's Piece, Cambridge's great park – an army encampment since the outbreak of war – and the distant expanse of the rail yards, which stretched north into the Fens along the river.

The Wellington Arms, at the corner of dead-end Earl Street, was packed with soldiers, most of whom were bivouacked in bell tents on the nearby park. The manic buzz of conversation, the raucous laughter, spoke of anxiety and excitement in the face of the news of war; Dunkirk had gone, Paris had fallen, and now air battles raged over the Home Counties, and everyone talked of the imminent threat of invasion. No day passed without hysterical 'sightings' of German parachutists, reports of shadowy fifth columnists sabotaging the war effort from within, or radio reports of spies spotted landing on the South Coast, or – worse – the East.

The sense of danger found its physical expression in the gas masks on every table, hanging from chair backs or flung over coat hooks, within reach should the dreaded attacks materialise.

Edmund Grandcourt, Brooke's batman during a very different kind of war, was at the crowded bar getting his beer. In Palestine during the 'last lot', Brooke had relied on his stoic common sense. After the war Brooke had pulled strings to secure him a position in the university's engineering department, in charge of stores. Diligent, honest, organised, an encyclopaedia of everyday knowledge, he'd thrived. Most nights, when the sirens wailed, Grandcourt was on duty as a voluntary warden at one of the public air raid shelters on the park. But tonight there had been no siren, the first such reprieve since an attack earlier that summer which had left nine dead and a terraced street reduced to rubble. No more bombs had fallen since, but the sirens had sounded nonetheless, sending the city's weary residents below ground, or out into backyards and gardens to the damp delights of Anderson shelters and the horrors of the chemical toilet.

But not, it seemed, tonight. The clouds, masking a bomber's moon, promised a brief return to a normal life.

Since Brooke's return to Civvy Street he'd often relied on Grandcourt when a case proved intractable. The Borough, the city's miniature police force, had just two inspectors, while its rank-and-file had been sorely depleted by the demands of war. Retired officers had been drafted back onto the streets, but the Borough's ability to preserve law and order was often stretched to the limit, if not beyond.

Grandcourt's other priceless asset, besides his common sense, was that he could be found at night. Brooke treasured the company of nighthawks. In the desert he'd been captured by the Ottoman Turks: staked out in the sun by day, interrogated before the silvered lamp by night. His eyes, damaged, had never recovered. He wore tinted glasses of various hues to alleviate the pain of photophobia – an extreme sensitivity to light. They ranged from jet black – for direct sunlight – to a calming brown-yellow, although here, in the dim, smoky bar, he'd abandoned even these, so that for a few moments he could let his blue eyes enjoy the world in true colour.

Brooke took off his hat and rested it on the tabletop, pushing thick black hair back from a high pale forehead. Since he'd come home, and joined the Borough – when it was clear his injuries made further study for his degree impossible – he'd built up a network of such nighthawks dotted across the city, individuals who had to work after dark, or who shunned the light, or simply thrived when the rest of the busy world slept. Brooke's damaged eyes were the outward sign of his injuries. The inward sign was acute insomnia. So the night, and the people of the night, had become his half-lit world.

Grandcourt came back with the beer. He'd not been able to wait and so his moustache was decorated with suds.

'So what's this, sir?' Grandcourt was almost part of the family, familiar with Claire and the children, but the 'sir' never faltered, although its note of deference had faded over the years.

Brooke had placed a small bottle on the table. It was made of

14

clear glass, with a stone stopper held in place by a brass lever. The liquid inside was a subtle colour, a pale blue, an echo of Brooke's unshielded eyes.

'Go ahead,' he said, as Grandcourt manipulated the bottle, testing the release on the stopper. 'It's not a precious object. It's what's inside that's got me foxed. I came across it in the river.'

'Swimming, sir?'

Swimming, and particularly the full extension of the legs, had been part of his life since he'd been treated at a sanatorium in Scarborough after his ordeal in the desert. His Turkish captors had shot him twice in the left knee, hoping that he'd die where they had left him, at their camp near an oasis, just east of Gaza. Despite torture, he'd failed to tell them of General Allenby's plans for the forthcoming battle. When the fighting started and it was clear they'd been duped, they had turned angry and scared, a combination that had resulted in their attempt at vengeance. Claire, a nurse on his ward in the sanatorium, had supervised his first attempts to loosen the damaged knee in the basement pool, and later in the lake, which ran away from the old hospital. Swimming had become part of his life, especially at night.

Grandcourt produced a clean linen handkerchief to uncork the bottle, took a sniff and sat back, repeating the exercise several times, as if gauging a fine wine. He used his cuff to clean a metal ashtray into which he poured some of the mysterious liquid. He lit his pipe and dropped the match, still alight, in the dish. The flame leapt, the combustion almost complete in the instant, so that all that was left was a drifting cloud of thin vapour.

It reminded Brooke of the ceremonial lighting of the Christmas pudding.

'Where did you say you found it?' asked Grandcourt.

That evening at sunset Brooke had slipped into the water at

15

his secret place, beyond a locked door where his old college kept its punts, and he'd swum against the current up into the languid channels on Coe Fen. The heat of the day had still been oppressive, and in retrospect he should have heeded the warning smell as he reached the deep pool beside the corn mill at Newnham, a spot overlooked by a riverside inn.

'One minute I was in cool, still water and then I heard it – a distinct *pop!* like a gas-ring lighting. Then I saw the fire burning on the surface. A blue flame, almost a film, just a shimmer, beautiful actually, like a layer of icy fire.'

Grandcourt raised his eyebrows at the poetry and took a fresh gulp of India Pale Ale.

'It was moving,' continued Brooke, leaning forward, dropping his voice. A group in the corner had started singing show songs and the decibel level of conversation had risen to counteract the racket.

'The edge of it, where the flame was, came right for me. So I went under and looked up, through the fire, at the sky. That's a sight. I could see the burning line moving over the surface. Walking pace, or cycling maybe. A few seconds and it was past. So I came up and got out quick on the bank by the inn.

'There was a couple there, on the grass, on a picnic rug. They looked a bit shocked. The young man admitted he'd just finished a cigarette and had thrown his stub in the water. So that's what did it.'

Brooke took an inch off his beer.

'It's petrol, surely?' he asked, resetting his pint on a dirty mat.

Grandcourt was examining the colour again. 'Maybe. But it smells odd, and looks odd. Petrol on the coupons is colourless. Extra fuel – for business, farmers and that – that's red. Rust red. Nothing like this.'

16

'Can you ask about?'

'I can try, sir.' Grandcourt lit his pipe and was promptly obscured by smoke. His position in the department of engineering gave him access to considerable expertise – and a wide network of 'oppos' – his opposite numbers – in other disciplines. The deployment of so-called forensic science was currently the domain of Scotland Yard, and the Borough's methods were largely old-fashioned, but Grandcourt gave Brooke access to the university's collective scientific brain. It was a priceless asset.

A radio on the bar suddenly filled the room with the sound of the time pips: it was ten o'clock precisely.

The silence in the pub was church-like, as everyone braced for the worst. Brooke wondered whether Churchill's broadcast of the previous week, in which he'd lauded the Spitfires and the Hurricanes, had hit the right note. It certainly sounded confident, assured. He'd listened to it in this very bar and in the silent beat after the final words a collective breath had been taken, before they'd all cheered.

The news broadcaster's voice hit a similar upbeat note.

A man in the corner, filing a pipe, looked up at the radio.

'The War Cabinet has just issued a short statement. Late last night upwards of one hundred bombers of the RAF conducted a successful raid on Berlin, dropping high explosives. The target was the German capital's Tempelhof Airport. There were no British casualties . . .'

The cheer drowned the rest out. Brooke kept to his seat, wondering if it was wise for the RAF to bomb their capital, when the defence of their own was problematic. Grandcourt, seated too, nonetheless raised two small clenched fists beside his ears and grinned widely.

The cheers faded, but the radio was left on, playing a big band number, possibly in the hope of drowning out the chorus in the corner.

Despite the barroom clatter, Brooke's ears registered a minute compression, a sense in which the air in the bar thickened slightly in those final seconds. The shell fell unseen through the night sky above the Kite, hurtling towards its point of impact. It was only in the final second that Brooke detected the high-pitched scream; a second in which he could think but not move, his blood still. Grandcourt had heard it too, possibly a beat before Brooke, and his mouth hung open, his pipe in his hand, his eyes lifted to the ceiling.

CHAPTER THREE

Brooke never remembered the moment of the blast itself. The first thing he could recall was that the windows of the Wellington Arms were gone, but there was no immediate sense that the outside had flooded into the bar, much more – it felt to him – the feeling of being inside had intensified, solidified even, pinning them down in their seats. The air itself was thick with debris, drifting slowly, dictated by some mysterious current. Like a stationary snowstorm it obscured all things, comprising particles of dust, of glass, of wood, of skin, of hair, and some strange thread-like substance somehow distilled from what had been present before the bomb.

All this moved sluggishly across the bar, in mid-air. For a sickening moment Brooke felt that it was he who was drifting away, sliding past a reality that had been shattered. The sounds of the crowded bar had gone, leaving a distant dull bass soundtrack, made up of a thrum, which Brooke deduced was the diminishing echo of the explosion itself. And, belatedly, he could hear a distant air raid siren.

The most disturbing element of the scene in those first surreal moments after the impact was that some people who had been in the bar, particularly the man sitting on a stool by the door, had disappeared, while others, such as Grandcourt, were sitting where they had been and appeared untouched, except for the gradually accruing ash-white layer of dust. His friend's face had a shocked blankness, while his eyes were full of fluid, his lips parted, his skin very tightly stretched over the bones beneath so that there was a real intimation, a disturbing one, that Brooke could discern the skull below.

Grandcourt was blinking slowly, and shaking slightly, but otherwise seemed uninjured.

While so much was intact – the bottle of mysterious liquid, for example, still stood on the table – there were several incongruous objects which had simply materialised: a window, carrying an etched image of a cricketer at the wicket, stood against the bar, the glass hardly cracked. A pair of curtains was wrapped round a light fitting over their heads.

The dull cotton wool of the soundscape parted for a second and he heard the rich heady swing of the big band on the radio, which still stood on the bar, although the barman had gone, as had all the bottles and glasses, and the tankards and cigarettes, which had been on the wooden shelves behind.

A man in a black uniform with ARP written on a tin helmet walked into the pub and looked around. Fresh-faced, he seemed oddly unimpressed by the scene of desolation. He said something, the sound muffled, and then – instantly – Brooke found himself *outside* the pub in the street, aware that time had jumped forward, although he was not in any way personally disorientated by the leap, because at precisely the same moment the real world of sound was back on, at full volume, and he was talking to a group of people, including the warden and a woman in a pink nightdress which was lightly sprayed with blood.

Several casualties lay on blankets in the street. All seemed to be alive, being comforted by strangers, and he recognised the barman. A fire engine stood in the middle of the street, from which a hose had been unfurled so that water could be played onto the roofs of the houses. The Wellington Arms looked derelict, with no lights, the white ash drifting out through the windows. Grandcourt was helping two men out into the street. A crowd had gathered, watching a squad of civil defence men ferrying bricks into neat piles.

Brooke was aware that he was suffering from shock caused by the blast, and that it was loosening its grip, but only by degrees. He was being asked questions. The ARP warden was demanding something but Brooke couldn't latch onto the meaning.

'Everyone's accounted for on my list,' said the warden, holding the woman in the nightdress gently by the arm. 'But this lady says the couple in number 36, that's the Pollards, might not have gone to the shelter like they usually do. So they might be inside.'

He pointed at a house which had clearly taken the brunt of the blast. The facade was black, the windows gone and the roof torn away, while white smoke drifted from the wreckage.

'That's right,' said the woman in the nightdress. 'Arthur and Nora are fed up with it, dossing in a bloody shelter at their age. They said they might sit tight and get a decent night's sleep for once. Arthur snores – he's in the front room. Nora's in the back. And Arthur'll have the dog with him; they're never apart, him an' Pickles.' She looked at the blackened house and covered her mouth. 'But there's not a sound, is there?'

The ARP warden took off his hat and pushed fair hair out of his eye. 'It's smouldering but the auxiliary fire boys say it's out. Mind you, the whole lot still looks pretty rickety. It needs propping up. If the old dears are inside they wouldn't have had much chance, but like I say, it's your shout. Someone said you're with the Borough. So you're in charge.'

CHAPTER FOUR

Brooke had decided to enter the house, and had borrowed the warden's tin hat, when a soldier approached, the bomb disposal insignia on his cap catching the light.

'Witnesses say they heard several bombs falling,' he told Brooke, not bothering to cite his rank or name. His voice was bored, matter-of-fact.

'Well, there was one here for certain,' said Brooke, pointing at number 36. 'I reckon it came down behind, in the yard, and it's blown out the windows, and the roof's gone.'

'You police?' asked the soldier.

'Inspector Brooke – the Borough.'

The officer made a careful note with a pencil in a small book before slipping it into the breast pocket of his uniform.

'There may be others close by, Inspector. Bombs which haven't gone up yet. Do you understand me?'

He stepped closer, rapidly transferring a cigarette to his lips from the same pocket which had taken the notebook. Brooke caught a whiff of shaving cream.

'They might not go off if they're faulty, or they might have time-delayed fuses; that's the real danger. It's a devil of a thing. They reckon one in Portsmouth took out twenty people when it finally went up – medics, nurses, relatives.' He checked his watch and marched off. 'The most common delay is one hour. That's twenty minutes away in this case. You need to clear the area. We'll check it out by daylight, but not before.'

Forty minutes lost? Brooke felt sick, aware that a slice of his life had simply been wiped from the record.

'I brought this, sir. I thought it might help.'

Brooke turned round to find Detective Sergeant Ralph Edison at his shoulder holding a loudhailer.

Relief flooded his blood stream like morphine.

'Can you clear the street, Sergeant?' said Brooke.

Edison had been in uniform for thirty years, the public face of the Borough, manning the duty desk at the Spinning House, the force's headquarters. He'd retired before the war but had been recalled in plain clothes. Despite the loss of his uniform he still managed to radiate its authority.

Edison used the loudhailer to usher sightseers away, and then briskly ordered back the other emergency services. He gave them a five-minute deadline to leave the street, implying by tone of voice alone that failure to meet this target would result in a night in the cells.

Slowly the street began to clear, but not before a young woman in an ill-fitting khaki uniform pressed a mug of tea into the hand of the woman in the bloodstained nightie. No more than seventeen or eighteen, she held the old woman by the hand and told her to drink up, that it would do her good, and that she should come to the local relief centre, which had been set up in the primary school in the next street. And she should find a nurse for the cuts on her arms.

'They're clearing all the streets, dear. You can't stay,' she said. 'You need to find a comfy spot at the LRC – that's at St Joseph's.'

Sometimes Brooke felt the war had ripped apart all the words in the world they needed to survive, leaving them with these useless acronyms: LRC, ARP, AFB, HE, BCC. He imagined the little tiles of a set of Scrabble being blown up in the air. But he could see the logic of it all. The organisation, the fussy officials, the application of rules and procedures inspired a sense of purpose, a steady reminder that everyone could cope.

The WRVS girl (*There we go again*, thought Brooke) was trying to get him to take a mug of tea too, while Edison was bearing down with the hailer to chivvy her away to safety.

Finally, the street was clear, and it took on a more dismal, threatening aspect. Smoke drifted out of the ruined house, while all the rest stood empty, windows shattered, dark and cold. Somewhere a dog barked rhythmically, without any sense of urgency.

Then time changed again.

Brooke found himself standing right in front of the stricken house, beside his sergeant, who was wiping his face with a large, immaculately ironed handkerchief.

The bomb, it appeared, had indeed fallen in the rear yard and ripped through the interior from the back, blowing the curtains out of the windows. The front room on the ground floor was visible through the gaping frame, blackened by smoke, but otherwise

25

largely untouched. The wallpaper, which featured roses entwined, was still just visible.

Brooke checked his watch. He had fifteen minutes before the hour was up. The old couple might be dead, but they might not. They might have gone to the shelter. Or they might be trapped under falling bricks and rafters in bed. It was his duty to make sure they didn't die in a second explosion, or in a collapsing house.

'I'll be as quick as I can, Sergeant. You get back to the barricade and make sure nobody strays close.'

The front door had been blown off its hinges and stood at an angle. He squeezed through, but by nudging the door dislodged it, and it fell with a crash, and the whole house seemed to shudder. Dust and ash drifted from above, and there was a fresh shower of falling glass in an upstairs room.

Halfway down the hall he got to the door into the kitchen, where supper plates were set on a table, smeared with vinegar and brown sauce. A single sliver of cod skin revealed the menu.

Brooke turned to go up the stairs and was surprised to see Edison standing on the doorstep, with his back to the house, bravely ignoring his previous order to retreat to the barricade.

A soldier appeared; not the bomb disposal man, but a captain in a pressed uniform.

'What's going on?' he said.

'The inspector's taking a quick look. We're in charge here,' said Edison.

The soldier took a step backwards and surveyed the front of the house.

'It's his funeral. Bloody thing could come down any moment. We need to get engineers inside and put some steel supports up once we've got the all-clear: if it goes over the lot could come down.'

He looked at a map. 'This is Earl Street, isn't it? Who

said you could close it off?' He shrugged because it was clear Edison's authority precluded answering peremptory questions. 'Alright. Have it your way. Tell me when you're done. I'm at the barricade.'

He marched out of sight, leaving Edison, who set his feet squarely apart as if he'd settled down for a nice quiet shift on point duty on Market Hill.

Brooke took the first three steps up the stairs and instantly felt the whole structure move an inch or more to the left, and then lurch back to the right. He stopped, waiting, desperate for the movement to stop.

Looking down he could see into the front room. A blackened dresser stood open, the shelf empty. What had it held? A piece of crockery? Porcelain? Down-at-heel family treasures? Had they been incinerated in the blast, or blown out of the window? There was a circular clear patch of wallpaper over the dresser, but no sign of a precious shattered plate or a broken mirror.

He felt the first stomach-tumble of unease. He took the next step up, and this time nothing moved, so he pressed on. The carpet and bannisters were untouched by the blast, but as he looked up he could see the night sky through a hole in the roof, the low clouds illuminated by a distant wandering searchlight.

Gaining the top landing, he felt much safer. It was an oddity of these bombs that the pressure wave simply blew out the main fire before it could start. The only danger other than collapse was a cracked gas main or shorting wires. Brooke stopped on the landing and sniffed the air: nothing, except the metallic dust, and the chemical edge of the explosives, and the dampness from the hose. Water was running down the walls, the stairs, and over the brass rods which kept the carpet in place.

He pushed open the door of the front bedroom.

27

The old man was in the bed, shuffled up against the back wall. He held the dog in a casual embrace. They were quite dead, Brooke could see that. There was no blood, or sense of violence, which was typical of blast victims. It looked as if the old man had turned inwards in those last seconds after the scream had become audible, possibly to protect the dog.

He took a moment to check the room. There was a chest and all the drawers were pulled out – not higgledy-piggledy, but by almost exactly the same distance. Brooke's eyes scanned the room for further evidence – a rectangle of clean wallpaper had once protected a picture, and he could see the frame and the broken glass on the rug, but no canvas.

Out on the landing he noticed the gloves for the first time. They were a man's leather driving gloves, and they'd been draped over the bannister rail carefully, so that they were balanced – fingers on one side, cuffs on the other. It seemed a miracle that they had preserved their position despite the blast, unless they had been left after the explosion had torn through the house. Brooke picked one up, and caught a faint whiff of petrol, so he held it to his nose and breathed in the fumes.

The coincidence made him stop. For a half-second he was back in the river watching the chemical burn on the surface with its poetic light. The street was silent, and somewhere a clock was ticking, so he moved on to the back room.

An elderly woman lay on the floor. She'd got out of bed, and the bomb had knocked her down, so she was lying along the skirting board. She had hardly any hair, but what there was lay under a hairnet, and her face was turned to the wall. From her thin legs and slightly fleshy arms, Brooke guessed an age of seventy to eighty.

Like the others she exhibited no mortal wounds. But there was a trickle of blood at one ear.

It was her hand, stretched out, which caught Brooke's eye.

His uneasy guts tumbled at last, recognising the crime for what it was.

The left ring finger and the middle finger beside it had both been severed neatly below the bottom joint, probably with a hacksaw blade. The mutilated stumps still bled. Brooke envisaged the act itself with a brutal clarity. The thief had come prepared, with his gloves, a bag perhaps, and the tools of his trade: a gemmy, a knife, a torch. Rifling through the wrecked rooms he'd taken anything of value, before finding Nora on the floor. The rings had been held fast by swollen joints. Desperate to get out before the emergency services arrived, he'd taken the fingers so that he could remove the stubborn jewels in his own sweet time.

Looting was an ugly word, and only ever whispered.

Brooke fled, pocketing the gloves.

CHAPTER FIVE

Once the stroke of the hour had passed and the area was judged safe, it fell to Brooke to 'preserve the scene of crime', as recommended by the Borough regulations. The offence itself demanded a serious response. Looting was listed under the Emergency Powers Act, the sweeping catch-all legislation which gave the government such draconian powers that its word was – literally – the law. The stipulated penalties for looting ranged widely, and there was plenty of room for leeway, but culminated in the gallows in the worst instances. Brooke was determined to follow the book, in case the powers that be decided it was time to make an example of the thief of Earl Street. The desecration of the body was, incidentally, an offence in itself.

The ARP rescue corps removed Nora Pollard's corpse (her hand discreetly covered beneath a sheet), and that of her husband Arthur, and the dog – Pickles. On the way out of number 36 they met the RSD on the way in; Rescue, Shoring and Demolition needed to prop up the house, in order that its collapse did not threaten the entire street. Brooke, using a Borough radio car, requested a police photographer from County to take shots of the upstairs rooms, once the RSD had made it safe, while he prepared to make a thorough search of the house and organise an inventory. A constable was despatched to the local school to begin interviewing friends and neighbours. Had anyone seen the thief?

But then the bomb disposal officer reappeared and announced that military headquarters at Madingley Hall, on the outskirts of the city, had sent a messenger with orders to evacuate a quarter-mile sector of the Kite in case the time delay on the mysterious unexploded bombs (if they existed) might be two hours, or six. In this case military authority comfortably outranked the Borough's, and so the crime scene would have to fend for itself until the next morning at the earliest.

Brooke's writ could run no further until the area was safe.

He met his sergeant at the barrier.

'You alright, sir?' asked Edison, yawning.

While Brooke was a nighthawk his detective sergeant was partial to his bed, a Rip Van Winkle in fact. He had been known, while duty sergeant before the war, to sleep standing up at the Spinning House front desk.

'I'm fine, Sergeant,' said Brooke. 'A bit of shock from the blast but I think it's passed. Why don't you go home to your bed? We can't do anything until they're sure there isn't another bomb – although where it's supposed to be hiding I've no idea.'

He stepped closer, dropping his voice, and told Edison about Mrs Pollard's injuries and the thefts. Edison became very still, a sure sign – Brooke had learnt – that his detective sergeant was thinking.

'In the overall scheme of things a little thievery is neither here nor there, Sergeant. But looting the dead is an inflammatory crime. It may ring alarm bells. So let's do our jobs, and keep mum for now if we can. We don't want vigilantes on the streets.'

'It's the kind of thing that gets about, sir.'

Brooke nodded. 'I've asked the ambulance crew to be discreet, but you're right, gossip is a national sport, especially now the government has shut down the racing and the football.

'Let's make an early start. I'll see you at seven at the Spinning House. And, Edison . . .' Brooke produced the leather gloves he'd found draped over the bannisters at number 36 from his greatcoat pocket. 'Mrs Edison must have a Kilner jar – or similar – to spare?'

Edison was a keen grower of fruit and vegetables. He ran an allotment on the edge of town. Jam, and other preserves, was his wife's speciality. Air-tight glass jars were a crucial tool. One of which would preserve the evidence perfectly.

'She's dozens,' said Edison. 'We've got raspberries and strawberries to bottle. We'll be living on it by Christmas.' Rationing was now in full swing and home-grown produce highly prized.

'You've come in the car?' asked Brooke.

Edison nodded. His pride and joy was an elegant Wolseley Wasp. One of the perks of rejoining the Borough was a regular supply of petrol coupons to keep it on the road.

'Then take these now,' he said, handing over the gloves. 'They were at the scene. Pop them in a jar and bring them in. As I say – seven, my office.'

His sergeant smelt the gloves. 'Our man's a driver? I doubt the residents have a car – it's a decent street, but they won't own a car unless it's for trade.'

'It may mean nothing. As you say, Mr Pollard may have been a mechanic, or a bus driver, or work in a factory – who knows. But they might be the thief's. Just keep them safe.'

He watched Edison drive off in his Wasp, its ruby red paintwork covered in a thin layer of ash, a plume of exhaust hanging in the night air.

The residents were being moved on, to friends and neighbours in other parts of the city, or the shelters, or the rest centre at the school, where tea and sandwiches were promised.

Brooke elected to walk home. It was now a fine summer's night and a crowd had gathered on Parker's Piece, watching smoke drift over the rooftops from the bombsite. News of fatalities had clearly spread, for as Brooke strode past he sensed the hushed whispers, and noted that while several people had brought their children out with them they held them close, in tight family circles. Soldiers stood smoking by their tents. The all-clear had sounded, and a few cars, headlights swaddled with regulation tape, crept past the scene, and on into the heart of the old city.

Brooke followed, the metal Blakeys on his leather shoes cracking out a *rat-tat-tat-tat* on the pavements, following the kerbs, painted white to help pedestrians in the blackout. Claire always said she could spot him a mile away by the walk: his body seemed to narrow to his feet, which trod a line, the pace always metronomic and brisk. She said that at rest, if he stopped to light a cigarette, especially with his ever-present hat, he looked like a nail driven into the ground.

He passed the Borough's headquarters at the Spinning House, a medieval pile which had once been the city's workhouse, judging that he could do little at such a time to begin the search for his cold-hearted thief. He'd planned to rest at home, but felt instead the need to talk, and catch his breath.

The street ahead was deserted, the blackout creating a narrow canyon of shadowy brick and stone. Even without a siren the city was plunged into this Stygian gloom every night. In the shadows, above the gates of Trinity College, Brooke saw that the hideous stone figure of Henry VIII had lost its royal mace yet again. Students stole it on a regular basis, then left it to be found, so that it could be laboriously returned by a bowler-hatted porter atop a ladder. With the outbreak of the war student japes had been outlawed by the proctors – the university police – but it seemed that, like the rest of the population, undergraduates felt that with so many men away in the forces the leashes of adult authority had slackened. Crime, particularly petty crime, had become a national pastime.

Brooke paused in a doorway and lit one of his precious Black Russian cigarettes. His father had slipped a packet in his kit bag – alongside a copy of the *Iliad* – when he'd seen him off at the station in 1917. The brand was difficult to get but a fragrant pipe shop off Market Hill ordered them from Sobranie, the makers. He let the nicotine circle his lungs, and for the first time since the blast felt a slight dizziness dissipate. His mind focused on the image of Nora Pollard's butchered fingers. Looters were another symptom of social disintegration, the weakening of public discipline. With so many capable police officers now in military uniform Brooke felt acutely the weight of duty, for in a real sense he was the force's sole senior detective, given that the other inspector oversaw the uniformed branch. He thought he had as much chance of finding his looter as catching the oik who'd lifted Henry VIII's mace.

Opposite Trinity's gatehouse, an alleyway ran down the side of the university bookshop. A roadster, an old man judging by the grey hair showing at the collar of a dirty macintosh, lay curled up by a line of bins, a cat sitting upright beside him, as if on guard. Vagrants were common now on the streets, as the mild nights stretched out, despite the city bomb shelters which were open to all. Brooke understood their wariness, for the public shelters were run with brisk formality by what they were beginning to call 'the authorities'. Rules were listed on printed sheets with the imprimatur of the government's local potentate: the regional commissioner. Brooke had some sympathy for those who complained of the overbearing nature of the wartime government because he'd always despised fussy regulations, and those who made them.

Twenty feet down the alley, a fire-escape ladder led up three floors. Brooke scaled it with confidence, then crossed a flat platform to a second ladder, which decanted him onto a further level, from which a short set of ironwork steps took him to the apex of the roof. Here, on a prefabricated ledge, the Observer Corps had set a lookout post. A low wall of sandbags protected the edge, which gave a 180-degree panoramic view of the Backs – that great sweep of river where the colleges ran down to the water. Set back by a chimney breast, a conical hut had been constructed in steel, and contained a Primus stove, a bunk and – vitally – a military landline telephone, linked exclusively to what they were all now instructed to call the BCC, the Bomb Control Centre.

Jo Ashmore, in her smart OC uniform and tin hat, was standing at the fixed mount for her field glasses, the ghost of a smile on her newly made-up lips. Brooke always got the impression that she arranged herself by way of greeting: the short haircut to within a millimetre of her collar, the gas mask set on the hip, but the truth was she was always what Claire called 'smartly turned-out'.

'Ah. The night detective. Tea? Or something stronger?'

The conical hut hid a bottle of malt whisky.

'Just tea,' said Brooke, looking out over the rooftops.

Ashmore had noted the condition of Brooke's greatcoat. 'Good God, Brooke. Have you been rolling in the gutter?'

'I was in the pub on Earl Street when the bomb came down. Fifty yards the other way and I'd be in pieces.'

She studied his face. 'You should see a doctor.'

'I'll see Claire. It's shock. I just need to sleep.'

They both laughed. His chromic insomnia was a constant source of conversation at the OC post, with Jo proffering possible solutions, while he thought of reasons why they wouldn't work.

Brooke told her about the casualties at number 36, and the evidence of looting, although he asked her not to put anything on the grapevine until the news got out.

'I'll get tea,' she said, removing a single piece of light debris from Brooke's shoulder.

The cluster of lights and drifting smoke in the Kite were just visible to the east. The searchlights, stationed at the ack-ack barrage on the hills to the south, swung round in search of lone raiders, casting circles and strange distortions of circles on the low clouds, as if agitated by having failed to locate the deadly bomber until too late. Otherwise the city was as it almost always was: silent, tense certainly, but not in any way greatly disturbed from its ancient customs. Raids such as the one that had destroyed the Pollards' home were extremely rare. For the most part Cambridge felt itself on the far reaches of the conflict.

The town clocks began to strike twice, marking the hour.

'I've added some Dutch courage,' called Jo from the hut. 'You look as pale as a ghost, Brooke.'

Ashmore had grown up in the villa next to the Brooke family

home at Newnham Croft, where the water meadows spread out into the headwaters of the Cam. Here a pair of Victorian homes had been built, their gardens running down to the towpath. She'd played with Brooke's children, Joy and Luke, running amok in the fields and along the banks. The two families had become intertwined, sharing high days and holidays, Sunday lunches, and even days at the distant beaches on the Norfolk coast. The children had given Brooke a wide berth. The hero of the desert war – who'd served, it was whispered, alongside the great Lawrence of Arabia – was a figure of legend. Ashmore had recently confessed that Brooke had cut an intimidating figure behind his array of exotic glasses. The sudden appearances in the river, hauling himself out to limp up to the house, were another source of mystery. Luke, his son, had confided to the other children that on winter nights El Aurens himself would appear at the house, uninvited, and whisk his father away for secret talks with the Fenland Bedouin, presumably camped out around a fire of bog oak.

Ashmore's own story was racy. She had fallen in with what was called the 'fast set' before the war. There had been parties in London, a married man, a scandal averted. Her father, a professor of history with hardly a trace of humour in his overbred personality, who had been largely absent from the family home for decades, had demanded his daughter pursue a low profile. His own academic career, and the eventual mastership of his college, hung in the balance. She'd promptly volunteered for the Observer Corps and dedicated her nights to keeping alert, but aloof. She'd just met a young pilot, a patient at the local burns unit, and the romance seemed to have put a light back in her eyes. Brooke wondered if the meddling professor would demand to vet the young man's reputation if he were unlucky enough to be taken home to meet his sweetheart's father.

They drank their hot toddies.

'You do look dreadful, Brooke. Why don't you sit down?'

She fetched a metal stool and he slumped, gratefully, an elbow on the sandbag ledge. He didn't feel dizzy, but he did feel exhausted.

Brooke took one of Ashmore's Craven As.

'Did you clock the bomber itself?' he said. 'There was no siren.'

She nodded, a hand resting on the metal sighting table with which she could plot incoming EA – enemy aircraft. Once she had a bearing and a height she rang it through to the BCC.

'Not until it was too late. Clever, actually. All that cloud cover you'd think they'd just drop the bombs and skedaddle, or not bother. But they flew in low and must have picked up something – the road maybe, or the river, or the railway.

'I had the report in ASAP. Not quick enough, obviously. The ack-ack had a go from Coldham's Common after she'd made her run but she was too fast. A Heinkel. It's just a one-off raid to show they can do it – boost morale, that kind of thing.

'They were aiming for the railway station again – that's the intel. Hoping for a bit of luck. They won't be back for a while.

'Your bomb was the fourth. They wasted three along the river on their run-in, and then dropped the rest on the shunting yards, on the way out. There's some damage but they reckon the mainline will be up and running by the end of tomorrow. Odd, isn't it? In peacetime the whole network collapses if a signal breaks. These days they perform miracles without exception.'

'And no second run?'

'Nope. Once the ack-ack picked them up they were on borrowed time.'

They sat in companionable silence watching the runway lights at Marshall airfield flicker into life to welcome the return of night fighters, presumably sent up to chase the raiders away.

'How's your flight lieutenant?' said Brooke, trying to find a bright note.

'The skin graft didn't take,' she said.

'Sorry,' he said.

Flight Lieutenant George Wentworth had been trapped in his Spitfire by an electrical fire after making an emergency landing in a field of hops outside Canterbury. He'd suffered third-degree burns to the left side of his face. The hospital unit at Ely, north of Cambridge, had a reputation for patching up the injured and getting them back in the air. Brooke had met Wentworth: the burns were bad, but only to one side of the face.

'Least they tried,' she said. 'Next stop's Queen Mary's; that's south of London, in the hills. Last time round they rebuilt people's faces, plastic surgery they call it. After the Somme, and Verdun. If anyone can help it'll be them.'

She filled her lungs with night air.

'It's a pig of a drive, and I don't have the coupons to make regular trips. I'll have to take the bloody train. It's out in the Surrey Hills. It'd be quicker to walk.'

'You could get a posting nearby,' offered Brooke, smiling.

Unkindly, Brooke imagined her rather enjoying the mercy-dash by train, climbing up into the pine trees of the Weald to some lonely halt, then getting a taxi to a Gothic pile, to see her wounded lover.

'No. I'll make the trip. George says he doesn't want me throwing my life away. Whatever that means.'

'It means he's a decent man.'

Brooke stood, leaning over the parapet and looking down into the street. The door set within the gates of St John's College opened and a porter in a bowler hat and coat stepped out in a rectangle of golden light, and then was gone, swallowed up by shadows.

Ashmore smoothed down her uniform.

'Word is . . .'

This phrase, heard widely in this second year of the war, was generally code for any bit of gossip which could be dressed up as real information. Ashmore's sources were, however, better than most. Madingley Hall sent regular notes on military dispositions, and Brooke knew that the OCs across the city swapped and cross-checked information.

'There's nothing in the papers or on the radio but the *word is* the Luftwaffe's switched tactics,' she said. 'They were going for ports, shipping, convoys. They wanted a peace deal then. Now it's going to be the RAF on the ground, then industry, infrastructure – so oil depots, railways, factories. And all this on a big scale, Brooke, not lone bombers.

'They hit the Midlands the other night, a big tyre factory apparently. OC in Birmingham city centre saw the smoke and it's fifteen miles away. And Bristol, and Hull, and loads of places around London – Croydon comes up a lot. And the East End, and Portsmouth. And . . .' She dropped her voice to an unnecessary whisper. 'One of the pool drivers for Civil Defence says they've been trying to knock out the masts along the coast – the radar. No luck so far, but if they take that down I won't be getting early warnings any more. Mind you, I didn't get any tonight so what's the difference?'

She rested a hand on the black Bakelite telephone.

'They reckon we'll hit back hard,' she said. 'That's what this Berlin raid's all about.'

She smoked her cigarette with elegant poise. 'One of the messengers from Madingley knows a bloke who's got a sister in Holland. She says they flattened Rotterdam to get the Dutch to surrender. All gone, he said – not a brick left standing on a brick.

Just some church left in the middle. And fifty thousand dead, Brooke. Think of that. Think of it here.'

Brooke didn't want to think of it. His son Luke had been caught up at Dunkirk. He'd made it back in the hold of a coal ship, and had then mysteriously disappeared, being sent north to an undefined 'posting'. His letters were oddly vague and Brooke couldn't shift the suspicion that young Luke had done what his father had expressly forbidden: he'd volunteered for something.

'Cambridge should be alright,' he offered, watching the army patrol boat sliding past on the river below, where a gap in the college roofs gave a view of the water.

'I tell you what is alright,' said Ashmore. 'Oxford. Know why?'

Brooke stood, shaking his head. 'Go on, why?'

'Hitler's got it earmarked as the new capital when he's won the war. He wants it as it is, in one glorious piece. So they're safe. But I doubt if we are.'

CHAPTER SIX

Brooke put the sleeping pill Claire had given him on a dish beside the bed and stretched out on the sheets. Through the open window he could hear the river trickling past at the bottom of the garden. The old house was silent, from his mother's 'Japanese' bathroom in the attic, with its eagle-clawed tub and screens, to his father's old laboratory, moth-balled now, embalmed in the basement, the dust long settled on Bunsen burners and fume cupboards, and the professor's private library of medical textbooks, experimental data and student theses.

Sir John Brooke had been absent for most of his son's

childhood, even after his mother's sudden death when he was six. A housekeeper had been installed to cook and serve solitary meals, and he'd been left to walk to and from school across the city, filling his spare time with exploring its alleyways and courts, which had become in effect an inanimate sibling, a playmate, a landscape for a lively mind and his own private paracosm; a parallel imaginary world.

His father had appeared each morning at breakfast from the cellar, lively and talkative, keen to discuss the news in *The Times*, before setting off for his rooms in college. He'd had a day bed installed below. When, occasionally, the laboratory door was left open, Brooke had sniffed the air, detecting tobacco, chemicals and old books. It had only recently been suggested to Brooke that his father had suffered from insomnia. The idea that his own disability might be partly genetic, and not solely the result of his mistreatment in the war, had been oddly sustaining. The only sad note was that his father's early death, at just sixty, had robbed him of a potential nighthawk.

He bunched the pillow behind his head, staring blankly at the plasterwork in the ceiling above, trying not to think about sleep, feeling instead the house around him, full of memories.

The silence was broken by a thin cry on the edge of hearing. His daughter, Joy, had the new baby in her room down the corridor. The baby: he still struggled to think of the child as Iris, the newest member of the family. The cry was followed by a soft whisper which might have been a soothing word. He'd told Joy not to worry about the noise. It was an extraordinary truth that once you were not directly responsible for a child its cries went almost unheard. Worse, there was a sense of smug schadenfreude, exquisitely apposite, as the sufferer was his own one-time torturer.

There was very little light in the room, despite the open window, but when he turned over he could see the dish, and the pill. He didn't want to take it: he'd resisted sleeping pills for more than twenty years. The risks of addiction were acute, the side-effects debilitating. His wife had wondered, often out loud, right here in their bed, whether there were worse things than such a habit. She conceded that barbiturates were dangerous, but that the soporific effects were beneficial if the dose was managed. She had gone to some lengths to procure him a supply of pills if he needed them, or wanted them.

She hadn't let the argument end there. She'd persisted: had he not become addicted, in his own way, to his affliction, a life lived after dark? Had he not grown to rely on the insomniac buzz of adrenaline, the sense of riding on the edge of the moment, of imminent collapse or adventure? In recent years she'd noticed a slight dissipation of his usual manic energy, as if he was a piece of clockwork winding down. His obsession with the night seemed to be taking its toll. Brooke, at forty-one, replied that it was simply the onset of middle age.

Earlier, after leaving Jo Ashmore's precarious post, he'd found his wife in the children's ward at Addenbrooke's, the city hospital. Sister Brooke ran the Rainbow Ward at night, having in the end found it easier to switch to his regime of time zones, rather than persist in her own.

He'd promptly described events on Earl Street and his symptoms: memory lapses, mild lack of eye focus, sporadic hearing loss, a little dizziness.

'But it's all gone now,' he said.

'It's still concussion,' said Claire, holding his head like a precious casket. 'You should see a doctor, right now, Eden. It is a hospital, you know.'

'The treatment's sleep. Even I know that. So I've got a problem, especially as I don't want to start taking your pills.'

He wanted to hold her close at that moment, but a child with measles was ten feet away and watching them keenly, sensing perhaps from the body language that something interesting was about to happen.

'One sleeping pill cannot be addictive,' she said. 'Go home. Lie down. Sleep. It's a cocaine derivative, so believe me, it *will* work. And they're not *my* pills, Eden. It's your life, and your decision.'

Claire had been brought up with five younger brothers. She spent most of her time organising other people, making sure that they were happy, comfortable and alive. She carried out these tasks with a brisk efficiency which had never calcified into anything authoritarian. She was a remarkable person, not least in making it quite clear she had never felt any pity for Brooke's condition. He was otherwise healthy, rather handsome, occasionally dashing and the beneficiary of a first-class education, and had inherited a wonderful old house by the river. Now he was blessed with two children and a granddaughter.

He'd kissed her, looking into her neat face, crowded with large eyes and a wide sensuous mouth.

'See you later in bed,' he'd said, and she'd pushed him away with a smile.

Now, remembering the sight of her, Brooke reached out, picked up the pill and held it up, noting the name etched in the white tablet: VERONAL. Claire had explained that the pills were in short supply as they were German-made, adding that the scientist who'd developed the drug – and this was hearsay – had decided that the Italian city of Verona was the most peaceful city in Europe. A byword for sleepiness. That had been at the turn of the century. Brooke thought that two world wars would most certainly have stirred Verona from her slumber.

There was another, darker, explanation for the shortage of sleeping pills. Anxiety and insomnia were rife as the nation waited for the bombs to fall. And worse still, hundreds – possibly thousands – of families were stockpiling them, particularly Jewish families. The threat of invasion, and what would follow, had driven them to contemplate suicide. If the Germans came, they wanted to be ready. Claire said there was a thriving black market in the drug, and that the hospital was too short of funds to secure a supply. She'd cheerfully pointed out that the upside was that if he did become dependent, it wasn't a state that could last.

He took the pill. It wasn't true to say he never slept. He often slept, it was just that these sudden plummeting descents into darkness were difficult to predict, and rarely lasted more than an hour. At the Spinning House he slept in the cells if he could. At home he tried to follow a regime of exercise, food and rest. Yet despite such routines he was constantly defied by a restless mind, or awoke sweating in expectation that a violent light was about to burst into his brain through his defenceless eyes.

The drug must have reached his brain because in those first few seconds he knew Claire was right, and that he would sleep. The moment was wonderfully close at hand. He heard the baby cry again down the corridor and thought of the child's father. Ben was a submariner, or rather had been a submariner, before his boat (he'd been most clear on this point at Christmas: it was a boat because it couldn't carry other boats, which was what defined a ship) had developed engine trouble, and then caught fire, and drifted towards the north German coast. They'd scuttled her in the end, as a Kriegsmarine patrol boat appeared on the distant horizon. He was now in a POW camp, and they were hoping, soon, for a first letter. There had been a brief telegram from the Red Cross confirming that he was alive and well in Stalag Luft I and that the broad terms of the Geneva Convention were being followed. The silence since had begun to grate, and privately Brooke worried, while assuring his daughter that Ben was safe: the Germans looked after our officers because they wanted us to look after theirs.

Brooke imagined Ben now, lying on a bunk, in a hut lost in the woods, trying perhaps in his turn to imagine what it would be like to hold his child. And wondering, surely, whether it was a boy or a girl.

And then Brooke was asleep, immersed in a nightmare, in which he was climbing the steps at number 36 again, but they led on upwards, in an endless giddy series of turns, until he was left clinging to the bannisters, looking down on a burning city, watching the dark shadows of bombers flying over the fires. He awoke with a shout, but the narcotic was so powerful that he fell instantly back into unconsciousness.

This time he had a dream he'd had many times before. Its roots were in his memory of real events, but its power lay in its fictional elaboration. This was a feature of his dream world, that it merged reality and nightmare. He was in the desert on the outskirts of a town on the Sinai coast road in 1917. They'd driven the Turks out of the settlement and one of his men had been caught, red-handed, amongst the remains of a mud-built house. He'd got his hands on a fine metallic, painted pitcher, a set of three silver plates and a sumptuously bound Koran, and some dry beans and vegetables, as well as salted beef and a disc of unleavened bread. To make matters worse the owners of these treasures were local Arabs who – returning to their liberated home – had found the British soldier with his knapsack full of stolen goods, sitting by the hearth, calmly chewing the bread.

The situation was tense. All Brooke wanted to do was get Grandcourt to return the stolen goods to the aggrieved family, with some fresh bread, while he made sure the culprit – a malingerer called Orton – was put in a hard labour gang back at Port Said, digging trenches for the rest of the war.

But the villagers wanted Brooke to shoot Orton. And they had a point. The area was under martial law, and a published list of capital offences included looting. The relevant regulations had been printed on a poster and stuck on telegraph poles from Cairo to Haifa. The fact that Orton wore a British uniform ought to make no difference.

The villagers had surrounded Brooke's temporary headquarters: a ruined water pumping station. It was quite clear what the right military decision was: Orton needed to die. He was a petty thief, a hungry petty thief, but he'd chosen the wrong moment to succumb to animal instincts. If the mob lost control there would be casualties: soldiers, and locals, amongst whom were women and children.

In reality he'd left arrangements to the regimental sergeant major, who'd chosen a firing squad and taken possession of Orton's effects. Brooke had stood by while the execution took place, the villagers lined up to witness retribution, which had been swift and, as in all such cases, oddly deflating once the final echoes of the salvo had died away. Orton slumped to his knees, supported by a fence post, around which a rope had been tied.

Yet this was not how the dream ended. In the dream version of reality Brooke had been forced to cajole the men, and even then had found himself one short of the stipulated six. He had therefore to take up his own rifle and join the line. Orton, tied to his post, loudly proclaimed that he'd gone into the house because he was hungry. He said there had been no rations for five weeks, which was true. There was a dangerous murmur of assent from the assembled troops.

Brooke called the men to arms and issued the order to fire.

Only one bullet was live and it found its mark. But Orton wouldn't die. He simply refused to succumb to the shot which had pierced his heart. The squad was issued with five blanks and a live round, and fired again, and again. The condemned man bled, and Brooke recalled grey eyes, which never left his own, pleading to a figure of authority to be released from a life reduced to a never-ending series of ineffectual deaths.

CHAPTER SEVEN

In the kitchen at Newnham Croft, Brooke had pinned up the latest set of tide tables issued by the port authority at King's Lynn, forty miles downriver, where the waters of the Cam finally slunk out into the sandy wastes of the Wash. As well as providing vital nautical information the tables listed the times for sunrise and sunset, broadly correct within a minute for his present location. It was dark outside, and the clock read 5.05 a.m. – forty-three minutes short of dawn. He was due to meet Edison at the Spinning House at seven. The hunt for the looter could begin then. He'd had some sympathy for Orton, who'd died so many times in his nightmares, but he had none for the man who'd cut through the finger bones of Nora Pollard. Greed, allied to brutality, was unforgiveable.

However, the pursuit of the culprit would have to wait two hours. Which left Brooke time to deal with the riddle of his poisoned river. Could he find the source of the mysterious chemical which had spilt into the Cam? Was it a threat to public health? Was the supply of drinking water safe? If someone was dumping oil in the headwaters, he had the powers to prosecute. And there was that tantalising possible link with the looted house. Was it just imagination that seemed to match the odour of the bluish oil in the river to the gloves he'd found at number 36? Coincidence always made him uneasy. He believed, as the scientist he once was, that the world was governed by order and logic, not happenstance.

He fetched his coat and hat, left a note for Claire and slipped out of the house, pulling the door to behind him with a satisfying, oily click.

The world smelt fresh and clean. Following the towpath, he crossed Coe Fen and skirted the Mill Pond at Newnham village, where he'd encountered the strange, flickering flames. He knelt, cupped a hand in the dark stream and smelt the water as it trickled away. It reeked of weed and peat, and damp grass, and nothing else.

At Silver Street Bridge he was forced to abandon the towpath, as the river swept on in its stone canyon, sandwiched between the colleges, and take instead a route through the silent streets, emerging finally beside the Great Bridge, where a few early workers were trudging into town in the grey light before dawn, and where he could pick up the towpath again and head north.

A brisk march brought him to Jesus Lock, beyond which a line of barges stood waiting to slip their moorings and head seawards. The light had begun to seep into the sky, and he could see smoke trickling from stovepipes on the boats, and lights flickering within the cabins. The forward barge was laden with sugar beet and the captain was happy to give him a lift downriver, after Brooke had shown his warrant card.

He accepted tea, but declined a seat in the narrow confines of the stern cabin, a sort of cast-iron shed, which hummed with the heat generated by a coke stove. He was given permission to ride instead in the prow, where a nest of sandbags provided a comfortable perch. He smoked his first cigarette of the day, and felt a common illusion: that he was stationary, and that the landscape itself – the riverside boathouses and poorer cottages, the towpath and the rough water meadows – was sliding past, chugging south to leave him in its wake.

The tea was steeped in tannin and cleared his head remarkably well.

The river, growing wider, looked greasy and sluggish. His father, who liked to quote the classics, had often called it 'this oozy Helicon' – a reference to Byron, who'd contemplated the river of classical legend. But young Brooke had learnt early to check sources, and while the reference was true it was hardly what his father had in mind. The Helicon was famed for its odd trick of disappearing underground, into chalky caverns, only to reappear nearer the sea. It was the rationale for this party trick which had fascinated Brooke the child: the women who killed Orpheus had tried to wash the blood off their hands in its waters, and the river had gone to earth to avoid implication in the crime.

The Cam looked innocent of any such violence, but certainly

oozy, sliding sedately seawards. Beyond Barnwell the captain, briefed earlier by Brooke, swung the barge towards the bank so he could simply step off onto the stone wharf.

Here one of the city's great landmarks dominated the skyline. Barnwell Pumping Station boasted a 150-foot-high brick chimney, and was belching steam into the morning sky. Even at a hundred yards Brooke could feel the visceral pounding of the great engines within.

Inside, through open metal doors, stokers threw coke into a series of open furnaces, which pained Brooke's eyes, so that he was forced to select his blue-tinted glasses. As he tried to get used to the murky interior he was astounded to see, high above his head, the four great pistons of the engine turning in the shadows below the roof, reaching out smoothly, one after the other, only to return in a graceful arc. Every few seconds a plume of steam obscured the machinery from view.

Even here, within feet of the moving iron and steel, the sound was muffled and smooth, although the vibrations in the concrete floor were now distinct, and the bones in Brooke's inner ear buzzed in time.

He was pointedly ignored by the labourers until a man appeared, briskly wiping his hands with a cloth, in a smart set of blue overalls.

'Can I help?' he asked, checking a pocket watch. The man didn't look at him, but that wasn't rare, as many people seem to find the tinted glasses oddly disturbing.

'Inspector Brooke – from the Borough. A small matter, but I had a few questions . . .'

The man led him past the stokers to a brick shed beyond the machine hall. It had no door, so the heat of the engine kept it torrid. It was an office, with rotas and notices on a board, and maps and plans spread over a long table. On a separate trestle a piece of machinery stood in a metal tray of oil. It looked like a great valve, perhaps from the heart of the pump itself.

'The third shift finishes in an hour, then it's the first back on. We never stop, you see. I'm the night engineer. You had questions?'

He began making tea without asking if Brooke was thirsty. His name was Gore. His son, he explained, was in the Royal Navy. He pointed out a picture of a young rating on a dockside. Now that the war was in its second year, Brooke had noticed how freely people talked to strangers about their private lives and families, as if they needed to take every opportunity to share their fears, and their hopes.

'Back on leave next week, God willing. I wish I was out there with him. They wouldn't have me, I'm too old now. But I'm proud of the boy because he volunteered.'

Gore said he'd worked at the pumping station since 1919, when he'd come home after the Great War, during which he'd served in the navy in the Mediterranean. For a minute they swapped reminiscences shared, of steamy Port Said and insanitary Gibraltar.

Gore was proud of keeping his ship's engines going despite the heat, and equally proud now of the pump house. 'I know every nut and washer, Inspector. It's all about the details. And care and attention.' He cleaned his hands of oil. 'Sorry, you had questions?'

Brooke described the chemical spillage at Newnham village, the strange blue-tinted fluid, and swimming under the flames. He said he wanted to find the source of the spill, but had no idea where to start.

Gore looked taken aback. 'You're a swimmer then. I never learnt. Used to get me in a panic.'

He gave Brooke a mug of tea, mashing the bag with a spoon and adding condensed milk.

'If you're partial to a dip you'll know the river's clean as a whistle. Has been for fifty years. This'll be a one-off. Not like the bad old days. All the city's sewage – everything from every house and shop and all the gutters – it all comes here by underground pipes, then we pump it out to Milton to treat it. It's a miracle really.'

'What about drinking water?' asked Brooke.

'That's separate. It comes up from the chalk out at Fleam Dyke; cleanest in the country, we even sift out the calcium, then pump it into houses through pipes. Nothing to do with the river, you see, so she's pretty much spotless.'

Brooke took his hat off and held it loosely in his hand. 'I'm having it analysed, a sample of the oil; I can assure you it did happen, Mr Gore. Surely it's dangerous – what about children? I learnt to swim in the river as a kid. We all did. It can save your life. The river's a gift for children. That was down along the Snobs – you know it?'

The Snobs was a shallow channel off the main river, not far from Newnham. On summer days it was crowded with thrashing children, overseen by attendants provided by the council.

'Like I said, I never learnt the knack,' said Gore.

Brooke looked up at the picture of his boy. 'What about him?'

Gore shook his head, picking up the picture. The air of breezy confidence had suddenly dissipated.

'The river's important,' said Brooke. 'The children won't learn if we don't look after it. It's a slippery slope, turning a blind eye. Has this happened to the river before?' he asked.

Gore looked uncomfortable, then shrugged. 'It's bound to happen, like I said. But it's rare.' He filled his lungs and then let the air whistle out. 'Last time it got downriver, towards Fen Ditton, there's been dead fish in the swim – carp, perch, tiddlers – that was a week ago.'

'A week? What's been done?'

'The boss here, and his bosses, they've got the regional commissioner breathing down their necks: can the water supply withstand a bombing raid – a big one? That kind of thing. The war's the priority. So everyone's stretched, so the word was that we'd ignore it, and it'd probably go away.'

'Well it hasn't,' said Brooke. 'I'm not sure turning a blind eye ever constitutes wise practice, especially when people's lives are at stake.'

Gore nodded, the blood draining from his face.

'I need to find the source,' said Brooke.

'Could be anything on the upper river – it's a maze, miles and miles of streams and ditches,' said Gore quickly. 'Garages, factories, farmyards – only takes a fuel tank to leak, or an acid bath to overflow. It'll have got in the river directly, as I said, not through pipes.'

Brooke settled his hat, and gave his mug back. 'If you hear anything – if it happens again – ring me.' He jotted down the Spinning House number on one of his cards.

Gore pinned it up on the board. 'Right you are.'

Then he grabbed his cap off a hook. 'You better see this as well,' he said, leading the way out to a small dock next to the pumping station, where a couple of flat-bottomed river boats, half filled with green water, lay stranded. Gore unlocked a pitch-blackened shed.

It was dark inside so Brooke took off his glasses.

'Good God,' he said, taking a step back.

'Hundreds – all dead,' said Gore. 'Same time as the fish downriver. Maybe we'll get more now with this new spill.'

The shed was full of rats, piled up in a pyramid. The naked tails, which looked like worms, were intertwined. The illusion that the grey corpses were moving, sliding one over the other, stayed with Brooke all day.

CHAPTER EIGHT

Brooke found the Kilner jar on his desk, the leather gloves within, and a note from Edison saying that he'd gone to Earl Street to organise door-to-door enquiries as the military had unexpectedly ruled the area safe. The shoring-up squad, he reported, had moved in a second time as there were concerns for the safety of the houses on either side of number 36. Several other houses in the street were badly damaged, and so he'd sent a constable to the local school – the designated LRC – to interview those unable to return home, and he'd try to compile a list of those items missing from the looted house. The Pollards' next of kin had been informed.

Not for the first time Brooke felt grateful for Edison's painstaking thoroughness. He sat down and typed a one-page report on the Earl Street incident, using two fingers, at rapid speed, so that the sound resembled a machine gun. Then he put the Kilner jar on a high shelf, grabbed his hat and ran down the stairs to the duty desk, handing over the report for delivery.

The sergeant shook his head. 'Sorry, sir. You're wanted in person upstairs.'

'Upstairs' was a euphemism for the attic office of Detective Chief Inspector Jean Carnegie-Brown. Her door was always open, but Brooke waited on the threshold. Despite having made enough noise clattering up the stairs he still had to cough to make her look up from a set of files. She wore glasses on a chain, which she now positioned on her nose.

'A moment, Brooke, and I'll be with you,' she said, indicating a straight-backed chair.

A Scot, she'd made the long journey from Glasgow to secure promotion. She'd made the Borough her own fiefdom through grinding work, and brisk – almost brutal – man management. Her known vices encompassed a silver cigarette box and a set of fishing rods. Brooke, on his late evening swims, had spotted her several times on the riverbank out beyond Newnham Croft, by the riverside inn, in full Highland outdoor gear, with a pint of beer to hand. Once, out with Claire on the riverbank at Ely, they'd stumbled on her in a nest of reeds, a glistening pike in the catch net, splashing. They'd mumbled something about the big Fen sky and then fled, as if they'd caught her sunbathing naked. She was more commonly associated with a bleak efficiency, which had – it was said – caught the attention of Scotland Yard. There were persistent rumours of a move to London, and a further rung up the career ladder.

She closed the file after a minute, and let the glasses fall from her hand.

Brooke placed his report on her desk.

'Report on last night's bomb, ma'am. There's evidence of looting.'

'Is there indeed,' she said, picking up the sheet of paper, automatically flipping the lid on the cigarette box with her other hand. She'd smoked in secret for a year, using the window which looked out on the high walls of Emmanuel College, but now all pretence had fallen away.

'We've enough paperwork to keep us busy without unnecessary addition, Brooke. A bit of petty theft in the blackout hardly calls for more reports, does it? Bumph is more likely to lose us the war than the Luftwaffe.'

'I think in this case the devil's in the detail,' said Brooke.

She held the sheet at arm's length and read the three hundred words in fifteen seconds. He'd left the gruesome details to the last line.

'I see,' she said, her nose wrinkling in disgust.

Brooke balanced his hat on his knee.

'Severed fingers – there's no doubt? It couldn't be a blast injury?'

'None.'

'If I send this to the Home Office there will be repercussions, Brooke. We may even warrant a flying visit from the Yard and we both know how unpleasant such assistance can be. It's a hornet's nest. Do we really want to poke it with a sharp stick? Looting is a sign of social disintegration. Common thievery is one thing. Mutilating a corpse, stealing from the dead, crosses the line.

'You were in the last lot, Brooke. War does strange things to otherwise sane people. I don't need to fill in all the spaces. If the bombing gets worse we need everyone to pull together, and keep on keeping on. Most of all, people need to think that life will go on. The everyday things. Getting up, work, family, a home, a pet dog, a pint of beer, an allotment. Looting is a crack in the facade, Brooke.'

It was the closest thing to a speech he'd ever heard from a woman largely restricted to one-sentence orders.

She paused, perhaps surprised by her own sudden passion, looking out of the open dormer window as a breeze shuffled through a line of London plane trees in the college grounds on the far side of the street.

'Looting now, today, tomorrow, sets precedents, it loosens inhibitions, it invites imitation. It will not be tolerated, Brooke. But what to do?' she asked, leaning back in her chair now, exhaling smoke. 'We can hardly publicly acknowledge the crime. That's the kind of shock that puts people out on the streets. Taking the law into their own hands. The official line is that we should avoid sensational reports.'

'It is – potentially – a capital offence,' said Brooke.

The chief inspector stubbed out her cigarette. 'The last thing we want is some petty thief swinging by his neck in Castle Yard, Brooke, simply because he stole a pensioner's tin of loose change from a wrecked house. Think of the obscene crowd outside, Brooke.'

'We can't ignore the crime,' he said.

'The view for now is that we do our best to limit the situation as discreetly as we can. Unless . . . Unless the line is crossed: organised looting will be met with the full force of the law. But we would need evidence that it really is organised looting, not opportunism, however brutal. Is there any such evidence, Inspector?'

Brooke shook his head. 'Not really. We've had half a dozen cases – but nothing to link them, and they've all been petty theft. However, none of the stolen goods have reappeared locally. We're checking further afield – markets, shops, known fences, in Norwich, Peterborough, Bedford. So far nothing. But it does suggest cooperation amongst thieves.'

Carnegie-Brown pushed her glasses to the bridge of her nose. '"Suggests" isn't good enough. Let me know if that changes. In the meantime, if we catch a few light-fingered roadsters in the process of stealing from a bomb crater, they can answer to the magistrates. Prison certainly, but all low key.'

Brooke felt the familiar urge to confront authority. 'But this case, ma'am – the mutilation of the body is an offence in itself, of course, if I recall my sergeant's exam. *Profanare de morminte.* And it's a potential obstruction of justice.'

'Sawing the fingers off an old woman to get her rings is despicable, Brooke. Let's deal with the specific charges when, or if, you make an arrest. Why don't we leave the gory details out of your report? Let's just call it theft. Omission, Brooke, that's the trick of it. No lies. Let's bide our time. We've enough on our plate.'

Brooke lit a cigarette without asking for permission, a mild form of insubordination, but one he always found effective. The chief inspector's attitude reminded him of Gore's superiors at the pumping station.

Carnegie-Brown slid the one-page report back across the desk and dismissed him with a nod.

CHAPTER NINE

Standing at the foot of Earl Street, by a corner shop and the windowless Wellington Arms, Brooke was struck by the extent to which a single bomb can transform a view, realigning the ribs and bones of a place, opening up undreamt-of vistas, redrawing the skyline. One bombshell had changed this little dead-end street for ever. The roof and part of the upper storey of number 36 had either collapsed overnight or been demolished by the safety crews who were even now winching wooden support struts off the cobbled road to prop up the facades of the neighbouring houses, which had been rocked by the blast. Opposite, the damage was far more extensive than had been apparent by night, the serendipity of bomb blast and air pressure sending most of the explosive charge across the street, tearing out windows, blowing in doors and bringing down hundreds of roof tiles. It was a miracle no one else had died.

The partial destruction of number 36 – the rotten tooth in the jaw – had changed everything, for it opened up a view of the backs of the shops on East Road, a bedraggled line of impoverished Victorian sheds and halls, pubs and the back end of a Methodist Chapel, all in ugly red brick. On the main road two buses were passing, curious passengers peering through the still-smoking gap into Earl Street, fascinated by this sudden, unexpected view of the Kite. It struck Brooke for the first time that carpet bombing – a new wave of Blitzkreig ahead of an invasion – might destroy his beloved city for ever. What had Jo Ashmore said about Rotterdam? That the city had been levelled, with just the cathedral left: *Not a brick left standing on a brick.*

Many of the inhabitants of the street, who had decamped en masse in the night to sleep elsewhere, either with relatives or friends or at the LRC, were now back, as Edison had reported, and the feverish activity reflected a very human urge to reclaim normality. The crowd worked steadily, sweeping away glass, hauling furniture and bedding out onto the cobbles, stacking bricks and tiles. The ARP warden had taken on a supervisory role, sitting on a doorstep smoking a cigarette, fair hair revealed now his tin hat was on his knee. The blast had fractured a water main and so a stream ran down the left-hand gutter, creating a widening lake. Children, school forgotten, were racing paper boats. The Wellington Arms, at the far end, had its doors open and tables outside. A few men drank mugs of tea and smoked; others sat on the kerb, their boots in the one dry gutter. Brooke thought they looked exhausted, beaten to some extent, and it reminded him of watching his own men march back along the desert road after the debacle of the First Battle of Gaza, every ounce of energy bleeding away into the sand.

Edison appeared from the throng of labourers working outside number 36.

'Sir.' The salute was Edison's best, reserved for public admiration. 'I've told them to bring out everything they can from the house. Anything of value. That way we might be able to work out what's gone.'

Brooke could see a uniformed constable conducting a doorstep interview further down the street. 'Anything yet on the thief in the night?'

'No, sir. Most people just blame outsiders; that's what everyone says, of course. Not one of us – that kind of thing.'

They watched a queue form at a dowser marked WATER – BOIL FIRST.

'The dead?' asked Brooke.

Edison set out their full names and details. Then he put away his notebook. He had an extraordinary ability to remain still amid chaos. A child's football rolled up to the sergeant's feet but the assembled urchins just stopped and stared, waiting for him to nudge it back, which he did without a word.

'I checked the files on the other incidents, sir. A motley bunch, with nothing much to link one incident with the next. There was a watch taken off a corpse at the Hills Road incendiary attack – that's the only one that catches the eye. Mostly it's just pilfering.' Edison rearranged his polished boots.

The constable who'd been conducting door-to-door enquiries appeared with a child in tow, wheeling a bicycle with a silver horn on the handlebars.

'Sir. This is Jack – he lives at number 40. He's a bit of a whizz on bikes – aren't you, son?'

The child nodded. He was about six or seven years of age, with a front tooth missing, wearing a large jersey which was several sizes too large.

'Tell the inspector what you told me.'

Jack's story was as vivid as only a child's could be. When the bomb dropped he was knocked out of bed and his mum was screaming, and kept on screaming, until his dad got them all down the stairs.

'We looked out the front but the street was full of smoke,' he said, clearly delighted. 'So we went out the back and saw the bomb hole, but Dad said we had to squeeze past.'

His aunt lived at number 21 so they'd set off down the back alley to see if she was alright. Jack had noticed a bicycle lying in the rubble of what had been the back wall of number 36. He knew Nora and Arthur Pollard because he played football in the back alley – a game called 'fives' – and they used to complain to his dad about the noise.

'Dad always told them running about is good for kids,' said Jack proudly.

The bicycle in the rubble was blue, with the brand name, Lucifer, in silver on the haft of the crossbar. Jack knew all the bikes in the street and he'd never seen one like it before.

'Lucifer's the devil, isn't it?' he asked.

'Yes,' said Edison, touching the top of the boy's head.

'But before he was the devil he was an angel,' said Brooke. 'The bringer of light. Was it a new bike, Jack?'

The boy shrugged. 'No – it was a bit tatty.'

'What happened next?' asked Brooke.

'We got to Aunt Joan's and I realised I'd forgotten Joey – he's my budgie – so I ran back and got the cage. The bike was gone.' The child fell silent for a moment. 'I got a thick ear off Dad when I got back, but Joey's alright.'

'So how long was it between the moment when you saw the bike, and the moment you saw the bike was gone?' asked Brooke.

'A minute?' offered Jack. 'I ain't got a watch.'

'One thing,' said Brooke. 'This bike, there wasn't a bag, or a holdall, or a pannier, you know, like a basket?'

Jack nodded. 'A wicker one – and it had a can in it.'

'What kind of can?'

Jack pointed to the water dowser in the street.

'Like Mrs Clarke's,' he said.

A woman was at the tap drawing water. She had an army-issue container. Everyone called them 'flimsies'. In the desert, General Allenby's troops had used them for water, but mostly they were used for petrol.

Edison patted him on the head. 'Well done, lad. You'd make a good copper.'

The constable said he'd write out a statement and led Jack away.

Brooke took off his hat and ran his hand through his hair. *So that's another possible link in the chain*, he thought: *the spill in the river, the gloves, and now the can in the bicycle pannier. Why did the thief need to carry petrol – if it was petrol?*

He lit a cigarette. 'So now we're reduced to trying to track down a bicycle in Cambridge, Sergeant. Some chance.'

Edison led the way to the Wellington Arms, where the snug bar, at the far end of the building, had been deemed safe, despite the fact that the ceiling looked like a cracked egg. A woman sat on a wooden settle beside a female police constable.

'This is Alice Wylde, Nora and Arthur's daughter,' said the constable.

'Could I have a drink?' asked Alice, before she'd let go of Brooke's hand. 'Just water. I don't hold with beer or spirits.'

She straightened her back. Brooke guessed she'd stand tall, and he could see she had large bones, and a slightly brittle, joyless manner. She was about sixty years of age, with a fine head of grey hair, tied with a black velvet band. But she might be much younger, because the war seemed to have aged everyone, anxiety and the night raids combining to line faces and dim the eye.

The publican, cleaning up debris behind the bar, produced one of the flimsies and poured a glass.

She took a gulp. 'Sorry. It's the shock. We weren't really close. We fell out over money, and my girls . . . We only live a few streets away but we hardly visit.'

She kept picking at the high neck of her cardigan, as if it was stopping her drawing breath.

'Dad was a drunk, everyone knew, so that didn't help.' She looked quickly around the pub, squinting at the greasy unwashed windows, the cheap furniture. 'He was in the last lot but he didn't lift a finger this time. Least I turn out for the WRVS – pour a few cups of tea. Mum spent half her life in 'ere as well. We're chapel – at least my Peter was. But he's long dead. Still, blood's thicker than water, I suppose.'

She examined her glass and took a second gulp. Again he noted the extent to which the war had torn down barriers. Everyone seemed happy to share their most intimate family stories.

'Dad loved that dog. Never without it. He used to kiss it for a joke.'

He let her talk herself into a silence, doubting that the family history would help them catch a skulking thief, but recognising that letting her ramble on was probably doing her good.

She said she had three daughters, all in work, which was a blessing because they were still short of cash, what with the rent to pay and no man to bring home a decent wage.

'Mind you, Mum and Dad never went short. They *owned* their house.'

With this final shot she seemed to run out of bitterness.

Brooke wondered whether she was regretting the family feud, because they'd never be able to make it up now.

'Mrs Wylde, I'm afraid there have been some thefts from the house and we're trying to track down what's missing. I wondered if you could help make a list?'

'Someone robbed them? When they were dead?'

'Yes. I'm sorry.'

'I can try to make a list. Like I say I didn't go round that much. The girls did, Mum spoilt 'em, so they were always there. It was no palace but there's a few bits and bobs which would sell.'

Brooke stood up. 'When you feel up to it can you go with my sergeant and have a look at everything they've brought out of the house? Then see if you think anything valuable is missing. The structure is unsafe so you can't go in – not at the moment anyway. Can you do that?'

She nodded.

'Mrs Wylde, one thing we do think the thieves took is your mother's rings.' Brooke hoped she wouldn't ask how he knew they'd taken them, otherwise he'd have to claim they'd seen the marks on her fingers.

She said that rings had been her mother's pride and joy. She looked Brooke in the face for the first time. He took off his tinted glasses so that she could see his blue eyes.

'Did they take the whole box?' she said.

'There was a box?'

69

'On her dressing table, large as life. I bet that's gone. Not just rings, but fancy stuff. Earrings, bracelets, the lot. Most of it was tat, mind you. Mum didn't have much taste as long as it looked shiny.'

'Can you describe the rings?'

Alice wasn't listening. 'She had cash too. When I was a kid she hid it in a tin in the loo cistern. She was always going on about her "nest egg" – my guess is it was five bob and a few buttons, but there we are.'

Edison made a fresh note.

Alice was nodding, catching up with the questions. 'Three rings. She wore three rings. All her life . . .'

She covered her mouth with her hand at what she'd said – *all her life*.

'She always said she scrubbed up well,' she added, recovering herself. 'When she went out there was a lot of sparkle in Mum, like I said. But not much class.'

She held out her own fingers, pointing. 'Wedding ring – plain band – on the ring finger. Below that her engagement ring, which was Dad's mum's. Typical, that. Mind you, it was gorgeous. Silver, with three little rubies. Peggy, my eldest, loved that ring when she was a kiddie. She'd talk Mum into taking it off and she'd wear it, dressing up and that. She's all grown up now.'

'And the third ring?' asked Edison.

'That was a "moving feast" – that's what Mum said. But always on the middle finger. She'd had all sorts over the years. When she'd done with them she kept them in the box . . .'

Edison asked if she knew which one her mother had been wearing recently.

'Last time I saw her she had on a Victorian one she'd picked up at Newmarket. Three shillings, she paid. They call 'em poison rings –

there's a little lid and it pops up if you press your fingers together, then you slip the arsenic in the drink when nobody's looking.'

She laughed briefly, finishing off the water. 'Maybe she had Dad in mind. She didn't need to bother, did she?'

It was a bitter thing to say and Alice set her jaw, as though resisting the urge to take it back, to say sorry.

CHAPTER TEN

Back at his desk after lunch, Brooke found a single sheet of typed paper on his blotter. The shoring squad at Earl Street had brought out what they could from number 36 and Alice Wylde had given them a list of what appeared to be missing, other than Nora Pollard's three rings.

Wedgwood plate. Wall mounted. Six inches diameter approx.
Pistol. Great War issue. Arthur Pollard's.
Fish knives and forks in box. Electro-plated steel.
Jewellery box. Bangles, rings, earrings etc.

*Silver salver from Great Eastern Railway. Engraved to mark
the retirement of Arthur Pollard.
Cut glass decanter. Silver stopper missing.
Framed picture. Moulin Rouge.
A football trophy. Possibly silver. Awarded to Crusaders FC
Under-12s.
A fur stole with a fox's head.*

Brooke felt that their best chance was the salver, so he'd rung
the railway office to trace the silversmith and get an outline of
the design and wording, which apparently included Arthur's full
name, and the date. Descriptions of all the stolen goods were sent
by motorcycle messenger to Norwich, Peterborough, King's Lynn
and Bedford, and added to the Spinning House's own register, but
with little hope of success.

The most disturbing discovery was made by one of the shoring
squad, who finally managed to remove the rubble in the back yard
and drag out the toilet cistern. The tin containing Nora Pollard's
'nest egg' was inside, but empty. Which strongly suggested the thief
had inside knowledge, or ample time to check out likely hiding
places, although young Jack's testimony suggested the culprit may
have been inside just a few minutes.

They'd send the tin up to County to brush for fingerprints but
to Brooke's eye it looked as clean as a whistle.

Tracking down the Lucifer bicycle seemed equally daunting.

Over lunch at the British Restaurant on Peas Hill with
Edison he discussed the case with little enthusiasm. The menu,
set by the government and relentlessly hearty, offered a dubious
shepherd's pie and a choice between kale and cabbage, with
mashed potato. The thin gravy made everything watery and
insipid. A former Masonic Hall, the building itself usually

inspired Brooke, with its intricate plaster work depicting compasses and moons, starbursts and hammers. Today the images seemed to mock him.

The Earl Street case left him feeling overwhelmed by profound frustration. Petty theft was common because it was random, so that no logical trail presented itself to trace the crook. Even the suggestion of inside knowledge on the part of the thief served only to reduce the possible suspect list to friends, neighbours and family. But the thief could easily have guessed that the cistern was a safe hiding place. It was hardly novel.

Edison did have a theory concerning the petrol can. 'I reckon chummy's out to nick a car, sir. There's been a spate in the blackout. A lot of vehicles are either low on fuel or pretty much empty. The coupons run out fast, and you only get new ones at the end of the month. So maybe he's got fuel in the can so he can drive them off.'

They agreed, somewhat forlornly, to press on with house-to-house enquiries and circulating descriptions of the stolen goods.

Back at his desk, Brooke turned his attention to his in-tray: reports on half a dozen burglaries, several cases of actual bodily harm related to fights in the city's pubs, three incidents of domestic violence, over forty notifications of criminal damage and eight cases of vehicle theft. Public nuisance reports ran to over fifty.

By mid-afternoon the sensation that he was merely going through the motions was debilitating. The Borough's investigative resources were meagre. There was a crushing sense that out on the streets, and in the houses and shops, crime was rife but largely unreported. There was no doubt that the war had provoked a crime wave of unprecedented proportions, particularly juvenile crime, and that the inability of the police to respond was now simply a recognised fact of life.

The wartime black market was thriving. Rationing had created shortages, and shortages boosted prices. A cash-based economy was developing quickly, bypassing regulations and official scrutiny. There had also been a marked change in moral outlook. Brooke felt that normally law-abiding citizens now felt that, given the sacrifices being made and the hardships endured, there was nothing wrong with a bit of casual crime. He'd even read a piece in *The Times* which blamed the lowered cultural tone on Hollywood – gangster movies were popular and tough guys were heroes, especially junior tough guys, like the ones in *Crime School* and *Angels with Dirty Faces*. And then there was prostitution: organised, informal or casual. It was a scandal that the authorities were trying hard to ignore, although the public health issues were alarming: the 'clinic' at the hospital was wildly oversubscribed.

By five o'clock Brooke had had enough. Besides, he had a regular appointment to keep.

He doffed his hat to the duty sergeant and checked his pigeonhole. There were several notes, which he stuffed into his pocket, because at this point in the day he had decided many years ago that for an hour at least he would let the Borough run itself. He strode out into St Andrew's Street, zigzagging by alleyways to the locked door of the Michaelhouse wharf, where his old college kept its punts. Here, in a hidden corner, he retrieved his bathing shorts from their wooden box, replaced them with his clothes and slipped into the river.

He struck out south, a gentle front crawl, under Silver Street Bridge, into the braided streams which trickled across Coe Fen, until he got to Newnham Pool, his nose at water level, trying to catch a ghost of the chemical and its related gas, but there was nothing. As Brooke trod water he could hear the sound – the unmistakable sound – of children in the water ahead, swimming in the Snobs.

As he entered the shallow channel he could see a scramble of youngsters playing in the blinding light of sunset. White water shot here and there, and out of the shadows on the bank a child came running, launching himself into the melee, limbs flailing. Two or three adults sat on the bank smoking cheerfully.

Brooke hauled himself up onto the bank, letting the water drain from his shorts, before padding over the grass towards the high banks which ran up to the main river. Here, in a shaded spot, stood Hodson's Folly, a miniature flight of fancy in the shape of a classical temple, just big enough for a small family picnic. According to the story related by his father, Hodson had been an enterprising college butler who'd run a fishery at the spot, and liked to sit and watch over his daughter when she swam in the river, from the splendour of his miniature palace.

Claire was already there. It was a favourite meeting spot because she could slip away from the hospital, which stood beyond the walls of Peterhouse college, only a minute's walk away. She'd brought bread and cheese and a bottle of beer, and a towel from the children's ward.

'It's not going to cover much,' she said, handing it over.

Over the years the romance of the spot had been overwhelming, and they'd sneaked off into the long grass of the Fen meadow. But tonight the howling boys were everywhere.

Brooke, half dry, sat close. They shared the beer from the bottle. They had not seen each other to talk to properly for several days. Domestic news led them to Ben, their son-in-law, and the fact there was still no word, and then to the baby, of which there was much: gripe and colic, eyes turning green, Joy struggling with shifts and worrying about leaving Iris with Mrs Mullins, a woman who took in babies to mind for working mothers. With so many men gone to the war Joy said the poor woman was overwhelmed, and that Iris might be neglected, but that she couldn't face not working, and being left alone with the child at home. And finally there was their son, Luke, of whom there was also no news, although he'd gone north to his posting and was therefore presumably perfectly safe.

'Come wintertime we'll leave the windows open and I bet Iris will sleep like a log,' said Claire. 'Luke did. It's a primeval reaction, to shut down and preserve heat. So I told Joy it's not an open-ended sentence, and that Mrs Mullins is diligent and honest, and that we couldn't ask for more.'

Brooke offered a résumé of his day, outlining the case of Nora Pollard and Carnegie-Brown's suggestion that they withhold the details of her injuries in order to avoid a bureaucratic reaction from London. He admitted that catching the thief was going to be a tall order unless they had some luck. The really depressing thought was that hardly anyone else in authority seemed to care whether the culprit was brought to book.

Then he told her about the chemical in the river catching fire, and the sample he'd given to Grandcourt – who'd left a message to say he'd found someone to analyse it but it would take twenty-four hours. Then he outlined his trip to Barnwell Pumping Station, but left out any mention of the rats. Claire, who never exhibited any signs of squeamishness, was nonetheless terrified of rodents of all kinds.

They fell into a shared silence. The dusk was deepening rapidly, the shadows shading to purple, like bruises. Brooke rubbed his arms for warmth. Nightrise, which was edging over them from the east, had brought out a star. 'The water's crystal-clear tonight,' he said. 'You've not seen anything up at the hospital, I suppose – no swimmers getting a mouthful of chemicals, skin burns, that kind of thing?'

Claire packed away the bread, brushing crumbs off her uniform.

'Nothing. We've had a spate of children with nasty stomach complaints but they were all from Romsey Town and the culprit was easy to find. I think we had four in and they told the same story: they'd all had chips. The Guildhall reckons it's contaminated cooking fat. Nasty, actually: swollen lips, raking coughs. They've closed the chippie down.'

They watched a barge slide past laden with firewood.

'We did have a swimmer in – from Byron's Pool,' said Claire.

'I thought they'd put a stop to that?'

'Looks like they're turning a blind eye.'

Byron's Pool lay south of the city, in the foothills of the chalk downs which fed the river. It was deep, and a wooden floating dock encouraged divers to the spot. Long before the poet had made it famous, students had indulged in a dangerous sport. Items of dubious value – old coins, a discarded cut glass, a silver dish, a tankard – were thrown into the pool. Retrieving the treasures required skill and courage. Children and the foolhardy were also tempted: there'd been accidents, and a distant fatality at the turn of the century. The college authorities had cracked down and the sport had died away, only, it seemed, to reappear now.

'You'd think people had enough danger in their lives,' said Brooke.

'They brought in a student. He'd passed out coming up. Hardly worth it for a battered old pewter cup. And there's weeds, and tree roots, and mud, and I bet it's nearly dark at the bottom. What makes them do it?'

'Glory,' said Brooke, which gave him an idea, like a flash of lightning in the dark, in which he saw a way of tracking down the elusive Lucifer.

CHAPTER ELEVEN

Swimming back down the river in the dusk, he heard the air raid siren as he approached his secret steps: the heart-stopping wail carrying easily on the breeze from the Guildhall. Changing quickly he locked the gate and raced along the narrow alleyways towards King's Parade. The siren was early, and there was an evolving tradition that it could be ignored, but last night's lethal bomb had been a reminder that the city was still a target. The pavements were crowded with pedestrians hurrying towards the shelters, lugging bedding and suitcases. He'd once asked Grandcourt if they ever opened the cases when they got to the shelters. He said he'd seen a few, and spotted documents, guessing they were deeds, wills and share certificates. Brooke had never stopped to think how afraid people must be that they might lose everything if a bomb struck: not just their homes, but their pensions, or their savings.

Brooke's Blakeys sounded their distinctive tattoo on the stone pavement as he strode down the rapidly emptying streets, glancing up to see a barrage balloon drifting serenely beyond the four Gothic pinnacles of King's College Chapel, caught in a nervous searchlight beam. A voice of authority, magnified by a loudhailer, was calling people into a neat line outside the entrance to the shelters on Market Hill. There was something nightmarish about the sight of so many people, so afraid, happy to take orders from anyone in authority.

At Silver Street Bridge a minor traffic jam had formed at the tight corner with King's Parade. Cars edged forward, their headlamps partly obscured by tape. Brooke paused on the whitewashed kerb, the street lamps flickered out and the blackout descended. Stepping back into a doorway, he let the last of the fleeing civilians run past, and used his torch to check the messages he'd picked up at the duty desk when he'd left the Spinning House: there was a note from a city centre cycle shop confirming that no sales of Lucifer bikes had been made that year, and a telegram from Madingley Hall informing him that Carnegie-Brown's request for help had been accepted and he was welcome to visit the city's Bomb Control Centre – located in the air-raid-proof bowels of the Fitzwilliam Museum – in the interests of liaison on the issue of 'petty theft from damaged domiciles'. He noted the pathological need to avoid the word 'looting'.

And finally an envelope marked from *DR HENRY COMFORT*.

The line inside was in the Borough pathologist's usual copperplate:

Brooke. Nora Pollard: if you can make the morgue by nine I can talk you through the prelim. A surprise.

Dr Comfort was a university man with a chair in medicine, a joint appointment with his role as pathologist, which went back to Victorian principles of efficiency. The city's murder rate was low. Violent, unexpected or unnatural deaths were common in the centuries of open conflict between town and gown, but much rarer in the age of gaslight. So the role of Borough pathologist was not demanding. Dr Comfort took it seriously nonetheless. He attended the scene of crime when he could, and the bodies were spirited quickly to his laboratory in the Galen Building – part of the medical faculty, one of the country's newest and most well-equipped scientific institutions – where they could await autopsy, and eventual release to the coroner.

The Galen was a brutal six-floor block in ice-cold white tiles. Brooke found a porter bolting the door.

'There's an air raid warning,' said the old man, a cigarette drooping from his lips.

'Dr Comfort?' Brooke showed his warrant.

The doorman nodded. 'Top floor. He doesn't believe in shelters. But I do – so he has a key. Go on up, but it's at your own risk.'

The interior of the building was dominated by a zigzag of rising concrete stairs. Comfort, a solid man with butcher's hands, was on the last landing putting on a black tie.

'Ah. Just in time, Brooke. I've hardly used the knife. I'll open her up tomorrow. But there's something of interest.'

The laboratory had windows on three sides which were all now obscured by blackout boards. The one solid wall held the metal boxes for cadavers. Each year medical students were assigned a body left to the university for scientific purposes, which was disaggregated by degrees in the interests of medicine, and then stitched back together for eventual burial. At any one time several such bodies were therefore in storage. Brooke had been touched by the annual ceremony which marked the students' final sight of the body they'd briefly made their own: prayers were said, and a letter written to the nearest relative expressing the university's debt to the family.

It struck Brooke as an unexpected dividend of burial delayed.

The laboratory held two mortuary tables in cold steel, one of which was occupied, the corpse beneath a white sheet.

Comfort shuffled the cloth neatly back from the face to the shoulders. Any semblance of life had long fled from the features of Nora Pollard. Despite two decades of confronting such sights in the morgue, Brooke was always astonished at the degree to which the ebbing away of life transformed the face. She was unrecognisable from the woman he'd found slumped in the back bedroom of number 36 Earl Street. Gravity had robbed her face of any semblance of intelligence.

'I won't bother you with the technical description of the internal injuries we expect to find,' said Comfort. 'Suffice to say that the force of the blast will have been sufficient to tear connective tissue, dislodging the major organs, rupturing arteries and veins. She would have died within minutes of the bomb hitting the house. However . . .'

Comfort, without looking up, reached above his head and found the handle of an angle-poise lamp, bringing it down to the victim and switching it round to illuminate the head. The brutal play of shadow and light made the old woman's features jump and shift.

'Just here – two small bruises on either side of the trachea . . .'

To Brooke they looked like inky smudges.

'I opened the back of the neck to examine the site of the trauma from within,' he said, turning away to a table and coming back with a kidney-shaped dish within which were two tiny fragments of a C-shaped bone, with the circumference of a florin.

'The hyoid bone. Classic indicator, Brooke. I found fractures to the cornu and thyroid cartilage as well. She was strangled, you see, by someone standing in front of her like this . . .'

He put down the dish, took a step towards Brooke and raised his hands, presenting his thumbs forward towards the detective's Adam's apple. Brooke's heartbeat had picked up, and was mildly erratic. It was what Claire always called his 'jazz heart'.

'And there's these . . .' added Comfort, turning the old woman's wrists to reveal bruises on the knuckles.

Brooke actually felt the physical presence of the unsaid word itself: *murder*. Ironically, it brought the world alive, as it always did, making him adjust his tinted glasses to focus on the wounds.

'I'm amazed, considering the effects of the blast, that she put up a fight, but she clearly did. It can happen. You see road accident victims walking away from wrecked vehicles and then just falling down dead. It's as if everyone has enough energy left to escape, or at least to try, but no more.' Comfort had produced a small cigar, which he lit up.

'So you think she fought with the thief in the bedroom as he tried to take the rings?'

'That's your department,' said the pathologist, slipping a black dinner jacket from a hook and swinging it expertly around his shoulders.

'Or perhaps she cried out and he had to silence her,' added Brooke.

The pathologist set the sheet back over Nora's head before walking to the wall, turning off the lights and opening one of the blackout boards so that they could see the city spread below, bathed now in moonlight.

'It's a conundrum, Brooke,' said Comfort. 'Out there – to the south, in France – soldiers are dying, have died, in their thousands. Civilians too. But here we are worrying about a single death. An old woman killed in a seedy burglary.'

Brooke nodded. 'That's war. This is murder. I'm done with war – or it's done with me. A thousand dead in battle – that's a statistic. One death is a tragedy. This killer thinks we're too distracted to care, too distracted to bother. I'm going to prove him wrong.'

CHAPTER TWELVE

They parted company on the steps of the Galen, Comfort striding away in a cloud of Havana smoke while Brooke doubled back towards the river, along Trumpington Street, towards the pale, soaring mass of the Fitzwilliam Museum, home for 'the Duration' to the city's Bomb Control Centre. His father had always called it the Fitz, exhibiting as always an easy familiarity with great institutions. His mother had been a trustee, and had often taken her son round, filling in biographical detail on the 'moderns' – having no interest in anything painted before the turn of the century. Family anecdotes were rare in Brooke's childhood but the great ball held at the Fitz was an exception. Brooke's grandfather – an academic pathologist – had been there to celebrate the installation of a new vice-chancellor. The invitations to this great event had been much sought after, fought over, even forged. The building, a towering statement of self-importance in Portland stone, had been half finished, but a grand ceremony was required. There'd been no gas, let alone electricity, so they'd put wax tealights on high niches. His grandfather claimed six hundred guests had danced the night away. There had been champagne and glittering conversation. The dripping wax left blotches on the bare shoulders of the ladies. His grandfather noted, with a medical man's eye, that the result was not dissimilar to the early stages of leprosy.

Tonight the building, a vision more at home on the slopes of the Acropolis, looked deserted, the entrance lost in the impenetrable shadows below the towering portico. The two lions set to either side, as big as those in Trafalgar Square, were lost in shadow, but must be there, because Brooke had climbed on them as a child and knew every etched claw, but they were invisible at their posts. Legend suggested they came to life each night and ambled down into the street to drink from the wide stone gutters, built to bring fresh water into town and save it from disease. Brooke heard a clock strike ten, then strained to hear the lions creeping away, but there was nothing but silence. As he peered into the dark, the image of Nora Pollard's taut throat, bruised by the killer's thumbs, seemed to loom into view. The case had altered: looting and desecration had become murder, and the weight of the enquiry to come seemed to press down with the weight of the night.

'Who goes there?' asked a voice, which made him start.

A soldier materialised from the shadows. Brooke held out his warrant card and a torchlight suddenly blazed.

'Through the doors, down the stairs.'

A sign over the double copper doors read *BOMB CONTROL CENTRE by order of the REGIONAL COMMISSIONER*. According to the note he'd picked up at the duty desk, the BCC had been instructed to help the Borough in tracking down the looters, assistance Brooke felt he now desperately needed.

The museum's entrance hall was deserted. Above, the glass circular dome let in starlight, while the marble staircase led up in splendour, a pair of caryatids flanking the entrance to the galleries where his grandfather had danced. To the left and right smaller staircases led down to the lower basement.

Brooke took the steps down to the right, flanked by Assyrian sculptures of bird-men and gods. Most of the museum's treasures had been packed up and moved to a country house in North Wales, watched over by a rota of staff who were banished for the purpose. The upper galleries were empty, although a series of special exhibitions did attract crowds – especially of bored servicemen. The lower galleries had also been cleared, although a few of the larger Egyptian and ancient works were too big to move. As Brooke emerged in the gloom he could see dust sheets over mysterious objects.

A chair was set on the stone floor, beside a small table, on which stood a telephone. A soldier in fatigues sat stoically, illuminated by a single lightbulb which had been slung over a beam above.

Brooke wondered if the guard had fallen asleep, as he sprang to his feet, dropping his rifle, and while trying to pick it up battled to refasten the buttons on his tunic.

'I'm expected,' he said. 'Inspector Brooke, from the Borough Police.'

He was told to wait on a stone bench.

Left alone, he found the shadows unnerving. He could see the legs of a monumental stone figure which ascended into the dark, its torso and head unseen, and the upright lid of a sarcophagus.

'Eden?' said a voice, making him jump for the second time. A soldier emerged, a major's crown on his epaulettes catching the light. 'Did I startle you?'

The face which emerged was more in keeping with the hidden Egyptian artefacts than the British Army: large brown eyes, sallow olive skin, the sharp architectural lines of the face of a pharaoh.

It took him a second to realise that it was a face he knew.

'Good God – Edmund,' he said, shaking hands warmly.

'Yes. I've just arrived. I was going to look you up. But you can rely on fate. It is really good to see you. Come on in. There's tea. There's always bloody tea. It looks like a false alarm by the way – the siren – yet again, but after last night we can't relax. That's why you're here of course, Madingley gave us the heads-up, bit of mischief in the Kite, I hear . . .'

Beyond an arch, a corridor led towards a distant light. Brooke followed the outline of his old friend's familiar silhouette.

Edmund Kohler had been the battalion quartermaster in the desert, in sole charge of supplies. This required an ability to deal with highly complex situations, a gift for what was now described in the modern army as 'logistics'. Kohler's father had been a senior Egyptian diplomat, who'd studied at Oxford and married into the minor British nobility. In the desert Brooke's men had called his son 'Johnny Turk' behind his back, exhibiting cheerful ignorance, but Brooke had told them many times that they owed their lives to Kohler's loyal skills, especially in the rationing and supply of water, and that Egypt was, after all, a British protectorate. Even so, the murmurs never ceased.

At the end of the corridor a steel door swung back to reveal the BCC in all its glory, safely tucked away behind the six-foot-thick stone walls of the museum's old vault. Here, each night, the authorities' response to air attacks was coordinated, under the theoretical direction of the regional commissioner.

One wall was floodlit and held a large map of Cambridge itself, while the wall opposite carried one of East Anglia, reaching to the sea. Bomb attacks had been plotted with pins holding flags. A trestle table stood in the centre of the room where six women in civilian clothes sat at an array of telephones. In one corner Brooke could see a radio operator, headphones in place. A telegraph printer chattered.

'It's not the Bristol Hotel,' said Kohler, bringing him a mug of tea.

In the desert war they'd set up battalion headquarters in Cairo's plushest hostelry. A vivid image came to Brooke of a large gin and tonic, with ice, served by a uniformed flunkey, marking the unit's return from the first battles of the Egyptian campaign.

'But it is pretty safe,' added Kohler, sipping the tea and taking off his cap. The lights were very bright, in contrast to the shadows, so Brooke slipped on his ochre-tinted glasses.

Kohler looked away briefly. 'Ask me, the whole bloody building's a monstrosity,' he said. 'But the floors are three feet thick and the walls would withstand a direct hit. So, ideal really, and we're opposite the hospital. All very handy.'

For a minute they swapped news, catching up on children and desert comrades.

'And Claire . . . ?' asked Kohler.

'Yes. She's fine.' Brooke realised with a shock that Kohler had been a guest at his wedding. The pleasant thought occurred that he might have stumbled on a new nighthawk, another friend condemned to work at night. 'And you're back in harness, Edmund?'

'Yes, sort of. Retired, at forty-five. Had to dust off the uniform when the call came. They wanted quartermaster skills. Otherwise,

I'm up at Celia's house in the Borders. You should come and see us, Eden. Six thousand acres, rolling away to the North Sea. You always were a great walker.

'The locals are in a real bind. I'm the lord of the manor, and despite the modern age there's a lot of forelock touching, but they can't help staring at my face. The children always give the game away. They don't know what they shouldn't see.'

There was a silence in which Brooke considered the extent to which the passage of time made it difficult to recover lost friendship.

He was going to cut to business but Kohler beat him to it.

'How can I help? I understand we may have an issue with civilian discipline,' he said coolly, watching one of the women taking a call, making a note. The radio operator was talking softly, without any sense of urgency. With each passing minute the moment for sounding the all-clear was getting closer.

'Yes. A case of looting,' said Brooke. 'One of the dead was a woman who'd had two fingers hacked off to get at her rings. But I'm afraid things are much worse than we thought. I've just come from the mortuary. The pathologist is certain she was strangled. She put up a fight despite the lethal injuries of the blast.'

Kohler's eyes widened slightly.

'It changes everything of course. A bit of light-fingered theft in the ruins of a bomb site is one thing. We could have let the mutilation of the fingers pass. Now I've got a murderer to catch, and I need to catch him fast. But as you can imagine I have few leads . . . So I need your help, Edmund.'

'How?'

'I need to understand how all this works,' said Brooke, which wasn't really an answer to the question.

Kohler nodded, but there was disappointment in his eyes, as if Brooke had let him down.

'I see. Right – well, let's take a typical raid.'

The normal sequence of events had a chilling inevitability. The radar stations on the East Coast – Chain Home – were the front line, unless reconnaissance aircraft managed to spot incoming bombers over the North Sea. Radio and military landlines were used to alert BCCs inland, which in turn alerted Observer Corps and local airfields.

'Newmarket's our key forward post,' said Kohler. 'They've got radar up on the downs, and ack-ack guns, and a flight of searchlights. If they pick up anything at all they tell us pronto. Then we have a pretty simple decision to make. If the information is credible, and there's any realistic chance of a raid, I ring the Guildhall and the siren goes off.

'We also contact Marshall's and local RAF stations so they can try and put something up to make things difficult for the bombers. The barrage balloons are flying already, of course. They do a job – no doubts about that.'

Once the siren had sounded, explained Kohler, the local emergency services placed themselves on standby for a location to be released by the BCC. The city had six Observer Posts with trained operatives able to track incoming bombers and calculate bearing, speed and height. That information was 'short-circuited' direct to the ack-ack guns. Once a bomb fell, any of the recognised services could ring in the location, or they could rely on the Observer Corps again, as all the posts had direct landlines to the BCC.

'Once we know what we've got on the ground we dispatch what we think they'll need. Each of the services – fire, bomb disposal, ambulance – have their own dedicated telephone lines. And we've got six motorcycle messengers on duty at any time.'

Brooke surveyed the map of the city he knew so well.

'You didn't mention police,' he said, smiling.

'I'll ring the Spinning House if there's an issue – closing roads, keeping back the sightseers. It's not a priority, I'll grant you that. Once a bomb's dropped your boys seem to be there within minutes anyway.'

Brooke nodded.

'Anything else?' asked Kohler.

Brooke shook his head.

'Give me a minute,' said Kohler, breaking off to chat briefly with the telephone operators and the radio man. After examining a telegraph tickertape, he picked up one of the phones and dialled a number.

Kohler raised his voice. 'BCC here. Major Kohler. Today's code word is "yellow". You can sound the all-clear.'

The radio operator lit a cigarette and one of the girls stood up, stretching, and asked if anyone wanted a cup of tea.

Kohler headed for the doors, waving Brooke to follow.

They passed the guard and climbed up to the atrium, under the circular glass dome. The stars were brighter, but the silence profound, until they heard the thin wail of the Guildhall siren.

The sense of the space above them, big enough to accommodate a church, was oddly threatening.

Brooke put on his hat, adjusting it.

Kohler smiled, offering a silver cigarette case. 'It's alright, Eden. I've worked it out for myself. Nothing personal.'

Kohler lit his cigarette and jerked his head to one side to avoid the cloud of sulphur. 'There's a Russian fable about a man who goes to a museum – one just like this, I think. He notes all the details – every exhibit, every carefully inscribed note under every cabinet. Later he tells someone about his visit and when he's finished his friend says, "What about the elephant?" He'd missed it, you see – a stuffed mammoth, in the middle of the main gallery.

'Never overlook the obvious. That's sound military intelligence. It's likely, isn't it, that our looter, or looters, our murderer, is in a uniform. ARP, WRVS, OC – the police, doctors, nurses. I think we're telling them where to go, where the bomb's struck. So you're not here for help at all. You're here to track down your man.'

Brooke nodded. 'Sorry. I should have been straighter. You're right; no one suspects a uniform. And it doesn't have to be bona fide, of course. They might be fakes – it's pretty easy to run up an arm band and paint a few letters on a tin hat.'

'But dangerous,' said Kohler. 'What if you get challenged? ID cards make that kind of malarkey very risky. And why bother? We're after volunteers. We pretty much take anyone.'

They smoked in silence, creating a column of grey fumes which rose up to the dome.

'But what to do, Edmund?' Brooke asked.

Kohler examined his polished boots, which reflected the dome above. 'You've been to a bomb site, Eden. It's chaos. The problem is that the priority is saving lives, not spotting opportunist thieves or charlatans.'

Brooke stepped closer. 'If it's possible I'd like a list of the volunteers we have on the street – auxiliary fire, wardens, messengers – the lot. Is that possible?'

'I can try, Eden.'

'And could you have a quiet word for me? Ask each of the services for help. You'll know who to talk to. Tell them to keep an eye out for anyone suddenly spraying cash about. The woman on Earl Street had a stash, all cash apparently. Ask them to have a chat with those they trust. Is there anyone they don't trust? If they've any suspicions just get me the name and the service. The Earl Street bomb in particular. There were all sorts there. Bomb disposal, regular army, WRVS. And yes, it might be a woman. With the men away, cash is short. Strangling an old woman already mortally wounded doesn't require a lot of brute strength. Can you see what you can get? Also, anyone who travels to the scene by bike.'

Kohler stretched, head back, looking at the statues guarding the upper galleries.

He laughed. 'Ironic, isn't it? Here we are trying to track down murderous looters in a grand museum full of looted treasures: Egypt, Assyria, Babylon, Greece. "Collected", of course, in the interests of academic enquiry, but often at the point of a sword or the barrel of a gun. But what's the real difference, Eden?'

CHAPTER THIRTEEN

As Brooke threaded his way through the city, families were appearing from the underground shelters in the city centre, clutching baggage, hauling along children half awake, heading home. The siren had released them all from the dank basements below the Guildhall. No bombs had fallen, but the drone of RAF fighters up from Marshall airfield was oppressive, circling overhead. Despite the hour Brooke felt even sleepless rest was beyond him, especially as a further opportunity was at hand to track down his murderous thief.

Ducking down All Saints' Passageway, he entered the maze

of streets which had once constituted the city's Jewish ghetto. As a child he'd memorised its twists and turns, courtyards and alleys, until he could find his way in the unlit, narrow, cobbled streets by touch alone. His route, Braille-like, led to the doors of Michaelhouse college – his alma mater – where he administered the now-standard coded knock with his signet ring: two raps, a pause, two raps. The lock on the small 'Alice-in-Wonderland' door, set within the great oak, turned smoothly.

Doric, the night porter, led the way into the lodge. Behind the counter and an array of pigeonholes was a panelled room, with a coke fire which never seemed to go out. On a griddle, a kettle steamed. The night was warm so Doric was in shirtsleeves, the cuffs held back by garters. On the hearth, three pairs of shoes lay waiting to be polished.

Doric was Brooke's longest-serving nighthawk. When Brooke had got back to Cambridge in 1919 from the sanatorium in Scarborough, the condition of his eyes had ended his studies for a degree in natural sciences. Joining the Borough had offered some moral purpose, and an intellectual challenge, but first he'd had to endure a year on the beat in uniform. A kindly mentor, a senior detective, had at least secured him a night beat to protect him from the pain in his eyes. It had been a blessed relief. His disability – photophobia – was in danger of transmuting into heliophobia – an irrational fear of light. He needed a settled routine, a worthwhile job, and Claire's support to keep the demons at bay.

Doric, an old acquaintance of his student days, had offered patient company and the unspoken sympathy of an old soldier. Privately Brooke had maintained his studies, and regular visits to the college allowed him to pick up the latest journals from his pigeonhole, kindly selected and rerouted by his former tutors.

'Did you get a note?' asked Brooke, taking a seat. He'd rung from the Spinning House before he'd gone for his swim, and left a message with one of the day porters.

Doric straightened his back, examining the room's vast clock, upon which the daily routine of the college relied. It was ten minutes to ten o'clock. 'He said he could make the hour, Mr Brooke. Burns the midnight oil, does Swift. He'll be here.'

As a student, Brooke had often taken refuge in this room, a kind of landlubber's cabin, which provided an escape from the schoolboy japes of Formal Hall. He'd found the bread-throwing cacophony of the undergraduates unbearable. Instead, he had shared Doric's supper, gleaned from leftovers and supplemented by any wine which had been opened but not drunk.

Tonight there was a plate of cold beef, some Dauphinois potatoes and a decent chunk of Stilton.

Doric set an opened bottle of Bordeaux on the hearth.

'What's afoot?' he asked, standing with his back to the fire, bouncing on his toes. A veteran of the South African wars and various Indian skirmishes, he had formed a bond with Brooke which had rarely relied on extended conversation. They often shared a companionable silence, in which Brooke remained still, while Doric exhibited his usual restless routines.

He began to polish one of the shoes.

'I need young Swift's help,' said Brooke. 'He wanted something from me, and I said no. Now I want something from him, so I'm prepared to say yes.'

Doric spat on the toecap of the brogue. 'What does he want?'

'Immortality,' said Brooke, tapping a Black Russian on the arm of the chair. 'Or glory,' he added. 'It's not uncommon, is it? The university is full of brilliant men. They wish to be successful, to carry off the glittering prizes. A place at the

Cabinet table, or the bench at the Old Bailey. Or a bishop's mitre. If they can't get one of these treasures they make one up instead. It's prizes for everyone.

'There's Byron's Pool, of course. Dive to the bottom and recover a silver cup and you're famous amongst your peers. Or the Great Court Run. Belt round Trinity's courtyard in less than what? Forty-five seconds, or forty-four, or forty-three, and you'll be lionised. An immortal, Doric. Just like Lord Burghley.'

Brooke had seen the feat. A crowd had gathered to see the annual race, held on the day before the matriculation dinner. The challenge had been set: to run 400 yards in the time it took for the college clock to chime midday. Brooke had always felt this was a cheat, because Trinity's clock sounded the four quarters first, and then the hour twice – hitting a low note first, high second. And if they forgot to wind the clock it took even longer. And Brooke guessed – being a natural scientist – that the atmospheric pressure affected the delicate mechanism of the flywheel. So who really knew the time?

Doric slurped his wine. 'Easier before the last war, a course. They started in a corner back then, so they only had to run round three corners. Now they start by the gate.' He shook his head at the blind stupidity this revealed. 'So they have to run round four. That's what slows 'em down.'

'Yes, but Burghley has his glittering prize,' said Brooke. That day, with him cheering along, the young athlete had beaten the final chime. The first man to achieve the feat.

'Young Swift wants his own such prize,' said Brooke.

For half an hour Brooke read the porter's evening paper and an article on the geology of Swaziland, while Doric produced a luminous shine on his black shoes.

When Vin Swift appeared he looked every inch the 'captain'

he was: about five foot ten, Brooke judged, with a very small torso but extended limbs – great levers turning on fulcrums of cartilage and bone. His head was small and round, with his hair oiled back, so that it was difficult not to see it as deliberately aerodynamic. He stood before them in his college suit, shifting from narrow foot to foot.

Brooke cut to the chase. Vin Swift was captain of the Clarion Club, a cycling fraternity, originally springing from radical political roots in the 1930s. It had a reputation for mild disorder, its speeding peloton thundering through quiet villages or round the city's parks. The year before it had applied to the Borough for permission to establish an annual race, loosely based on the Great Court Run. A route had been suggested, comprising the Backs, Trinity Street, King's Parade and Silver Street Bridge. The time target was to be set by Great St Mary's chimes, between the hour and quarter past.

'The Clarion race,' said Brooke. 'There's still interest?'

The official request, asking for the streets to be closed, had been turned down by the Borough. It had, in fact, been an intervention by the county force, based in the Castle, which had scuppered the project. A note had complained of the risk that 'rowdy' behaviour would lead to public disturbances. In a city with a long memory of violent disorder, the warning had won the day.

Brooke was sure he could get Carnegie-Brown's approval for a change of heart.

Swift, who'd unfurled his limbs and slid onto a window seat, said the race was still an ambition, and they talked of it often, as the club was thriving, full of young men keen to be fit for service.

'A lot of us are doing shorter degrees, starting early. So we've less time, but that just means you pack more in, make the most

100

of it. And we let in townies, if they can ride, and if they train. So numbers are up.'

Brooke jettisoned the Black Russian into the embers of the coke.

'We can let you have your race,' he said. 'No promises. Let's just say the Borough's behind you. But we need something from you. A quid pro quo. How many members in the Clarion?'

'Sixty – a few more.'

'How many bicycles in Cambridge?'

Swift shook his head, laughing. Doric, taking up position on the hearth, blew out his cheeks.

'Ten thousand?' offered Brooke. 'A few more, a few less. I make that one keen Clarion man to every one hundred and fifty bikes. They're not all on the street, of course. Not all the time. Hallways, college bike sheds, maybe, but mostly railings, walls, alleys. Factories too, thousands there, in bike sheds. At the station, too.'

Brooke stood. 'I want you to find one bicycle, Mr Swift. But it's a rare one.'

Edison had collected an advertising flyer from a new cycle shop at Mitcham's Corner.

Vin studied it with a light in his eyes.

He turned out to be a minor expert on the brand. The Lucifer was sold in Paris, through a department store called Mestre & Blatge, which had an outlet in London. But the bike was rare. He'd never seen one in Cambridge.

'Two hundred and fifteen francs,' said Swift, nodding. 'A nice machine.'

Brooke nodded. 'This one isn't brand new. In fact it's battered – probably second-hand. It's blue, and it'll have that badge that's on the flyer – the name, and the sunburst of light.'

Brooke felt a bolt of impatience. It was likely the killer didn't yet know the bike had been spotted, but gossip, and the search, might raise the alarm. They had to act quickly and track it down.

'If you find the bike, send someone to the Spinning House straight away,' he said. 'Don't do anything else. Don't approach the owner – but keep tabs. Find me Lucifer, Vin. Then you can have your moment of glory.'

CHAPTER FOURTEEN

Helmut Bartel, and his one-time best man Walther Schmidt, stood outside the main hanger at Waren airfield, thirty miles north of Berlin. It was late evening, and the stars overhead stretched from the woods in the east to the woods in the west. The scent of damp pine needles was almost hypnotic. They smoked with little enthusiasm, cradling cups of chestnut coffee, contemplating the Heinkel, which was being serviced by the ground crew within the hangar, while connected to a fuel bowser – a tanker on tractor wheels – by a long snaking articulated pipe. The lights by which the men worked spilt out over the grass.

The Heinkel, up on blocks, had been scarred by its encounter with ack-ack fire over Cambridge two nights before. The dorsal fuselage was pitted with shot, and a charcoal-grey stain marked the area of the port wing that had briefly caught fire. Damaged fabric had been stripped from the fuselage frame to reveal the struts, a disturbing vision of the skeleton within, which looked impossibly fragile. They had returned at dawn, limping back, trailing smoke – and when the ground crew had got inside the aircraft they'd found Muller, the top gunner, dead in his harness, hanging like a pheasant or a partridge from a butcher's hook.

'She's almost ready,' said Schmidt, nodding in the direction of the aircraft. 'Another few hours, a coat of paint, and we'll be back in the air. Perhaps tomorrow, or even tonight? Why a briefing at this hour?'

A note had gone up in the mess after dinner informing them that the commandant would brief the crew at 20.30 hours.

Relaxed, even jovial, Bartel's friend nevertheless now lived on his nerves like the rest of them. The Cambridge raid had sucked any sense of adventure from the crew. They'd been lucky to survive. Since their return there had been no leave, no communication at all with wives and families, and so the idea that they had in fact *not returned*, but were held in some forest purgatory, had enveloped them all in a gloomy lethargy. At night, at precisely this time, Bartel wondered whether his wife and daughters even knew if he was alive at all. Or did they imagine the Heinkel falling to earth, or arrowing into the grey waters of the German Ocean?

'This tastes of ash and nothing else,' said Bartel, throwing the stub of his cigarette to the ground with a look of self-disgust.

A bomb rack was approaching, towed by a tractor, and the ground crew had opened the doors of the 'bathtub' – the low-slung cabin through which the crew climbed aboard, and through which the payload would be winched into position behind the glass cockpit and the nose cone.

'My money's on tonight,' said Schmidt, looking away, towards the dark forest. While they were all depressed by inaction, the idea of flying again made Bartel's guts twist.

'Perhaps,' he said. 'Let's wait for the briefing. You know as well as I do, Walther, that it depends on the decisions of others, on the weather, on the target, but most of all on the much-lauded grand strategy.'

It was remarkable how quickly they had all become cynical about the abilities of the high command.

'They're throwing everything at London. We may have to join this great armada in the air. Or we may be a lone wolf again with our own target – the docks at Hull, perhaps. It is out of our hands, my friend. So why worry?'

London was the talk of the mess. Maps and diagrams of the capital's docks had been pinned up in the bar. There were rumours in Berlin, relayed to Waren by the cooks and the cleaners, the barman and the farmer who brought them milk, rumours of a 'knockout blow' ahead of an invasion. And there was talk of revenge for the RAF's first daring raid on the German capital, of which there was still no news concerning casualties or damage.

Bartel had his eyes on the commandant's quarters, a squat rustic bungalow with its own picket fence, which stood beside the gates on the far side of the runway.

'Here he comes,' he said, removing tobacco from his upper lip.

Oberst Fritsch had appeared, striding out across the grass, a folder loosely held against his chest.

Bartel buttoned up his tunic to the throat, and they walked to the briefing hut. The night was soft and the dew had begun to settle. The hut – at one time a small sports pavilion when the airfield was set out during the Great War – had a veranda and decorative woodwork. Bartel always thought it looked like a house from a fairy tale set in the woods, which made him think of his daughter Helga, and her invariable demands for a bedtime story. The baby – Ellen – would no doubt follow suit. If he lived long enough his life would be full of children's stories.

It was clear that Oberst Fritsch's story would be less of a comfort to his men. By the time Bartel and Schmidt had joined their crewmates on the stiff chairs set out in a row, their commanding officer had pinned up a series of aerial photographs on the ops board.

'These have arrived from Berlin in the last hour. They are taken from thirty thousand feet,' said Fritsch, swelling slightly, his polished buttons straining. 'But pin-sharp.'

Bartel's heart sank. All the shots showed the same landscape. A river running north, shadowed by a railway line, which crossed the water on a girder bridge. It was their one-time target in Cambridge: Bridge 1505.

'There is no doubt, I am afraid,' said Fritsch. 'Despite your optimism you failed to destroy the bridge. You must return. This is now a target of the utmost importance.'

Fritsch's weakness was cognac, and once he'd had enough, he was happy to regale his men with tales of his heroics in the Great War, when he had been a pioneer in the new science of aerial photography. At the Somme they'd attached cameras to balloons to get a view of the battlefield. Then to rockets, launched from behind the lines. But very quickly the pre-eminence of the aeroplane had been established. The necessary technical breakthrough had been the heated camera, which had allowed the aircraft to operate at high altitudes, beyond the range of fighters, or shells. Fritsch had piloted such craft into the stratosphere, and wore the Iron Cross as proof.

'Bridge 1505,' said Fritsch, leaning over and tapping a pointer on one of the pictures, revealing a shaving accident visible just below the line of his lumpen jaw, which he'd staunched with cotton wool.

'This was taken this morning shortly after dawn from 30,000 feet. Note the approaching goods train to the south. Sixty trucks. Empty. And here,' he added, pointing at the next picture. 'This shows the same bridge, but in a second pass over the target two minutes later. The same train, now to the north of the river. So our bridge still stands, still functions, gentlemen. See for yourself – *Leutnant?*'

Couched as an invitation, it was in fact an order, an act of ritual humiliation.

Bartel stood and walked forward, taking a seat at a small table, upon which Fritsch set two apparently identical photographs. Bartel thrust his head into the aperture of an instrument set on the table which resembled a double microscope. It provided two magnified images of the photographs, allowing Bartel's brain to merge them stereoscopically to form a three-dimensional image. The result was shockingly clear: the bridge stood, the river glittered beneath, the train thundered confidently north. On the river he could even see the fragile outline of a boat, an 'eight' – he'd rowed himself at home and noted the perfectly aligned oars. On either side of the river lay water meadows, and the mathematical grid of a set of small-holdings, *Schrebergärten* – allotments.

'We must go back. We must go back soon,' said Fritsch. 'The key is the weather. There are at present no clouds to provide the cover we require. So not tonight. We are not – yet – in the business of flying suicide missions. Rest, or play football if you must, but if anyone breaks a leg I will personally sign their transfer permit to the Kriegsmarine and they can fly paper kites off a rolling deck for the rest of the war. You must enjoy the country air because there is no leave to Berlin. Everyone is confined to the base.'

There was silence then, as if he was daring them to complain.

'Is it the raid?' asked Bartel. 'There are rumours of devastation, of casualties.' His rank gave him this privilege, to ask the questions the others didn't dare. 'The cook says the RAF bombed the southern suburbs, and that the U-Bahn took a hit.'

Fritsch bounced slightly in his polished boots. 'The cook should keep his mouth shut and concentrate on not boiling the potatoes to mush.' He held up both hands. 'The raid was a blow. But the damage was restricted. Yes, there have been casualties, but the city goes about its work and play as it always did. You will have leave soon.

'Be patient. You are confined to the base, gentlemen, because I do not want anyone to go AWOL. The mission is of the utmost importance. A night in the bars of Berlin, or worse, the whorehouses, is not ideal preparation for such duties. And now. Pay attention.'

They took notes as Fritsch talked them through the flight plan. This time they would fly further north and approach from the coast of the Wash, that great gulf of sand and shallow tidal creeks which ate into the coastline of East Anglia. The river would lead them to the target again. Anti-aircraft fire was concentrated to the south and east. If they flew low, and fast, the fighters would still be on the ground when they struck. This time they must leave Bridge 1505 in ruins.

CHAPTER FIFTEEN

Brooke walked home along the towpath, exhausted now and desperate for rest, if not sleep. He'd done all he could to set in motion a murder enquiry: the hunt was on for the mysterious Lucifer, with the help of the Clarion Cycling Club, and Major Kohler would even now be making discreet enquiries with civil defence and the emergency services; if the brutal thief was hidden behind a uniform he might well have given himself away – a spending spree, perhaps, or an over-diligent search of a bombed-out house. Tomorrow, he'd go back to Earl Street and interview neighbours, friends and the oddly dysfunctional

Pollard family. For now he planned to take to his bed, and wait for Claire to finish her night shift at the hospital.

Heading south, he reached the wider water meadows, where the path was marked by superannuated gas lamps, set out by the Victorians to illuminate starlit skating. They reminded Brooke of winter, but only briefly, because the warm soft night spoke only of the summer's day that had gone: cloudless and hot. His Blakeys cracked on the gravel path, alerting a herd of ghostly white cattle, prompting an exodus through a gate towards a shadowy barn.

A quarter mile further brought him close to home, a cluster of old villas hidden amongst willows and ash. Here the main river took a tight looping horseshoe curve, and ahead of him on the path, on the 'inside' bank, he saw distinctly a man, on a camp stool, beside a glow-worm light, by which he appeared to be sketching. Brooke stopped, undetected, and watched for a moment.

The moon was just a sliver rising feebly over the trees, so Brooke took the opportunity to jettison his glasses at last, feeling with a sense of relief the cool air on his eyes. (His actual vision was 20:20 – although everyone who saw the tinted lenses assumed he had the sight of a mole.) The figure by the river stood and Brooke saw it was a man, and recognised the way in which he set his stout legs squarely apart as he consulted a book by torchlight.

The air was extraordinarily still, and every sound seemed uncannily clear: the trickle of the summer river, the distant *brr! brr!* of the nighthawk, so that when he whispered the word it felt as if he'd launched a shout: 'Peter?'

The man turned in his direction. 'Eden? I thought you might come past one evening. I hope this is evidence that you are following my regime and going home to bed?'

As they shook hands Brooke produced his packet of Black Russians and they both lit up.

The lantern was set on a riverside bench so that it illuminated an open sketchbook, which was dotted with numbers and hieroglyphs and a grid of data. Dr Peter Aldiss had shared college rooms with Brooke before the Great War. A natural scientist, he was currently engaged in a series of experiments investigating the mysterious forces of circadian rhythm – nature's extraordinary ability to match day and night to the needs and appetites of the animal kingdom. The work had caught the attention of Whitehall and the military, keen to find ways of keeping soldiers and sailors, not to mention pilots, alert during the long watches of the night. Aldiss was one of Brooke's fellow nighthawks, and he'd often spend an hour in the scientist's laboratory, watching over scuttling cockroaches, glowing fireflies or whispering hamsters.

This was a departure: science outside the laboratory.

'Let me guess,' said Brooke, watching the moonlight pick out the thread of a current in the river. 'Is it owls? Are you monitoring their flights and mapping them against the progress of the moon?'

'A change of tack,' said Aldiss, lowering the light in the lantern. 'I'll show you – take a seat, and let your eyes get used to the shadows.' He offered Brooke a metal box to sit on as the grass bank was already shiny with dew.

They sat diligently, the light shielded, their eyes switching to night vision. Brooke contemplated his friend, who sat with his hands on his lap as if they were dead weights. His intelligence was undoubted, but not apparent. People who met him were initially underwhelmed, guessing perhaps that he was a not very bright county solicitor. Dr Aldiss thought slowly, but with deliberate care, and often devastating logic. He was a master of patient experiment.

'See?' asked Aldiss at last, nodding to the far side of the narrow river, which lay in the shadow of a steep bank. 'The question is, what makes them bloom now?'

Brooke stared into the darkness and saw nothing. Then one pale disc appeared, then twenty, then a hundred, until finally the colour was perhaps just discernible: a hint of yellow?

'*Oenothera biennis*,' said Aldiss. 'Evening primrose to you. I'm trying to work out if it's the moon that makes them bloom, or the temperature, or even the humidity. It's a mystery. In broad daylight they're shut up like clams.'

'But why?' asked Brooke. 'Why bloom at night?'

Aldiss held out a small tin and flipped the lid. Inside was a large moth, pinned to its cushion. Brooke felt a distinct sense of sadness at the sight of such a delicate life, skewered to its nametag. Not for the first time he forgave his desert torturers for robbing him of a career in the natural sciences.

'The sphinx moth,' said Aldiss, which made Brooke think of Edmund Kohler, in his major's uniform. 'It pollinates the flowers, and it's nocturnal, or possibly crepuscular – that's another small mystery. Just like your good self, Eden. It thrives at dawn and dusk.'

Brooke's condition had provided Aldiss with a living experiment, and a laboratory specimen he could interrogate.

For a few minutes Aldiss made notes. There were also plants on this side of the river, opening close to their feet, and he knelt down with a micrometer and measured the degree to which the petals had opened.

Eventually Aldiss closed the book. 'I must get back to the lab. I may even sleep. Then it's back at dawn.'

He began to pack up his gear with practised efficiency.

'And how is the new regime?' he asked Brooke, folding the footstool. 'I trust you've followed it to the letter.'

Brooke's sleeplessness had prompted the scientist to proffer a cure: Aldiss had been the one to set out the daily routine for him to follow, including at least an attempt at going to bed at a regular hour, after food and a hot bath, and an early walk in the light.

'Do you want the numbers?' asked Brooke.

'Of course.' Aldiss worked to the classic pattern: hypotheses were all very well. But in the end it was the hard numbers that really mattered; the very stuff of science.

'In the last thirty days I have slept through the night twice.'

'Compared to?'

'In the previous thirty – once. In the thirty before that, none at all.'

'There you are then. It's very slow progress, but progress nonetheless. You may find that the odd night's proper sleep is eventually habit-forming. Give it time.'

Brooke was thankful for the two nights, and much else, because it was Aldiss who'd first suggested that his insomnia – while undoubtedly prompted by his torture in the desert – might actually be to a degree inherent. This idea, that in some way his disability was a gift of birth, had made it easier to sleep, or at least easier to fail to sleep.

'Go to bed, Eden,' said Aldiss, shouldering his knapsack. 'Or do you have a case that can't wait for daylight to be solved?'

Brooke contemplated the river flowing past. The peaceful scene, the gently flowering primroses, jarred badly with the concept of murder, so he told his friend instead about the river catching fire, and that Grandcourt was even now seeking out the best brains in chemistry to analyse the liquid. He told him that the 'authorities', as such, had turned a blind eye to an earlier incident, and seemed happy to turn a blind eye to this one too. And he told him about the apparently coincidental links with the looting on Earl Street.

Aldiss seemed to absorb the information, and Brooke felt he

could almost hear the wheels of his mind turning, processing, ordering, storing.

'It's in delicate balance, a river,' said Aldiss. 'Pouring petrol in it won't exactly enhance its subtle rhythms.'

'Will you keep an eye out?' asked Brooke. 'Or rather a nose?'

'I will conduct a survey,' said Aldiss. 'I will take a sample each night, at the same time, and keep a record because I am a scientist. Police work seems to consist of guesswork and chance.'

Brooke laughed. 'On a good day.'

'I have three research sites for this experiment – here, and two more up towards Audley End. So that's three lots of data. But I can do better than that. I've inveigled two of my undergraduate students and Dr Sutton from chemistry to lend a helping hand. All of them have three sites, and all upriver. Even more data, Eden. We'll have enough to put forward a sound hypothesis. We'll find the culprit. It's probably a farmyard leaking fuel from a storage tank.'

'Thank you,' said Brooke. 'If they find anything, let me know – the Spinning House will take a note if you phone.'

He was going to leave it at that but the niggling coincidence, the possibility of a link to Earl Street, made him pause. 'And Peter. Tell these students of yours that if they do spot something, just come to me, or you, with a location. Don't investigate. Don't snoop. It's not worth it, and it might be dangerous.'

CHAPTER SIXTEEN

Brooke slept intermittently until dawn, when the first anxieties of the day ahead began to snare his overactive mind. Claire lay beside him in a deep slumber, so he slipped out of bed and made tea in the kitchen, taking a mug down to the riverside, where the Cam had been transformed into a channel of threaded mist, just an inch above the surface. Then the sun rose above the trees, a pale disc, and the heat burnt off the vapour, to reveal the green river beneath a blue sky. The temptation to take a swim was almost overwhelming, but he had a murderer to catch, so he left a note on the kitchen table, and fled.

By seven-thirty he was in Carnegie-Brown's office, where he delivered a résumé of Dr Comfort's preliminary results. The chief inspector's judgement concurred with Brooke's: the likelihood was the killer was an opportunist thief. There was no reason to believe organised looters had launched a brutal campaign to rob and kill the dead, and therefore no need to alert the Home Office, or more pertinently Scotland Yard. The press would be told that an elderly woman had been killed and robbed, but the mutilation of the body would remain confidential. The chief inspector would contact County and request uniformed assistance for door-to-door enquiries and other footwork. Brooke was to be afforded all the assistance necessary for a murder enquiry.

Back in his office he found Edison, and two young women, sat on his 'Nile Bed' – the day cot he'd brought on the quayside at Port Said, which was decorated with images of green rushes and white exotic birds.

Edison introduced them as Elsie and Connie Wylde, two of Nora Pollard's granddaughters.

'You'd better repeat what you've told me, girls,' said Edison, standing with his back to the door. The sergeant's advanced years excused the use of 'girls'. He could be their grandfather. As to their ages, Brooke would have guessed Elsie was twenty, and Connie perhaps seventeen or eighteen. He couldn't be sure. Young people were always eager to look like adults, and the war had accelerated the trend. Sometimes there seemed to be no intervening developmental stage between childhood and middle age.

Elsie wore no make-up, had an untidy bob, and was dressed in brown overalls. Connie, the younger, had shoulder-length hair, and she'd made a half-hearted attempt to apply lipstick. She wore a skirt and polished black shoes. Both had lively pea-green eyes, and fashionably pale skin.

'Mum's worried,' said Elsie. 'Our sister Peggy's disappeared.'

Brooke recalled the stiff-backed matriarch Alice Wylde. He'd have to inform her soon – as next of kin – that her elderly mother had been murdered in her own home. It wasn't the kind of information he could blithely tell her daughters.

'Peggy's the oldest,' said Connie, and suddenly burst into tears. Elsie clung harder to her sister.

'Can you just tell me what's happened, in the order in which it has happened?' Brooke asked. He produced some cigarettes and both girls took one.

Edison fled to get tea. Elsie told the story, but Connie chipped in.

The Wyldes lived on Palmer Road, half a mile from Earl Street, but still in the Kite. The three girls had gone to work early on the morning after the air raid. Their mother was a charlady at some solicitors' offices in town and had left the house at dawn. It was only when one of the lawyers came in from court that she learnt that there had been casualties on Earl Street. She'd asked for an hour off and rushed back to the Kite to check if all was well at number 36. Brooke had interviewed her in the wreck of the Wellington Arms.

By that time the three girls were at work. Connie had been behind the counter at Robert Sayle, a draper's and department store a few doors away from the Spinning House along St Andrew's Street. Elsie worked at a factory along the river which turned out utility items, such as cheap chairs and tables, to meet the growing demand. Peggy had cycled off to work at Marshall airfield, where they trained RAF pilots and patched up the planes. Peggy worked in the 'fabric' shed, repairing wear and tear on the aircraft.

The girls always met at four-thirty at a tearoom on Peas Hill, a treat after work. Alice decided to join them and tell them the bad news, although the rumour mill was already buzzing with gossip about casualties in the Kite. Alice arrived late, hoping they'd all be there, but there was no sign of Peggy. She told the two sisters what had happened, then they waited an hour but Peggy still didn't appear, so they went home.

Edison came back with tea and the girls each took a cup.

'Peggy never turned up, she's just vanished – hasn't she, Con?' said Elsie. They had an odd sisterly habit of talking to each other without looking at each other.

'When was the last time she was seen?' asked Brooke.

'Harriet, who lives down our street, works in the same shed,' said Elsie. 'She says she had lunch with Peggy – well, they sat out on the apron of the airfield and had their sandwiches. She said that by then the gossip was that an elderly couple had died in the Kite. Peggy was really worried it was her nan and grandad, but Harriet told her it was daft to worry because there's hundreds of houses, and it was just gossip. Peggy told her she'd be seeing us at the tea shop as usual. At clocking off, Harriet saw her ahead in the line and then she disappeared.'

'Time?' asked Edison, who'd started making a note.

'That's four o'clock,' said Elsie.

The day was already hot and Edison opened the window, carefully avoiding lifting the blinds, which kept the light levels low. The distant sound of children in the playground at the nearby school flooded in, and it seemed to make everyone relax.

'How old is Peggy?' asked Brooke.

'Twenty-one,' said Elsie.

'So she's old enough to do what she wants. Is there a boyfriend? Maybe she's upset – maybe she found out what had happened and she's with friends. Does she ever stay out overnight?'

'She gets moods,' said Connie. 'She's got friends she doesn't tell us about. She stays out sometimes with girlfriends, but it sends

Mum mad – she says she's Wylde by name, wild by nature. There's loads of boyfriends. And she's talked about running off, leaving home and that, finding a new life that's not boring. But she'd never do it without telling us.'

'And there's been absolutely no word?' pressed Brooke.

'Not a thing,' said Elsie. 'Mum went round last night to relatives and that. And to neighbours – everyone. She rang the factory from the box on the corner this morning and got the charge hand. She's not turned up. We share a room and she didn't come home at all. She's just gone.'

Brooke took off his glasses and gently massaged his eyes, contemplating the coincidence: Nora Pollard is murdered after the bombing raid, and her granddaughter goes missing the next evening. He was perfectly aware that such chance occurrences happened in real life. It was just that he was, he felt, paid to make sure they were really coincidences. He had a murderer on the loose, and now a missing girl.

'Where is your mum now?'

'Out looking. She's taken her bike and she's checking round again. Once she's got the bit between her teeth there's no stopping our mum.'

Again, the conspiratorial family smile.

Brooke told Edison to take a statement while he got the duty sergeant to put a call into Addenbrooke's Hospital. 'That'll be it, you'll see. Your sister's come off her bike and she'll have had concussion and got her leg up in a sling.'

They all got to their feet.

Brooke reached for his hat. 'I want you to give my sergeant a description of Peggy – and get a picture from home of your sister too,' he added. 'What was she wearing?'

'A blue dress,' they said in unison.

'Sky blue – that was her colour,' said Elsie. 'And it had a white belt.'

'That helps. Anything else of note? Shoes? Gas mask?'

'She's a bit of a film star is our Peggy, so she decorated her gas mask with sequins and it had tassels, didn't it, Elsie?'

Elsie nodded.

'And her bike?'

'Red,' they said in unison.

'It's old – it was Mum's first,' said Elsie. 'Is it a BSA or something?'

'That's it,' said Connie. 'Dad used to say they made rifles in the war.'

'British Small Arms,' said Edison, making a fresh note.

'We'll get the *News* to run an item, saying about the dress, and the gas mask, and the red BSA bicycle,' said Brooke.

'Why do you need to do that?' asked Connie.

'We need to find her as quickly as we can, and make sure she's not hurt, or upset.' Brooke opened the door to usher them out. 'Don't worry. We'll find her.'

CHAPTER SEVENTEEN

Marshall airfield stood on the eastern edge of the city, a grass plain across which the wind blew straight from the pole in winter, until it tore at the Nissan huts or rocked the frail biplanes which clustered on the apron of the runway. In summer the bleak windswept note was still present, but at least the sun gave the vista a seaside air, as if the far green edge of the horizon might be a cliff edge.

A windsock flew briskly by the entrance gate where Brooke, leaning out of the car, offered his warrant card. After a morning cooped up at the Spinning House, issuing orders for door-to-door enquiries across the Kite and trying to rope in help from County, he was relieved to be outdoors, under an open sky.

The barrier bounced up and Edison drove them past a gaggle of workers – a few young women, but mostly lads in overalls, laid out on the grass for what looked like an impromptu elevenses.

A twin-engined biplane swept over the scene, banking to land into the breeze. The union flag on the art deco 'airport' terminal building blew fitfully from the south-west.

A bristling signpost directed them anti-clockwise around the grassy runway towards two large hangars and a small cluster of Nissan huts. They asked an idle young man smoking a cigarette for the way to Fabric.

'You want the girls, then . . .' he said, brightening, and pointed to one of the sheds.

With the doors open, the hangar revealed itself as a single hall, about the size of half a football field. Several aircraft – mostly Oxfords, according to Edison, but at least one Spitfire – stood in various stages of repair, their inner bones revealed, while the 'girls' worked to cover them in fabric. Some of the aircraft, finished, had been covered in the 'dope' that would dry, stretch and form a lightweight skin. The smell of the chemical was overpowering and left Brooke slightly dizzy.

He sent Edison to ask around in the admin building to see if they had a file on the missing girl, while he sought out the foreman. He stood by a forklift truck weighed down with barrels of chemicals, and tried to spot someone in charge, juggling a Black Russian out of its pack while searching pockets for his lighter, but was brutally reprimanded by a shout: 'Oi! Can't you read?'

A man with white hair, dressed in a set of black overalls, was advancing at pace, pointing to a sign painted on the wall which must have been ten foot tall and fifty yards long:

Brooke stashed the lighter and held up a hand in surrender.

'Sorry – didn't think you'd use anything flammable on aircraft . . .'

'The dangerous stuff is nitrate dope,' he said. 'This is butyrate dope. It's only less flammable. It'll burn, but slower. And there's air fuel. That goes up with a bang, so stash the fags, alright . . .'

Brooke nodded, making a mental note. Something on the air smelt like the sample he'd handed over to Grandcourt: was it the air fuel or the dope? He wondered whether any streams led down from Marshall to the Cam.

The man in black overalls was the foreman. He said he'd already heard that Peggy Wylde was missing, and added that she was a diligent worker, if a bit chatty, and she tended to attract young lads who hung around at tea break.

'Moths round a flame, eh?' said Brooke, recalling Aldiss's nocturnal pollinator, flitting between the evening primroses on the riverbank.

'Pretty girl,' said Hatton. 'And they're a bit thin on the ground 'ere. Mostly blokes – 1,500 of 'em. So she played the field. And it's a sodding big field. More like bees round honey. A swarm of the blighters. Any news?' he asked. 'Word is she's gone AWOL, run off with a fancy man, that kind of thing. Not been seen here since she went home yesterday evening.'

'There's a night shift, is there?' asked Brooke.

'No. Two day shifts. She was seven to four,' said Hatton, pointing up at the skylights in the curved roof. 'It's tricky work and the girls are good at it but you need natural light. If the balloon really goes up, who knows, we might have to work by arc lamps, but it won't be easy.'

'Girl was happy, was she? No reason why she'd disappear?'

Hatton shook his head. 'Ask this lot if you like – this is Peggy's flight.'

Five girls were working on an Oxford, repairing the tail fins. The picture they outlined for Brooke of Peggy Wylde was more nuanced than that offered by the foreman. Popular certainly, but she thought the boys were a bother. She'd gone out with one or two pilots. They'd taken her out on the river, or for a spin in the country in their cars.

'Any names?'

They all avoided his eyes.

'She reckoned the pilots were all after one thing,' said one. 'So she ditched them pretty fast. Bruno Zeri, that's her new beau.'

'Does he work here?'

'Canteen – he's a cook. His dad ran that restaurant by the bus station . . .'

'The Roma?' offered Brooke.

'That's it, he's an Eyetie, but he's alright. Born here I think, but she said he grew up in Italy with his grandparents and then came back to work here a year ago – so he speaks funny. They carted his mum and dad off to some camp – enemy aliens and all that. But Bruno's British, although he gets some stick . . .'

A voice, the speaker unseen on the inside of the fuselage, added, 'And he's drop-dead gorgeous.'

The rear gunner's hood slid back and the owner of the voice appeared. 'And he was waiting for her yesterday when she went home, just outside the gates. I was cycling behind.'

'This was clocking-off time?'

'That's it. Four o'clock on the dot.'

'Sure it was him?' pressed Brooke.

'Yeah. He stands out cos of the hair: black and shiny.'

Brooke took her name and said she might have to make a formal statement.

Then he walked to the canteen. A Nissan hut again, but newly painted, with clean windows. Inside, trestle tables and chairs were set out for hundreds. Pots and pans clattered from an open kitchen. Trays of what looked like liver and bacon were being slipped into ovens.

The head cook, a thin woman called Val Wright with mousey hair held back by a squadron of hair pins, told Brooke he was out of luck if he was looking for the missing girl's boyfriend.

'Bruno's gone. Found me in the office after his break yesterday and said he had to go, a day or two, a week, maybe more. Emptied his locker and off he went – no reason given, but said he was sorry if he'd left me short. I said the job might not be there when he got back but it didn't stop him.'

Brooke nodded, perched on a bench, and took out his notebook.

One of the passing cooks stopped beside them. 'Val's got a soft spot for the Eyetie. She likes a pretty face.'

'Which is why I've never liked you, Fred. Why not surprise us and do some bleeding work?'

Fred swaggered away, hauling a box of lard.

'We need to find the missing girl, so we thought we'd start with the boyfriend,' said Brooke.

'What's the panic?' she asked, snagging a stray hair and tucking it behind her ear. 'I know Peggy Wylde. She's a grown-up woman. She certainly knows she's a looker. Maybe she wasn't happy at home . . .'

'Her grandmother died in the Earl Street bombing,' said Brooke. 'She may be upset – frantic. We need to find her. We need to know if she met this boy, what she said, if she's still with him . . .'

'He wouldn't hurt her if that's what you're thinking,' said

125

Wright. 'Wish I had twenty like him,' she added pointedly. 'They give him a rough time. Fact is he can cook. It's in the blood.'

Brooke strove for patience. 'What time did he leave?'

'It was only an hour early – about three o'clock, three-thirty. He'd cooked lunch, so there was just cleaning up left for the next shift. Then he took his break with the rest of them.'

She'd been walking while talking, carrying a large pan to a set of shelves, beside an open door into what was clearly the staff room. A thin mist of cigarette smoke hung in the air, over a long table strewn with newspapers, comics and several sets of cards, splayed mid-game. Half a dozen men sat around, one of them with his head down on his folded arms, asleep.

Brooke asked the men if any of them remembered Zeri acting strangely the day before, especially during the break. Several of the men simply got up and went back to work, while those who bothered to answer said he'd kept himself to himself and spent most of his time reading newspapers.

Giving up, Brooke walked out with Wright into the kitchen. 'Friendly bunch,' he said. 'Where do the women go?'

'We've got our own room, thank God. This place is a pit. But it's their little kingdom,' she added, leading the way to her office. 'They don't like outsiders. Not even me – but then I'm a woman, and that seems to unsettle them. It's just smutty pictures, gossip, fags and cards. Pathetic really.'

'So he has his break and then comes and says he's off – just like that?'

'That's it. He was upset, you could see that.'

'How could you see that?'

'He looked pale, and his eyes were full of tears. I asked – you know – if I could help and he asked to borrow the phone, so I let him.'

'Who did he call?'

Wright shrugged. 'I left him to it but I heard him ask the switchboard for a Manchester number. I think they just gave him the line – that's what they usually do. He had his wallet out and he had a slip of paper ready with a number on it.'

'How long was he on the line for?'

'Two or three minutes, then he just came and said thanks, not to worry, that something had come up. He just had to go.'

'What did you think?'

'I thought it had all got too much for him – his parents being dragged off to a camp.' She paused to use one of the myriad pins to deal with a stray lock of hair. 'We don't pay much by way of wages and I know he was short of cash once the restaurant closed. Odds on he won't see his parents again if they keep them banged up for the Duration. Can't have been easy for him. He's only a lad. I think he just gave up. He'll be facing a call-up soon anyway. Maybe he took his girl with him. Maybe they're heading for Gretna Green while they've got the chance. That's what people will think.'

CHAPTER EIGHTEEN

The Roma restaurant stood on a narrow alleyway close to the city's bus station, a grimy backstreet of poor shops, cordoned off from the smarter streets on one side by the blind walls of Christ's College. In the distance, bustling St Andrew's Street echoed with footsteps as lunchtime prompted an exodus of shop workers. At the other end of the alley a wide vista opened off Christ's Pieces, a diamond of common land neatly crisscrossed by footpaths, which led into the Kite. The restaurant stood between a cobbler's shop – the window of which was so oily it was difficult to discern the interior – and a pawnbroker's, which was open and doing brisk business. A woman clutching a broker's ticket was just coming out, dragging a small child by the hand.

Brooke tipped his hat but she hurried away, ashamed perhaps that sudden poverty had forced her to part company with a winter coat, or a string of fake pearls, for the price of a meal.

The front window of Roma had been smashed. Whatever had been thrown had failed to penetrate the plate glass beyond a small puncture, but it had left a spider's web of cracks. A crude swastika had been painted on the door. Churchill's order to round up Italians, Austrians and Germans – to 'collar the lot' – had led to random cases of violence and damage. The Borough, with a skeleton force, had been helpless to provide protection.

Brooke rapped on the door and peered in through the glass. He could see half a dozen small round tables with chequered cloths, and the dull glint of cutlery, and a string of garlic bulbs hanging over a counter. Edison, standing back, examined the single upstairs window, waiting for the curtains to twitch.

A man put his head out of the door of the cobbler's.

'If you're after food, forget it,' he said. 'They've shut up shop. Now the old man's gone they're out of business. Lad's still there, he works out at Marshall's. I thought I heard him last night – but there's no sign.'

'We need to get inside. We're from the Borough.'

'There's a spare key with the landlord – that's Harry Thompson, guvnor at the Red Lion.' He nodded down the street towards the Kite, spat in the gutter and went back inside.

Brooke despatched Edison to get the key while he tried the back of the property. A gate gave onto a line of rear yards. The Roma's had two raised beds in which tomato plants thrived. There was a shed full of drying vegetables: mostly onions and ginger, garlic and what looked like chillies.

Brooke rattled the door, but it too was locked. Inside he could see the kitchen, dominated by a gas range and several very large tin pans.

Back in the lane he quizzed the neighbours. The cobbler had nothing to add to his previous summary, except that the Zeri family had lived next door long before he'd taken up the shop after the Great War.

'They were on the wrong side that time too. You'd think they'd bloody well learn.'

'Actually, they were on our side when it mattered,' said Brooke, touching his hat. 'In fact, I doubt we'd have won without them. By the way, how did the boy get about? There's no bike in the yard.'

The cobbler shrugged. 'Then he's out on it.'

'Don't recall the make? Colour?' asked Brooke.

'It was just a bike. Nothing special. There's thousands . . .'

The woman in the pawnshop was happy to provide brief biographical details: the parents – Leon and Rosa – had been taken away after Mussolini's invasions in Africa. They were both Italian citizens. They'd both been taken to camps in the North. There was a daughter who'd married another 'wop' and gone to live in Bedford.

'The boy's got no money. So far he's been in here with the silver spoons, a couple of serving plates and a fur coat. I think he sends what he can to the camps. Nice people,' she added, then ushered Brooke to the door.

Brooke stood in the street and tried to recall a visit to the Roma when he was a child. His mother had brought him here about a year before she'd died. So he'd have been six. It was the night something had happened between his parents but he had never been sure of the exact events. His mother and father had never argued, at least not in front of him or the cleaning lady. There had always been a sadness about his mother; she was gregarious, even glamorous, and Cambridge was perhaps a disappointment. She'd studied the history of art in London, where she'd met the studious professor at a dance. That night before the war, when she'd brought her son to eat fresh tagliatelle, she'd been dressed up to go out, in a fur coat and a sparkling necklace. She'd gone down to the laboratory in the basement at home and reappeared with glassy eyes, telling him to get into his school suit.

While the alleyway had always been down at heel, the restaurant was a romantic island: candles on tables, the linen crisp, an intoxicating buzz of laughter and chatter. They hadn't booked – which in retrospect had perhaps provided a clue. Where had she planned to go with his father? The City Arms, perhaps, or Formal Hall at Trinity, or a party at one of the villas in Trumpington. Clearly the professor's work had led to a late cancellation. So she'd taken her son to the Roma instead. They'd had pasta, then lamb, cut in thin chops and fried in a garlic batter. His mother had asked for it in Italian, and it turned out to be the house speciality, which had brought the owners to their table to serve the dishes.

Brooke recalled a thin, sinewy man, with very dark hair, and a dazzling smile. His wife had hung back, wringing her hands in an apron.

They'd finished with ice cream. His mother had drunk red wine from a carafe, which she'd finished, giving Brooke a splash in his glass. She'd had a spirit too, a white oily liquid laden with what looked like elderberries. She told him all the dishes came from the same part of Italy: the mountains beyond Genoa.

How did she know so much? her son had asked.

'Our honeymoon,' she'd said.

Brooke ditched his Black Russian in the street, wondering

if his inability as a child to understand the world of adults explained the satisfaction he enjoyed as a detective, unpicking the motives of others.

Edison arrived with the key. The interior of Roma was a tawdry version of Brooke's memory of that night so long ago. The restaurant had been closed for weeks, but the dust and threadbare rugs spoke of a longer decline. There was a large framed poster of some Italian mountains and a small village, and in one corner an ornate shield in enamel depicting a green tree, against a red sky, with white jagged mountains. A crown was set above the tree.

The legend read: *Comune di Patigno*.

Upstairs, Brooke found three bedrooms, one of which had been given over to dry stores: canned fruit, flour and tinned fish. The box room appeared to have been young Bruno's. The bed was made up, but in disarray.

Back downstairs he found Edison in the kitchen, gingerly lifting pots and pans. A meat-and-two-veg man at heart, he looked ill at ease in the presence of a string of garlic.

'There's something here, sir,' he said.

At the back of the larder, the cans and packets had been pushed aside to reveal a wall safe. The door was open, the inside empty.

'If he had any money, he's taken it,' said Edison. 'Maybe he's planning a long trip.'

'Or tickets for two,' added Brooke.

CHAPTER NINETEEN

Mrs Muir, Chief Inspector Carnegie-Brown's secretary, was an upright woman in perpetual tweed, who organised the telephonists but avoided their company, and that of almost everyone else in the building. She drank tea from a flask and went home for lunch. She took the seat Brooke offered her in his office but declined a cigarette, crossing her legs at the knee and settling her shorthand pad in place, adjusting a pair of flyaway spectacles. Poised, like some angular wading bird, she awaited Brooke's words.

Brooke's priority was to find Peggy Wylde and Bruno Zeri. The girl had gone missing the day after her grandmother had been robbed and murdered. She'd last been seen meeting her boyfriend at the gates of Marshall aerodrome. They knew he was short of money, and Peggy would have known about her grandmother's cash and jewellery, and that she spent her nights in the public shelter. Was Zeri the thief? Had Nora recognised him? The lovers had met the next day outside Marshall. Was the Lucifer Zeri's bike? Nobody seemed to recall the make, let alone the colour. Young Jack on Earl Street might have noticed the badge, but he had an eye for bicycles.

Mrs Muir fidgeted on her chair. Normally Brooke laboured away at his typewriter to produce notes and correspondence, but dealing with County demanded that the bureaucratic niceties be followed.

'This is for Inspector Joyce's attention at County, Mrs Muir – up at the Castle.'

The Cambridgeshire force covered the wider county, leaving the old city to the Borough. Its headquarters, once in the city itself, had been moved up to the old castle, a position of lofty grandeur more suited to the chief constable's ambitions. The ingrained antagonism between the two forces stretched back into the mists of time.

'It should be marked as urgent, please, with copies to Chief Inspector Carnegie-Brown and myself.'

Brooke cleared his throat.

'Dear Raymond. Here is the copy we discussed. I understand the chief constables are of one mind . . .'

Brooke lit a cigarette, turned his back on Mrs Muir and studied the half-open blinds. The evening light was soft and warm.

'This is an absolute priority. I'll leave design and typeface to your men with the know-how. A budget of £50 has been agreed. The poster bills should read as follows . . .

'WANTED in connection with incidents in Cambridge. Bruno Stefano Zeri, aged 18. Black hair, sallow complexion, brown eyes. Stands six feet tall. Slim build. Speaks with strong Italian accent. May be carrying cash amount, or other goods of value. Any information on the suspect's whereabouts to Cambridge Borough Police: Cambridge 6767.'

Brooke opened a file and extracted a passport-sized photograph of Zeri, taken by Marshall airfield for his security pass. The young man was handsome, olive-skinned, brown-eyed, with an engaging smile.

'Can you attach this to the note, Mrs Muir, and then pass everything along to one of the messengers?'

She began to gather up her things, but Brooke held up a hand.

'Sorry – an addition: MAY BE TRAVELLING WITH . . . Peggy Wylde, aged 21. Dark hair, fair complexion, green eyes. Approximately five feet two inches tall. Last seen wearing a sky-blue dress, with a white belt, and carrying a gas mask decorated with sequins and tassels. Smart, polished, black leather shoes.'

Mrs Muir closed her notebook. Outside they heard steps on the stairs, and then a tentative knock at the door.

'I'm hoping this is the other picture,' said Brooke, jumping up.

A young man stood on the threshold.

'I'm Ollie Fox, Connie's boyfriend. The girls are out looking for Peggy. Alice is in bed. So they sent me with this . . .'

Ollie still had some puppy fat, but the young man was emerging, and Brooke thought he'd be a fully fledged grown-up by the turn of the year, no doubt eager to get into a uniform. Short and stocky, he looked like he'd make a decent rugby scrum-half. In his large hands he held a brown-paper package.

'Come in, Ollie. This is Mrs Muir. She's organising a poster of Peggy so that we can track her down quickly before she comes to any harm.'

The boy was shy and kept his eyes down, looking at his feet. He gave Brooke the parcel, inside which was a framed photograph of Peggy Wylde. It had been taken in a studio and there was a backdrop of a country garden with a Gothic ruin. Brooke was struck by her beauty, which was founded on her wide cheekbones and even wider eyes. In fact, it was clear she wasn't 'pretty', in the fleeting sense often used, but rather 'beautiful', in the sense that her looks might well last a lifetime. It provided an unkind contrast with her sisters, who were bonny enough but hardly photogenic.

'Alice said it was alright to use it but not to damage it,' said Ollie carefully, relaxing slightly, as if he'd been relieved of some duty. 'They're all upset. Alice says Peggy's run off to live in sin,' he added, shifting his feet.

Brooke gave Mrs Muir the portrait and asked her if she'd carefully remove the image and attach it to the memo for reproduction in the poster.

'Can you make it clear we'd like both original images back, Mrs Muir, in good condition?'

Mrs Muir gathered up her things. She'd looked at the picture of the girl, and now she looked again, holding the frame at arm's length.

'You'd never forget that face,' she said. 'You'd think she was a film star.'

The boy shifted his feet.

'I'll take it up myself to the inspector at the Castle,' she said, and fled.

Ollie didn't know what to do with his hands, which Brooke had already noted were bony, and hung loose.

'Do *you* think Peggy's run off to live in sin?' he asked.

'I didn't know her that well,' he said. 'Me and Connie have only been going out a bit. I saw her and that – cos I work at Marshall's too, but she hangs out with the other girls at lunch and breaks – they put out a picnic and lie in the sun.

'That's how I met Connie. It was Peggy's twenty-first and word got round she was in The Propeller – that's the pub up by the airfield. We gatecrashed, me and my mate Johnnie, and Connie was there.'

Brooke nodded, lighting up a Black Russian.

'We're going to send a picture of Peggy and her boyfriend up to the police headquarters on the hill, Ollie. They've got a machine which can blow the image up and make a poster. Then we're going to send the posters to railway stations, and ferry ports, and docks, and to other police stations. That way we'll track them down.'

'Peggy's gone with him, then?' asked Ollie.

'Maybe. We just don't know, but it looks like it.'

'Bruno wouldn't hurt her,' said Ollie.

'You met him, then?'

'Yeah. He was alright. He was good to me right from the off because he's lost parents – they've been taken away because we're fighting the Eyeties. That's right, isn't it?'

Brooke nodded. 'Why did that make him a friend?'

'I don't have parents, neither. I'm a Barnardo's boy. Sid and Marjorie took me on, but I'm old enough now to do what I want. Bruno came and watched me box at the boy's club in the Upper Town.'

'Why did he do that?'

'He could use his fists. There's an old bloke there that they call the trainer but he knows nothing. It's just to keep us off the streets. We're tearaways, that's what they tell us. I told Bruno the trainer was a duffer.' He grinned widely. 'So Bruno came along and got in the ring and showed us. He was dead strong and fast with his hands. He gave the trainer the runaround an' all.'

One of the switchboard girls arrived with a tray of mugs.

'Teatime,' she announced and gave one to Ollie.

'Sit down, Ollie,' said Brooke. 'What else did he do? He was short of money, wasn't he?'

Ollie nodded. 'He said one day he'd have his own restaurant. He said that the Roma – that's the cafe – that was his dad's dream. He was gonna make a life for himself. Start up his own place. Be his own man. I'm gonna do the same too,' he said. 'You know, make something of m'self.' He slurped his tea, his face suddenly flushed by the revelation of his ambitions.

'Good for you,' said Brooke.

The girl had left biscuits on a plate, which the boy kept glancing at until Brooke said he could help himself.

'Did he say any more about his plans?'

'He said he had cousins, family, that they lived up North and that they'd promised, like, to give him a hand to get started up there. He was gonna call it Zeri's. It's a good name, isn't it?'

'Did he say where these cousins were?'

'Yeah – it was a funny name. He showed me on a map once, there's a big one at the Boy's Club cos they try to sneak in some lessons. I think he wanted Peggy to go with him too.'

He concentrated hard, and Brooke could see his lips moving as he tried to recall the name of the place.

'It was called Little Italy but he said its real name was Ancoats. Something like that. That's up North, right?'

'It's Manchester,' said Brooke. Which made sense, because the diaspora of the thirties had brought many Italians to the city to run ice-cream parlours, restaurants and cafes. And Zeri had borrowed the phone up at the Marshall canteen the day he'd left and asked for a Manchester number.

Ten minutes later he watched from the window as Ollie rode away, teetering slightly as he mounted his bike, while Brooke held the phone receiver to his ear, waiting for the switchboard to get him a line to Manchester police headquarters.

CHAPTER TWENTY

Brooke pushed himself off from the grassy steps into the river and turned against the current. The lock gates lower down the Cam at Jesus Green and Baits Bite must have been opened, for the river ran with a gentle, persistent force against him as he headed south with a steady stroke. By the time he'd reached Silver Street Bridge he could feel the big bass drumbeat in his chest, so different from the fluttering of the jazz heart.

He forged ahead, wary of punts and dinghies on a stretch of water often crowded at sunset. He lingered in the pool by the inn, his nose an inch above the placid water, but detected no note of petrol, or any dangerous chemical; nothing more pungent than rotting reed and – from somewhere close – the unmistakable combination of chip fat and vinegar.

Swimming on, he ran through a checklist in his head, making sure he'd done all he could to track down the runaway lovers. A chief inspector at Ancoats had taken Zeri's details and would circulate the poster within the Italian community in the city, while uniformed officers would visit restaurants, cafes and ice-cream parlours. Brooke had suggested that they keep the mood downbeat: the Borough wanted to talk to Zeri and Wylde about events in Cambridge. There was no point creating a panic, and driving the fugitives underground, by mentioning the possibility of links with looting and murder.

The regular swimming strokes inspired logical thought.

He slid past his house at Newnham Croft, noting that the French windows were open but there was no sign of Joy and the baby. Reaching the open water meadows, he turned onto his back and looked at the sky, paddling with his feet, his body otherwise still, held in a dynamic equilibrium, sandwiched perfectly between cool water and warm air. The sun was down, but its lambent light shone on the great billowing fair-weather clouds in the stratosphere.

He'd reached a bend, so he rolled over and swam on to where an overhanging oak provided branches for a rope and a tyre. Great trees dotted the banks of the upper river, and as a child he'd given these landmarks their own names, at one point inscribing them in ink on one of his father's Ordnance Survey maps – a crime which had invited immediate punishment: he was 'gated' for a month, a stinging reprisal which confined him to the house and barred him from the city.

This particular spot had always had its hanging heavy rope and was marked on his morbid private map as The Gallows Tree.

On the towpath beside it, a cyclist waited on a slim racing machine.

'Mr Brooke . . .' The young man waved, and he recognised Vin Swift, the cyclists' captain from Michaelhouse.

The young athlete carefully leant the machine against the tree and knelt on the bank. Meanwhile three small boys had arrived and had begun to swing in the old tyre.

'Mr Doric said you'd be on the river; I've been up and down searching.'

One of the boys threw himself skywards at the perfect moment in the trajectory of the swinging tyre, launching himself in an arc before plummeting into the water.

'We've not found Lucifer,' said Swift. 'But I think it's second prize.' He grinned. 'At Byron's Pool, sir. I'll meet you there?'

And then he was gone, slim shoes slipping into their racing brackets, the gears whirring as he sped south.

Brooke, circling the shouts and splashes below the tree, set off in pursuit.

Around a bend was a stone bridge, and beyond it the first glimpse of the blue whale-backs of the chalk hills which led on towards Newmarket's high downs. The stream narrowed, but deepened, and became colder and darker. After a few minutes he could hear the weir ahead, beyond which lay the pool. He recalled Claire's report that students had started diving at the spot again, despite college rules which banned the sport. And he remembered his grandfather, who'd looked upon the poet's time at the university with a jaundiced eye, insisting that the pool had thrived when he was an undergraduate, long before Byron's regular visits made it famous.

The weir, now within sight, was bypassed by a narrow channel provided for salmon and other fish, but it was too narrow and steep to swim, so he hauled himself out onto the towpath. Ahead he could see where swimmers were diving in, resurfacing with a whoop. The river widened here at the confluence with the Bourn Brook, and a wooden floating pontoon provided the perfect launch pad for revellers.

On the far bank stood a uniformed police constable, the high collar and topcoat making him look hot and overdressed. Brooke dived back in and swam across. Byron's Pool, like most of the swimming spots reserved along the river, was for men only, and costumes or shorts were not required – a rule which caused some minor scandal, because this stretch of the river, where it began to meet the countryside in earnest, was also popular with courting couples.

Brooke, in the water, called out, 'PC Clarke!'

Clarke was on the Borough, and had been for the best part of thirty-five years. He made Edison look like a pup. His short hair was white, revealed as he removed his helmet and brushed a forearm across a sweaty forehead. Clarke's record was unblemished by achievement or initiative.

'They found this,' he said, hauling up from the grass the dripping frame of a red bicycle. It was a BSA, a ladies' bike, slightly battered. There was no certainty, but it might well be Peggy Wylde's.

Brooke pulled himself up onto the towpath, dripping. PC Clarke, no doubt relieved to see his inspector in shorts, saluted.

Vin Speed arrived, carefully placing his machine against a fence post.

'Joleyn Forbes – one of our men – is a keen diver,' he explained. 'He told us you get bikes in the river so we did a search, mainly under bridges. We were looking for the Lucifer, but they got this instead, and we'd all seen the description in the *News*. It was in the pit – thirty feet down with all the usual stuff.'

'Reckon it's the young girl's, sir?' asked Clarke.

Out in the middle of the green pool, a diver surfaced, then three more.

'Something else, Vin,' shouted the first. Brooke was alarmed by the divers' faces, which were quite clearly tinted blue, especially the lips. All of them were breathing rapidly, saturating their blood in oxygen, before returning to the depths.

'For God's sake be careful,' said Vin.

The diver took a theatrical final deep breath and plunged vertically down, followed by his three lieutenants, leaving a whirlpool in their wake on the surface.

Brooke sat on the bank, starting to count, inserting the statutory pause after each numeral. At fifty he realised how dry his mouth had become. One or two other swimmers sat on the bank too, wrapped in towels, examining wristwatches with admiration. Vin had his feet in the river, swirling them about, but as the seconds ticked on he too became still, transfixed by the motionless pool, which here betrayed no current, the leaves on the surface idly circling.

One of the swimmers, now back in shorts and pumps, had climbed a stunted willow to look down on the scene.

'Here they come!' he shouted.

Strange shadows moved over the surface, and then the pool erupted as the divers arrived, gasping.

Two of them had a rope, which they took to the bank. Vin and half a dozen helpers hauled hard, until something broke the surface.

On the bank they pulled away some weed and what looked like discarded fishing tackle.

Brooke would have been disappointed at yet another abandoned bike, but for the engraved shield on the haft:

LUCIFER

CHAPTER TWENTY-ONE

Brooke ordered a malt whisky without ice, despite the waiter's attempt to interest him in a small printed card listing the cocktails available at the University Arms. The bar itself, once resplendent beneath a coloured dome of glass in art deco swirls, had been reduced by the blackout to a shadow of itself. The hotel had been fined twice for breaching regulations, and had resorted to swathes of dark cloth and dimmed lights. There were three other customers: two elderly men in suits who looked like salesmen, and a woman on her own reading a book while sipping sherry, who Brooke took as a visiting academic, perhaps, with an aversion to college rooms.

In peacetime the view was panoramic, embracing Parker's Piece to the Donkey's Common. Tonight, blind to the world outside, they could have been in a down-at-heel hotel bar in any British city. The all-clear had sounded at nine, less than an hour after the siren, without sight or sound of the enemy, but the excitement which had accompanied such a release in the early months of the war had dissipated, and now everyone was looking grey, and exhausted, and generally bad-tempered.

Brooke checked his watch: he was on time. He sipped the malt.

The discovery of the Lucifer and – almost certainly – Peggy Wylde's bicycle seemed to confirm the emerging view of the crime at hand. Bruno and Peggy had fled, possibly on foot and then by train or car, dumping their bikes in the river. The act seemed symbolic, a little ritual of separation, perhaps, between one life and another. And it had certainly served to shroud their enterprise in mystery. However, it worried Brooke as well, because it seemed desperate and final.

Brooke was about to order a second drink when a man came into the lobby and approached his table with brisk confidence.

He introduced himself as Dr Harold Bannister, from the department of chemistry. He'd once had red hair, which had almost all gone, but left behind freckles and what looked like sensitive skin – blotchy and flushed.

He sat down and snapped his fingers, a habit which Brooke had always found unbearable.

Bannister ordered a whisky crush and pointedly asked for a straw.

'Here's to Grandcourt,' he said, when the drink came, taking the straw out of his highball glass. 'Good chap. I understand we have you to thank for that.'

Brooke sipped his malt then set the tumbler down on the

glass-top table with a crack. 'Hardly. He's his own man. But I wrote his reference, if that's what you mean.'

Bannister wasn't listening. 'We're all doing government work now, of course. It has to *make a contribution* – that's the lingo they like. I've got flat feet – couldn't even get in the last lot. But as I say – the department has several projects in train to assist the Ministry of War, and the Ministry of Supply. My field is petrochemicals.'

He took out of his pocket the small glass jar Brooke had given Grandcourt. 'So this didn't present too much of a problem once it got to my lab. It's adulterated petrol. About one part kerosene to three parts commercial fuel.'

Bannister picked up the straw, mixed his drink with it, swallowed the lot and ordered another. Brooke had taken against him, not because of his boorish behaviour, but because he represented perfectly an emerging class of men who worked vicariously for the state in shadowy, ill-defined roles.

'What's the point of adulterated petrol?' said Brooke, sharply.

'To make money on the black market,' said Bannister. 'You take vehicle fuel – which is rationed – and mix it with a lower-grade petrochemical. It'll run an engine, but inefficiently, and it'll probably damage it in the long run. But your profits go like that . . .'

He indicated with his hand the trajectory of an aircraft on take-off.

'We look at samples from all over the country. Almost always it's kerosene that is mixed with commercial petrol, which is doled out to farmers and hauliers and police stations. It's coloured red.

'This stuff of yours is standard rationed petrol that you'd get from a pump – but effectively diluted. We're beginning to see this much more often, especially in the big cities where there are so-called blackout gangs – they're just the same old thugs, but they've got a new lease of life with the war on. They steal the petrol, then mix it, then flog it on.'

A man in a dinner jacket had come into the bar. He sat at the piano, lifted the lid on the keys and began to play what Claire would have called 'spooning music'.

'How do they steal it?' said Brooke.

Bannister moved closer, taking up the straw. 'Well – not on any scale, Brooke. The ration system is pretty tight. Securing a supply would be tricky.'

The waiter had brought his fresh whisky crush. He took the straw and loudly sucked up a mouthful. The woman reading on her own looked up and coughed.

'We've had outbreaks of syphoning in London, Glasgow, Sheffield, Portsmouth. But anyone can do it.' He waved the straw. 'Ancient invention, of course. The Egyptians used rye grass. Then some Yank invented this – made a fortune. The Yanks are good at that; they take science, and they make money. We could learn a lot, but making cash is a bit *infra dig* at Cambridge.

'We think it's uncouth. A dirty word. But I'll tell you this, Brooke. The scientist who invented the plastic-covered straw sank a lot of the money into good works. Built modern flats for the poor workers at the factory. Toilets, running water, insulation – that kind of thing. If you don't make it you can't give it away – can you?'

Brooke sensed they'd lost the point of the conversation.

Bannister ordered his third drink, and Brooke joined him this time, thinking he may have misjudged him.

'The only difficult bit is getting the flow to start,' said Bannister, waving the straw. 'You drop in a rubber hose, suck on the tube, once it's running you're in business. But it takes practice – otherwise you end up with a mouth full of chemicals. Dangerous chemicals.'

'This is on the street?'

148

'That's it. The blackout's perfect. We've got engineers looking at lockable caps. A one-way flow lock. But it'll take time. There's a war on; this isn't the number one priority.'

'How'd it get in the river, do you think?' asked Brooke.

Banister shrugged. 'My guess is you've got an operation here in the city. They'll just be kids – or the usual petty thieves, or anyone who's short of a few bob.'

Brooke thought of Bruno Zeri and his debts, and his dreams, and the flimsie petrol can in the pannier of the Lucifer. And he saw looting for what it often was: an opportunistic extension of burglary and theft.

'To make it worthwhile you'd have to have a gang of them, syphoning and all that – but they'll be supplying a central warehouse or store. They'll add the kerosene and sell it on to a garage that's ready to offer it under the counter. Or better still, sell it to an operator in another part of the country, because when the engines start to cough you don't want to be available to take customer complaints. So best flog it miles away. No good trying to fleece regular customers because they'd soon spot the fuel was dodgy – backfiring, missing strokes, mechanical failures. So you need to offload it – a tanker full, a middleman, that kind of thing.'

'A fence,' said Brooke.

'Exactly. Someone in what we coyly refer to as "supply". Someone with contacts in the wider black market. Don't think this is just kids and ruffians. The production, supply, distribution – that's all organised.'

The drink was affecting Bannister rapidly, and his voice had risen several decibels, so that when he said 'black market' the pianist stopped playing for a moment, before ploughing on.

'The leak in the river is symptomatic,' he said, leaning closer, switching to a stage whisper. 'They had a case in Portsmouth.

They were mixing the stuff up in an old brew house. Gallons of it washing about. They tried to pipe it into a tanker and lost half of it down the drains. That's what I think you may have here, Inspector. Amateurs. But organised amateurs.'

He picked a bit of tobacco off his lip. 'Your problem – if I might say so – is that if they do establish a way of getting the stuff out into the black market, they're here for the Duration. The other problem is that we're seeing a proliferation of guns – you won't need me to tell you why. Every Tom, Dick and Harry brought back a pistol from the Great War. They're two a penny. The further you move up the supply chain the more likely it is you will encounter someone ready to use one. There've been casualties, Brooke. Fatalities. Be warned.'

The fresh drink brought its own cloud of minty fumes. Brooke thought of a mouthful of petrol, and the dizzying gas, and the taste of the rubber pipe. He thought of a throat burning, and lips parched by evaporating fuel, and what it might do to your stomach.

Bannister, expansive, produced a small cigar and lit up in a cloud. Then he stretched out his legs as if making himself comfortable for a long chat.

But suddenly Brooke had somewhere to go.

CHAPTER TWENTY-TWO

The night shift had just come on at the hospital and Brooke found Claire on Rainbow Ward, at the sister's desk, the downlight illuminating an open file and a green cup in a green saucer. The fringe of her neat bob hung down and for a moment he thought she might be asleep, propped on one elbow, but when she looked up the cat-like eyes were wide, and at the sight of him widened still, with a smile. Brooke always felt that unexpected meetings told you a lot about people, that in the first half second the face revealed the truth. He thought she looked happy to see him.

He pulled up a chair from beside a bed where a small child lay asleep on top of the covers.

'I thought lights out was seven-thirty?' he said, noting that several of the other children were reading by bedside lights: comics, newspapers, even a book, while one child sat on the edge of his neighbour's bed playing chequers.

'We've been getting the siren most nights; it brings its own routine. They're bleary-eyed in the shelter but if they do sleep they're wide awake by the time we get back to the ward. So why turn the lights off?'

'The boys with the tummy upsets. Presumably they all got sent home?'

Claire's eyes expertly scanned the right-hand rank of beds.

'Last bed on the right – he's the last left. Much better – but he was ill, really ill. They reckon the chip-shop owner was mixing some concoction up because he couldn't get the lard. Old Standish was in every three hours to listen to his chest – and the others. If the dodgy oil gets into the lungs it can present as pneumonia.'

'And the Guildhall analysis?'

'They didn't bother. They said the shop owner's up for a fine and they've carted off the "fat" to the sewage farm.'

'Charming,' said Brooke.

Claire flicked through a file at her elbow. 'Here it is. Albert Michael Smith – that's your boy. Aged thirteen. Address in the Upper Town, just off Honey Hill.'

A casual reading of the local paper would reveal that several of the defendants up in front of the local magistrates could claim addresses in the Upper Town, and especially off Honey Hill, a tenement warren whose demolition had only been postponed by the outbreak of war. Charles Dickens would have recognised the street, if not by sight then by smell.

'I'd like a word with the boy. A private one. Will you trust me?'

'That depends what you intend to do, Eden.'

'A little bit of gentle persuasion. Have you got a stomach pump to hand, Sister Brooke?'

The gastric lavage was not to hand, but was eventually uncovered in the store cupboard. The application of the hose down the throat, and the removal of the stomach contents, was so unpleasant as to require an anaesthetic. Its clinical use was generally discouraged, unless the patient's life was in danger from poison.

Young Smith was awake, reading *The Dandy*, his head moving hypnotically from side to side as he followed the adventures of Korky the Cat, oblivious of Brooke's presence in the ward until the curtained screen was run swiftly around the bed.

Brooke asked a few questions about Korky while setting the stomach pump at the foot of the bed.

Smith, Brooke judged, exhibited a certain amount of animal cunning in not enquiring into the purpose of the machine.

'So you're much better, lad. What do they call you – Albert?'

He shook his head. 'Bert.'

'Bert it is. I'd try another chippy next time, eh?'

Bert looked towards the ward's double doors, perhaps contemplating avenues of escape.

'There's another possibility,' said Brooke, sitting on the edge of the bed. 'Maybe the chippy was dodgy, but maybe you got poisoned by something else?'

Brooke took the rubber hose off the stomach pump. 'Imagine you've got something like this, Bert. Bit of garden hose, say. It's after dark – the siren's gone off again – you creep out into the Upper Town and you find a car. Then you twist off the petrol cap, slip in the hose, give a good suck until you get petrol in your mouth, then switch the hose to a bucket. If you don't know what you're doing – or if you have to try too hard because you've only got little lungs – you get a mouthful of petrol and it goes down your throat. Or down the wrong way into your lungs. It burns your throat, and your lips.'

The boy couldn't stop himself drawing in his lower lip.

'Which is a different story to the one you told, isn't it?'

Bert tried not to look at Brooke, which left him looking at the stomach pump.

'Luckily there's a way to find out the truth. The file says you've got some of this chemical left in your tummy – just a bit. So we can look at that, and decide if it's petrol or the dodgy chip fat. All we have to do is use the stomach pump.'

Brooke picked it up briskly. 'It's just like nicking petrol,' he said brightly. 'This goes down your throat and then the motor sucks everything out into this bowl. The nurse can do it.'

Brooke stood up. 'Unless you want to tell me – just between us – who you gave the can of petrol to?'

He watched Smith thinking this offer through. There was a glint of fear in the boy's eyes now, and for a moment Brooke thought he might actually vote for the stomach pump.

But then the defiant stare faltered. 'A bloke comes round with a lorry and said we could earn a few bob if we got the knack of it. I don't know his name. He gave us cans and said he'd be back on the corner the next day to pick 'em up. Sixpence for a full can. They reckon he's got people at it all over.'

'What kind of can?'

'The soldiers have 'em – for water and stuff.'

'Does it have a cap you screw off?'

'That's it.'

'What kind of lorry?'

Bert shrugged. 'Not that big, just a tarp over the back. But it's striped.'

'A striped tarpaulin? That's unusual. What colours?'

'Just black and white. It's a bit grubby.'

'How can I find this man?'

The boy shrugged. 'My mate Les says he ain't been back since we all got ill. I reckon he's got the wind up. We just thought it wouldn't do no harm. But it's harder than it looks.'

CHAPTER TWENTY-THREE

Brooke commandeered a bicycle from the Spinning House yard and set out for Marshall airfield in the midday sun. Edison had offered to drive him in the Wasp but he'd craved this modest adventure, and the time and freedom it gave him to think clearly. The airfield lay out on the edge of the city, but since the outbreak of war, and the ceaseless call to Dig For Victory, the countryside seemed to be invading the suburbs. In the car he'd have swept past, but now he saw that there was activity everywhere: wide verges were being planted with vegetables, front gardens and open spaces ploughed up, and once-peripheral land – where farmers had given up, waiting for a lucrative opportunity to sell for new housing – had been enthusiastically taken back up for crops. Cornfields ran up to bus stops. The front gardens of suburban villas had been turned into smallholdings. Further out, beyond the city boundary, the harvest was in full swing and several times he'd been overtaken by haywains, Land Girls perched on the ricks, with handkerchiefs around red necks. The sun was unrelenting, and Brooke had to stop and switch to his black-tinted glasses. The heat, intense, made the air buckle, and as he pulled up at the guardhouse the runway beyond was shimmering with a mirage of cool water.

As his warrant card was examined, he stood the bike against the wall and let his breathing return to normal. The sudden burst of exercise had set his heart thudding with its big bass drumbeat. He'd just come from Carnegie-Brown's office where he'd confidently set out the case against Bruno Zeri – a case now fortified by the revelation that a blackout gang was operating in the city, and pilfering petrol on a pretty impressive scale.

He'd found Carnegie-Brown eating, a neat lunchbox open, an egg sandwich half finished. There was an apple in the box too, and – sensationally – a small chocolate bar. Steam rose from an open thermos flask of tea.

'What progress, Brooke?' she asked, carefully adding evaporated milk to a mug from a tin.

Brooke said he felt confident he now had a picture of the crime. Zeri was part of a gang of small-time thieves and tearaways with an eye to burglary and scams, including syphoning fuel for the black market. In debt, desperately short of cash, he'd wanted to start a new life in Manchester with his girlfriend Peggy Wylde. Perhaps the cash at number 36 had always been in their sights. Peggy would have known that her grandparents usually took to the shelters, and possibly where her grandmother had hidden her nest egg. When the bomb hit Earl Street, Zeri had taken his chance. But number 36 wasn't empty, and he'd been recognised, and killed Nora, and then taken her rings. Now they were both on the run.

'Well, we'd better catch them then,' said Carnegie-Brown, reaching for the silver cigarette box while dismissing Brooke with a nod. Back in his office he'd rung Manchester but there was no news of any sighting of the runaway Italian. How hard were they trying to find the fugitive? He suspected that their resources were stretched even further than those of the Borough, but to a far greater extent. If there was no news soon he would commandeer Edison, and the Wasp, and they'd see if they could get results in person. Most immigrant communities survived in part on self-help, sticking together and maintaining an efficient grapevine. Surely they could flush the Italian out if they asked the right questions, in the right places?

But his real problem was the beguiling nature of the story he'd set before his superior officer. Was Zeri really their man? The airtight case he'd presented to the chief inspector was in fact less than compelling. He was asking Carnegie-Brown to believe that Zeri just happened to be in the area on his bike at the precise moment the bomb dropped. There was the presumption that he was part of a blackout gang based largely on the single petrol can in the pannier of the Lucifer. But the most worrying episode in the narrative he'd put forward was Zeri's movements after the murder. Why had he not fled that night? Why wait until his break in the staff room at Marshall to decide to go? He'd been upset, visibly upset. Why had his nerve failed at that precise moment?

Which is what had propelled him to Marshall airfield, with the help of the three-speed Raleigh. He found the canteen manager, Val Wright, in her office patiently checking and sorting small brown envelopes into order in a wooden tray. It was just after three o'clock and the cleaning staff were clearing up in the kitchens, a cacophony of clattering knives and forks and plates and pans.

'I'd like to ask a few more questions in the staff room,' said Brooke. 'The last time I was ignored. I put that down to indifference, or possibly animosity directed towards Zeri. Now I'm wondering if they've got something to hide. That time I was looking for a runaway thief – this time it's a murderer. My patience is limited.'

Wright checked a clock on the wall. 'It's knocking-off time for the shift but they'll all be there because it's payday. I usually make them wait half an hour but I'm happy to surprise them.'

She checked her face in a mirror by the door, and then led Brooke out across the kitchen, where a series of large tin pans were steaming on a range. Three women, their heads in white linen bonnets, worked chopping vegetables. The cleaning staff had fled. All the men were in the staff room.

When Brooke got to the door it wouldn't budge.

'It's locked,' he said, standing back.

Wright knocked smartly. 'Open up. Wages are here.'

They heard more scuffling, and whispers, and then the door opened.

Most of the cooks – a dozen men – were sat at a single long table. The only movement in the room now was the smoke drifting from cigarettes. On the table were several small piles of cash – pennies and a bit of silver. There was one newspaper on the table by the cash – a copy of the *Irish Times*.

'What's with the locked door?' asked Wright.

No one spoke.

'I'm asking the same question,' said Brooke. 'And I'll get an answer one way or another, here or down at the Spinning House. I need to know what's going on, and whether Bruno Zeri was involved. This is a murder enquiry and if anyone stands in my way they'll regret it – starting with a night in the cells.'

Brooke dragged out a seat and sat down, drawing the newspaper towards him. It had been open at the sports pages, where the runners and riders were listed for that day's meeting at Punchestown, outside Dublin, as were the race results from the previous day. Red circles in ink circled certain winners and losers.

A young lad stood by the tea urn, his tin hat in his hand, marked with a capital M for messenger.

'What's your name?' said Brooke.

'It's Billy. Billy Jordan.' The boy looked terrified. 'Bruno never joined in,' he said, and dropped his tin hat.

'Joined in *what*?' said Brooke. 'That's the last time I'm asking here. Next time it's down the nick.'

An overweight man with a chef's smock leant forward, rummaged in his pocket and put a handful of pound notes on the table.

'We have a flutter on the horses. Billy here runs the cash to a bloke in the stores. It's against the rules.'

'It's against the law,' said Brooke. The war had put an end to a lot of legal gambling. Racecourses had closed, football league programmes abandoned. There was moral outrage that while some men were dying others were frittering away cash in betting shops. Irish races were one of the few events left for the betting man.

'And the bookmaker who covers the bets. Where's he?' asked Brooke.

'We don't know any names,' said Billy, and everyone nodded in approval at this tactic.

'And you're all in this little syndicate, are you – but not Bruno?'

'He said he couldn't afford to lose,' said Billy. 'That he was saving up for stuff, and for his parents. They're in the camps. So he sat it out. He didn't join in anything, really.'

'He always had his head in *The Times*, the cocky sod,' said the chef. 'He sweet-talked a girl in the officers' mess to drop him their copy after lunch. We stick to the racing pages.'

'Was he reading the paper the day he left?' asked Brooke.

Another youngster piped up. 'That's it – he was sat there where you are one minute, then he gets up, tears a page out of the paper, takes his coat and bag from his locker, and marches out. We never saw him again.'

CHAPTER TWENTY-FOUR

Brooke had *The Times* delivered each morning, but usually read it after dinner, picking out stories to read aloud if Claire and Joy were at home, but when their shifts were early the papers piled up by his chair at home. Had Bruno Zeri read something in the paper which had prompted him to walk out on his job, and then leave the city? Brooke had the date; if he had the right paper, he might have the answer.

He was a hundred yards from Newnham Croft, and he could see the villa's brick chimneys, when he noticed a man in a sharp suit coming out of the garden, closing the gate behind him but looking back as if checking for signs of life in the windows. Claire must be out, and he knew that Joy had taken the baby to a birthday party.

'Can I help?' he said, when the man was a few paces away. 'I'm Eden Brooke. That's my house.'

The man smiled, revealing strong white teeth and a confident face.

'Hi. I'm Garret Burr – I was looking for you.' He had a rich, smooth voice and a strong American accent. 'I'm from the US Embassy in London.'

Again the smile. Brooke didn't like it one bit.

'I wanted to speak to Joy Ridding – the wife of Lieutenant Ben Ridding. I have news.'

'She's my daughter. She's out. Can you tell me?'

'It might be easier,' said Burr, which made Brooke's blood run cold.

Something about the man made him hesitate to invite him inside the house. It was pretty clear he had bad news, and somehow he felt it might be easier to bear if they were outside, under a wide sky.

'They won't be back – Joy and the baby – for a while. Why don't we sit in the garden?'

The lawn ran to the river and an iron bench, which had been there since Brooke's childhood. He thought it would be odd to sit next to the American so fetched a wicker chair from the veranda.

'What's this about?' he said.

'The US is the protecting power in Germany, so we're responsible for POWs. We're neutrals, an honest broker – you understand that?'

'Yes,' said Brooke.

'We visit the camps when we can, although we're run ragged as you can imagine. Since Dunkirk, and France, the system's pretty much collapsed. The Red Cross is taking over most of the work, and getting parcels through, so things should get better.'

He held up a hand, aware that Brooke's patience was being stretched.

'According to the Red Cross records, Benjamin Ridding was a prisoner at Stalag Luft I. They have what they call a "capture card" for him – which lists his details. I've phoned Geneva and they confirmed he was a prisoner there six weeks ago and that he was in good health. Did they let you know he was there?'

Brooke nodded.

'Well, he's not there now, Inspector. We made a visit ten days ago and our man got short shrift when he asked questions. We did manage to talk to what they call the "Man of Confidence" – he's elected by the prisoners to dole out the Red Cross parcels. He's a navy man – like Ben – and he's called Ted Peters. He said there'd been an escape, involving six men. The Germans are still building these camps, and escapes are common. In this case we think something went wrong.'

'What?'

Burr offered him a cigarette from a packet he'd never seen before, marked *Lucky Strike*.

'Peters said they heard shooting in the woods shortly after the men escaped. Later they brought back one of the men and he was in a bad way. He'd been beaten and they took him to a Dulag – that's like a special camp where they specialise in interrogation. That's not a good sign, Inspector.

'I'm sorry. We think they may have caught the men and shot them. It's not a common occurrence – so far the Krauts have played by the rules. But we do know there's been a lot of criticism in Berlin of the escapes, and that they want them stopped, so perhaps things got out of hand.

'We don't know anything for sure, but the Red Cross are going in with parcels again in a few weeks and so we may find out more then. I'll pass the case file to them, because Washington thinks the Germans don't trust us and we'll get turfed out and they'll ask the Swedes to step in, or the Spaniards. We don't want any cases getting lost in between. But I think your daughter needs to prepare for the worst. I'm sorry.'

Brooke couldn't help but think of Iris, and how she might never know her father. Joy would be stoical, but if there was no grave it might prove intolerable as the years passed, and it would take its toll in the end. Selfishly he realised that he'd always associate the iron bench with the bad news, and that would haunt him too.

'Do you think they'll mark the graves in the woods?' he said. He felt sick, and his own voice came to him as if an echo.

Burr was standing, smoothing down the suit. 'No. If they shot them we'll never know what really happened unless the survivor they sent to the Dulag lives to tell us his story. I'm sorry but that may well be unlikely.' The American checked a wristwatch. 'I'd better catch my train. As I say. Nothing is set in stone. The Red Cross may find out more. We'll keep you informed. Eventually there will be an official notification. But it may not say much more than I've been able to tell you today.'

They shook hands. Brooke forgot to say goodbye or to thank him for coming in person with the news. He walked him silently to the path and watched him diminish, thinking that he'd probably never see him again, but that he'd never forget him either.

CHAPTER TWENTY-FIVE

Brooke, in a daze, almost missed the map on the doorstep. It was wrapped in an oilcloth, with a note attached from Peter Aldiss in his careful scientific hand:

Eden.
The evening primroses have led me to the point marked on the map. There's a turn in the stream, doldrums, and I could smell your chemical I think. I took a sample, but I don't believe there's any doubt. You'll be right: petrol, or some other petro-carbon. The map points the way I think.

Even you will recall the principles of gravity.
Look upstream.
Peter

Brooke took the map into the kitchen and laid it out on the table. It was an Ordnance Survey map of Cambridge and what old-fashioned guidebooks liked to call its 'environs'. Aldiss had used a red pencil to trace over the spidery tributaries of the Cam, which rose south of the city in the chalk hills. Two streams came together just above Byron's Pool – the Rhee and the Granta – although Aldiss had also marked in the third source, the Bourn Brook, which slid into the main channel at the pool itself. The upper reaches of the river were spidery and complex, like a sketch of a lightning strike.

Brooke tried to concentrate but it was impossible. He'd have to tell Joy about Ben and the thought made his heart contract in his chest. The only salvation was that Claire would be home first. He could tell her the news, talk through the implications, and then wait for Joy and Iris to come home from the party. Brooke made tea, and opened the French windows, and sat down with the map again, trying to make himself concentrate on something – anything – which wasn't the image of Ben lying in the leaf litter of an obscure German wood with a bullet hole in his chest.

He traced his finger along the red lines Aldiss had inscribed on the map. How could one small river have such a maze of streams and channels? The complexity of the task briefly overwhelmed him, but then he remembered that this mattered: if he could find the source of the adulterated petrol it would get him closer to the blackout gang. Given the petrol can spotted in the pannier of the Lucifer, it might even get him closer to Bruno Zeri: could the couple still be in the city? Perhaps they'd ditched their bikes and were hiding in plain sight, or out in the country on the edge of town. Bannister, the chemist, had predicted there would be a 'factory' of sorts – somewhere they'd store the petrol, then mix it with the kerosene, then ship it out of town.

The 'X' Aldiss had positioned on the map was in red too. It was just above the junction of the two upper tributaries and indicated clearly that the source of the spill must be in the headwaters of the Rhee – which was a start, but still left the myriad headwaters to the west of the city.

Several villages nestled in the low, slow hills, Wimpole, Meldreth and Barrington being the main parishes. The river's spring lay at the village of Ashwell. Unbidden, a memory crystallised, of Joy on the weekend she'd brought Ben home for the first time, and they'd all gone swimming in the Rhee. They'd met boyfriends before but this was quite plainly a more serious relationship, because Brooke could see how proud his daughter was of the dashing submariner.

The sudden sense of despair was like a physical blow. He forced himself to take up the map again, studying the river's spidery route over the chalky hills. He knew all the villages well, and each one had its rural sub-station – a house, with a decent garden, and a blue lamp over the door. Later the constables would be at home for tea and he'd ring round and alert them to what might be on their doorsteps.

'What's that?'

Claire was at the door, smiling, but then she saw Brooke's face.

'What's wrong?' she said, walking briskly up to him and placing a hand flat on his chest.

'It's Ben,' he said, knowing he'd done the right thing, to make sure he told his wife, and that he didn't try to hide the truth. For the first time since Burr had broken the news he felt the constriction in his chest ease, as if he had been given leave to breathe more deeply.

She had a full shopping bag, and she hadn't put it down, but he told her everything, everything the American had said.

'So we don't know for sure,' he said at last. 'But at least we know what probably lies ahead. She'll be home in a few hours, but she'll have Iris, and it doesn't seem right to say it in front of the child.'

She shook her head. 'No, later. But tonight, Eden, at all costs. Joy wants to celebrate because there's a letter from Luke. Good news, thank God. She's taken it with her to reread if she gets the chance, but she wants you to read it out loud after supper because you've got the same voice. Let's get through that, and see Iris off to sleep. Then we'll tell her.'

They chopped carrots, leeks and onions and rolled some chopped rabbit in flour, but every now and then Claire came to a full stop, and just looked at her hands. Brooke poured them each a glass of wine, and they plodded on, and finally it was finished, and he heaved the dish into the oven. Brooke gave her a hug and was holding her head under his chin when they heard the rusty hinge on the gate squeal.

'There's a letter from Luke,' said his daughter, bursting in, Iris in her arms so that she could hand the baby to Brooke, although Joy always complained he held her like an unexploded bomb.

'I'll read it after the food,' he said.

'I'll change Iris and she can have her bath and some food,' said Joy. 'Then we'll have some peace and quiet if she'll go down, which she might, because Mrs Mullins said she'd been lively all day and hadn't had her nap.'

She lifted the baby up and addressed her seriously. 'If you're good, granddad will read you a story.'

It was remarkable, thought Brooke, how domestic routine

could smooth over crisis and grief. Joy disappeared upstairs and he remembered *The Times*. Trying to keep busy, he went to his chair in front of the fire where he kept the papers, but a brief search revealed the edition he wanted had already been used with the kindling. He checked his watch: it was too late now to ring the newspaper's library in London. It would have to wait.

Typically, Iris didn't sleep, so they let her lie on the floor in front of the hearth while they ate. After food they all trooped into the front room and flopped down in the old chairs, Joy rocking the baby.

Brooke washed up with Claire and then he read Luke's letter out loud.

His son admitted that he had indeed done precisely what his father had told him never to do: he had volunteered, and was now in field training. He was unable to say more. He didn't need to anyway, because he must have guessed they could provide their own detail. Churchill wanted commandos to launch lightning raids on the enemy. The newspapers had already carried accounts of such raids on Guernsey and the coast of occupied France.

It's certainly keeping me fit, wrote Luke. *We have to swim out into the loch in full kit, then come ashore, then hike ten miles along a line of telegraph poles. You have to run to the first, then walk to the next, then run to the third, and so on. Here's the devil. The whole platoon has to get there by the set time or you have to do it again. So if someone flakes out we have to carry the bugger.*

'"Loch" is clever, said Brooke. 'Just in case we hadn't guessed. Jo says the army's set up a training camp at Fort William for the commandos, up in the mountains at an old house. I hope he's gone by the time the winter comes.'

'I don't,' said Claire, bitterly. 'I hope he stays there for the

Duration.' She cast a glance at Brooke, which was intercepted by Joy, who looked away.

Brooke ploughed ahead with Luke's news: 'We're off soon. I hope I'm not seasick. After that I won't be able to write. Kiss Iris for me. Don't let Joy eat all the cake.'

Brooke folded the letter.

'She's asleep,' said Joy, looking at the baby.

Claire looked at Brooke.

'What is it?' said Joy. 'I know it's bad news. It's been as clear as day since I came home. Dad's got his blank face on and you won't look at me, Mum.'

'It's bad news about Ben,' said Brooke.

Two hours later Joy was in her room with Claire.

There'd been no tears at first, but when they had come, she'd given Iris to her mother to put to bed and Brooke had sat with her, holding her hand, trying not to say anything that was trite or might raise false hopes.

Brooke left a note saying he had to go to the Spinning House to make some calls. Then he shrugged on his coat, listened to the silence in the old house and, opening the door, slipped out into the night.

CHAPTER TWENTY-SIX

It took two hours to track down four village police constables on the upper reaches of the River Rhee: one was at home, one was out on a night beat, and the others were ARP wardens, on their rounds. Eventually he briefed them all, and managed to answer their questions – principally, what exactly were they looking for? Brooke said the fuel leak must originate at the point at which the gang was adulterating the petrol: a barn, a garage, a farm outbuilding. At some time regular supplies of pilfered petrol had to roll in – and the kerosene with which it would be mixed. There must be a workforce – perhaps two, three or half a dozen men. There must then be regular deliveries outward-bound, or lorries coming in to take it away in bulk. So – an 'operation' of some kind, which must be suspicious to those living nearby, which suggested a relatively isolated location. And then there was the tell-tale smell of fuel. And possibly local black spots in ditches and channels where spills would have killed fish, and rats. Brooke suggested they keep enquiries casual and low-key, but talk to gamekeepers, water bailiffs, farmers and postmen.

After two hours he could do no more, so he set off back home, walking away from the city centre. When he reached Newnham Croft, would Joy's light still be on? He felt torn between the need to be near her, and an understandable urge to keep grief at a distance. The street was silent, the release from his office a relief, so that he found he could no longer keep at bay more disturbing thoughts: what was it like to escape, and dream of seeing your family again, and then be captured, and for it to become apparent that your life was over? He imagined a woodland clearing and a summary firing squad, and Ben realising that he wouldn't see his wife again, or hold his child.

The city was so quiet, as he turned down an alleyway, that the burst of static – when it came – echoed off stone walls, unnaturally loud and close, as if he had the headphones of the radio cupped to his ear. He stopped, finding the contradiction disturbing: the city was dormant, nothing moved within sight, and yet this sound – and now he could discern the tumbling words – was upon him, and circling him, and then bouncing back off the high college walls.

'*Hauxton Junction, assistance immediate. Over.*'

Brooke heard this repeated three times as he ran towards King's Parade, his Blakeys clashing on the flagged pavement. At the corner of Silver Street he saw the radio car at last, parked in the cold canyon that ran between the high walls of Queens' College. The echoing stone had amplified the crackling radio signal.

The driver was a police constable, due for retirement in a few years, and way beyond service age. His name was Boyle and he'd been stout in his prime; now he was wedged between the seat and the steering wheel. He reported that a water bailiff had gone into the Blue Ball Inn on the water meadows beyond Newnham and asked the landlord to ring the Spinning House: he'd spotted several scraps of sky-blue material caught in the nets of a fish hatchery on the river. They looked like remnants of a dress matching the description of Peggy Wylde's clothes on the day she disappeared.

'Just scraps?' asked Brooke.

'Yes, sir. Floating on the surface.'

Brooke knew the fishery, and it was just above Byron's Pool.

'I can raise the local constable and get them collected,' said Boyle.

'I think we should attend, Constable,' said Brooke, sliding into the passenger seat and picking up the radio handset. His mind raced: had the tell-tale dress been swapped with something less distinctive as the couple made their escape? With each step in the case, the degree of premeditation seemed more apparent. He felt wide awake, and a trip out to the country was as good as lying awake on his bed.

A snaking lane, bounded by hedges, led from the edge of the town into the gentle hills to the south. After half a mile a line of poor terraced houses came into view, the pub in the middle, converted from an old cottage. The Blue Ball was a favourite of the city's porters and college servants because it lay beyond the city boundary. It provided a panelled, coal-lit snug – a home from home – but beyond the prying eyes of the proctors.

The landlord, a former colleague of Doric's from Michaelhouse, shook Brooke's hand and introduced the water bailiff, who was called Potter.

'I read the piece in the paper,' he said, kneading a tweed cap, 'and it looks to be what the girl was wearing, so I thought you'd want to know.'

Brooke thanked him and they set out in a line, tracking across a hillside and down to the towpath. Potter looked decrepit but he took the first stile with ease, using an old stick as a support. The river was hardly visible despite the moonlight, but quite audible as the current sucked at the bank, and turned in eddies around tree roots and sand banks.

They passed Byron's Pool – Brooke caught sight of the diving boards on the opposite bank – and then they were in open country, pale fields glimpsed between the hawthorn and willow.

A path branched off and took them towards a cottage. A light shone from the open door where a woman was waiting with a lantern. Beyond her Brooke glimpsed the interior of the house: a single room, a peat fire, eel traps hung from the rafters, and a bed of straw and blankets – a glimpse into the past, a lonely reed cutter's cote perhaps, on the eve of the Civil War. Between two poles in the kitchen garden, dead rats were hung up by their tails.

Potter fetched a long pole with a hook which hung from the rafters and a set of waders from beside the fire. Beyond the cottage a cut had been dug, a water channel which ran parallel to the main river, carrying its flow, trickling through cages and nets. Hauxton Junction lay ahead, the spot on Aldiss's map where the two main tributaries, the Rhee and the Granta, met to form the Cam.

The cut, which was about twenty feet across, plopped and

flopped with fish, held within their meshed cages. The silver-white splashes stood out starkly in the gloom. Brooke felt he could hear them too, scales clashing, air bubbles rising, tail fins splashing. It was a strangely disturbing sound because he'd always thought of the world beneath the river itself as rumbling and deep, but now he imagined the sounds as sharper, piercing and less peaceful.

Potter had hardly spoken since they'd met, but Brooke imagined he ran the hatchery – or more probably managed it for the colleges, which owned the upper river. At the end of the cut where it met the main channel, a set of poles supported a final net. Beyond that was the junction itself – a broad expanse of water filmed with algae, lit by reedy moonlight. Caught between the final poles were three pieces of floating material – all sky-blue.

'We've to be careful,' said the old man. 'If the poles break the nets'll fail and the pike'll by loosed in the river.'

This was clearly the real crisis: that the net might fail if they blundered in to get the evidence, and then the precious pike – an ornament to dinner tables at college – would swim free. He'd dined on the fish at Michaelhouse one evening and had found the flesh meaty and slightly muddy, while the dons had pronounced the feast first class. Brooke wondered if it was one of those delicacies lauded because of its rarity rather than its flavour. He did recall the teeth: serried rows, razor sharp, each one needle thin.

Potter sat on a log bench and struggled into the waders, then stepped into the cut, the long pole held over his head with both hands. The invasion caused a frenzy amongst the fish, which began to rise up, rolling over each other, mouths gasping.

Deftly the old man extended the pole and hooked up the nearest two pieces of cotton, ferrying them back to Brooke; the edges were torn, the material itself punctured with holes. The third piece was further out and clearly snared by a pole. For a minute Potter struggled to get it free. Then patience snapped and he used both arms to pull the billhook back with a violent tug.

His back was turned to them, but they heard him clearly. 'Christ Almighty,' he said, taking a sudden step backwards, his hands flailing in a sudden panic, so that he tipped into the water.

For a moment Brooke thought nothing had changed: the moonlight still caught the scrap of blue cotton, but then, like an oily, pale apparition, a body surfaced, turning turtle as it did, so that the pale neck and calves came into sight. The fish, sensing more danger, set about a chaotic thrashing.

The body, now free from its underwater snare, began to drift towards the open river, and the final net failed. The bailiff, recovering, managed to hook it back towards the bank, and they all dragged it onto the grass, while the pike scrambled for freedom in the wider river.

A single large eel followed them like a snake, inscribing a series of 'S's over the dark surface.

It was a woman, the sky-blue dress reduced to tatters. Brooke's eye caught the palm of one hand and saw the myriad lacerations of the pike's teeth. He knew that when the torch beam lit her face he'd recognise her in a particular way, because although he'd never seen her alive, he knew the family now so well, and the photograph they'd used for the WANTED poster had been pin-sharp and clear.

Peggy Wylde's face was extraordinarily pale, almost luminous, the colour of the eyes now hooded behind a glassy membrane. The odd detail which everyone would remember was the blood, which ran glistening in wet rivulets down her legs and arms and neck – freely, as if she were still alive.

Boyle knelt down to see if he could feel her breath between the blue lips, but the slightly bloated flesh, and the glazed eyes, told Brooke she'd been dead for several days.

The still-flowing blood told a lie. The pike had nibbled at the flesh but these wounds were puckered and bleached. The blood ran from black leeches which dotted her neck and legs, secreting their magic enzyme, which had stopped the wounds from clotting.

They stood back in silence as the cold corpse bled.

CHAPTER TWENTY-SEVEN

'You look like you could do with cheering up,' said Rose King, from behind the counter of her all-night mobile tea hut on Market Hill.

'It may never happen, you know,' she added, reaching for the metal teapot with one hand, her cigarettes with the other.

'Do you think I can fit you in?' she said, nodding to the city's central square. It was the dead watches of the night. Market stalls, locked up and shrouded in tarpaulins, stood in shadowy rows. The surrounding buildings – the stark new Guildhall, St Mary's Church, the narrow, gabled shops in neat rows, the college spires beyond – seemed to brood on the desolate scene.

There wasn't another human being in sight.

Mobile tea huts had popped up all over the city to cater for servicemen and civil defence workers, ARP wardens, fire watchers and the rest. Most were run by volunteers, like the WRVS, but Rose's stall was a family business, a feature of Market Hill since the last war.

'I'll join you before the rush starts,' said Rose. 'Bacon roll?'

Brooke took one of the chairs and slumped down. The Black Russian failed to raise his spirits. He'd had to wait an hour for an ambulance to arrive at the Blue Ball, where they'd eventually stretchered the body. Establishing cause of death would have to wait for Dr Comfort's mortuary: there was no point now summoning the pathologist because they'd had to move the body to the bank and so there was no scientific benefit to viewing the scene of the crime. Had the girl drowned? Had the girl *been* drowned?

The radio car took Brooke back to the Spinning House, where he'd typed up a brief report for Carnegie-Brown. The Borough's number one priority was to track down Bruno Zeri.

Sleep was out of the question. Dawn was just a few hours away. He felt himself in a familiar state of limbo – poised between night and day. There was a measure of guilt in his decision not to go home, apprehensive of what he might find. Iris had not slept through the night yet, and Joy would be struggling still with the news about Ben.

Rose's tea hut, en route to Newnham Croft, had proved irresistible.

She worked now behind the counter, griddling the bacon. The light flooded out around her, as if she were on stage. She had grey hair tied back under a bright red scarf, her face delineated by lipstick and eyeliner, a pair of earrings catching the eye. A platoon of soldiers suddenly clattered into the square and crowded in front of her, demanding tea and sausages, a cloud of cigarette smoke hanging over them. She began to slosh tea into mugs lined up on the counter. From the chat it was clear that they were a crew of gunners from the ack-ack barrage on the eastern edge of the city, stood down for another night.

They had taken refuge at Rose's stall, much as Brooke had done one evening in 1919. Back in Cambridge after his convalescence in the sanatorium it had become quickly apparent that Brooke's academic studies were over. His eyes could not take the strain of the books, or the laboratory observations that would have underpinned a career at the university. He'd turned to the Borough, and his first beat had brought him through Market Hill three times a night. Rose had been one of the first nighthawks. Widowed by the Western Front, she'd been left with three daughters, who all now helped run the business: the night shift had always been hers alone.

Having satisfied the soldiers' appetites Rose came round with Brooke's roll and a mug of tea and, ominously, her own large teacup. Rose was a devotee of the occult, of lore and legend and superstition, which Brooke tolerated with as much grace as he could muster. Rose had always treated him like a son, a complement to her daughters, and he tolerated her foibles with a filial affection.

'That's good luck,' she said, looking towards the Guildhall, where a sickle moon was falling towards the rooftops.

'In what specific sense?' asked Brooke, sceptical to the last.

'My mother always said that it was a bad omen to see the new moon for the first time through glass. We had to call her out into the street if we saw it – so she wouldn't just see a glimpse by mistake.'

Brooke watched the moon, trying hard to believe in good luck.

'Something's up, isn't it?' she asked.

'How could you tell?' asked Brooke.

'You look haunted,' she said.

At first he fobbed her off with a résumé of the last few hours: the discovery of Peggy Wylde, the silent procession carrying her body back through the moonlit fields. Then he told her the truth, about the visit from Burr, the American, bringing such dreadful news. He emphasised the degree to which there was still hope, and that the Red Cross would try to get answers from the camp commandant.

'I am sorry, Eden,' said Rose, putting a hand on his. 'Where's Luke? She'll want to speak to her brother.'

'You're right, but there's no chance. He's being trained up in Scotland. It's all hush-hush. We're just hoping on a last letter before he actually goes, anything really.'

Rose swilled her tea out into the gutter. 'That's a shame. My lot are as thick as thieves. They scrap like dogs over a bone, but take sides and they close ranks pretty quick, believe me. You can't get a cigarette paper between them. Luke would have been a comfort for his sister.'

It struck Brooke then that Rose had three daughters just like Alice Pollard. He wondered if Elsie and Connie had been close to Peggy, and how they'd react to the dreadful news of her death. For the first time it occurred to him that they might be harbouring a family secret.

The soldiers were laughing and joking, a hipflask being handed round to fortify the tea.

Rose examined the tea leaves left in her cup, delivering her opinion on the messages hidden within: justice, apparently, was going to appear with a halo of fire and wipe away an evil, while good fortune would follow a late-night knock on the door.

Brooke thought it was another instalment of the usual mumbo jumbo.

He ditched his cigarette and was about to set off home when he heard tyres screech as a van sped into Market Place. It came to a halt in front of a corner shop and the driver ran to the back, threw open the doors and heaved a pile of newspapers, bound in string, onto the step of a newsagent's called Hawkings'.

Which made him think about *The Times* and Bruno Zeri's abrupt departure from the staff room at the Marshall canteen. What had he read? Would the answer reveal why Peggy was killed? He realised suddenly that he didn't have to wait to find out the answer. A copy of the paper in question was actually close to hand.

CHAPTER TWENTY-EIGHT

The offices of the *Cambridge News* stood opposite the Spinning House. At this hour the facade betrayed no lights, and the 'front office' – open to the public – was locked. A side alley led under an archway and down a short incline to a rear yard. A lorry, loaded with a vast roll of newsprint, stood silently in the shadows. The rear of the building was dominated by the folding wooden doors marked *GOODS IN*. A cat was drinking milk from a saucer on a step, the door itself open.

The building inside was concrete, and cavernous, and contained the presses – a brooding mass of oiled steel and brass. Brooke felt the same thrill he always experienced in the theatre, the heady expectation that something was about to happen, and had happened in the past; that the presses would run, and the news would spill out on inky paper, to be rushed out to news sellers on street corners, standing beside bills which proclaimed: WAR DECLARED, or KING ABDICATES, or GERMANY SURRENDERS, or CUP FINAL HAT-TRICK.

He heard heavy, faltering steps, and an elderly man appeared in a grubby vest. He said he was the night watchman, and when Brooke explained that he was from the Borough, he wanted to know how he could help the police at that ungodly hour.

'Editor's not in 'til ten. The newsroom's early man is Cotter and he's supposed to be here at eight: supposed to be. But I know the truth, and he's hardly ever here by nine, and that's hours yet.'

Somewhere a phone rang.

'I wanted to see some old copies of *The Times*. Not that old. Three days ago. Do they keep 'em?'

'You need the morgue,' he said. 'They put all the obits in there – for the people who haven't died yet. Gives me the creeps. But they file the papers too. And cuttings. Follow me.'

Brooke followed the man's shoddy slippers up an iron staircase and through a heavy glass door. There was a very different atmosphere beyond, as a carpeted corridor led them past offices, then up a stairwell and through an iron fire door. And then everything changed again. The newsroom took up the whole floor, with windows on three sides. There were perhaps twenty desks, and two very long tables, and it was difficult to see anything clearly because of all the telephone wires hanging down, the pneumatic tubes for copy which ran horizontally above the desks, the metal spikes on every desk top, bristling with skewered paper, and the dangling telephone wires.

The 'morgue' was in a corner, behind a glass partition.

'I'll leave you to it,' said the old man. 'The obits are there,' he said, indicating a large filing cabinet. 'You'll want that lot,' he added, cocking a thumb at a desk, more cabinets, and an angled readers' desk on which the newspapers were attached to metal binders.

The desk was covered in eviscerated copies of the *News*. Brooke thought it must be someone's job to cut out all the stories and file them away, under various headings, like CHURCH, or FIRE, or CRIME, or COUNCIL, or RIVER.

The angled desk held copies of the *Cambridge News*, *The Times*, *The Telegraph*, the *Daily Mirror*, *The People* and the *Daily Mail*.

He extracted the right copy of *The Times* by unclipping the binder and took it out into the newsroom, realising belatedly that he was exhausted, and that he needed to sit down. The long desk, at the head of the room, had a big comfortable leather chair which swivelled, so he settled down there and spread the paper out.

The news for the day in question seemed unremarkable. Sporadic fighting had broken out in Somaliland as the Italian invasion continued, the evacuation of civilians from Gibraltar was continuing, and bad weather in the Channel had led to speculation that any invasion plans might be scuppered, while Brighton beach had been closed to allow the laying of barbed wire.

Brooke read everything twice, fighting off the urge to close his eyes. After twenty minutes he'd almost given up.

Then he found a small item on page 12.

TWO HUNDRED DEAD WASHED
UP ALONG IRISH COAST

Shipping Staff

Victims of the U-boat attack on the SS Arandora Star *on 2nd July, which was carrying more than 1,000 German and*

Italian internees to Canada, are continuing to come ashore on beaches in Ireland.

The official total so far is 256, as confirmed by a Gardai spokesman in Malin, Co. Donegal. Bibles, letters, papers and military identity tags have been used to identify the dead. Burials are taking place locally.

It is understood the final death toll of the disaster will be in excess of 850 and will include more than 200 British soldiers acting as guards on board for the transatlantic passage to camps in northern Canada.

HMCS St Laurent, first at the scene, was able to pick up more than 800 survivors. The wounded are still being treated at various hospitals in Liverpool and Glasgow.

Of the surviving casualties only one is still unidentified. An Italian male, in his late sixties to early seventies, has remained in a coma since being admitted to hospital, and is in a critical condition.

A spokesman for the Ministry of Health said that it is hoped relatives will come forward to identify the man. The patient was wearing a distinctive gold chain, carrying a silver disc, upon which was etched an enamel green tree, against a red sky, with white jagged mountains. A crown is set above the tree.

Descriptions of the silver disc are to be circulated amongst the Italian communities in the hope of finding the survivor's identity.

Brooke had seen this precise motif before, set in a framed map of the Apennines of Italy, hung on the wall of the Roma. Bruno Zeri's father had been interned. Had he been selected for transfer by ship to the new camps being set up in Canada? Was he fighting for his life now, alone in some hospital bed? There was little doubt his son thought so, because he'd walked out of Marshall that day, and Brooke knew now what had prompted his departure. What he didn't know was if Zeri's sudden flight had somehow led to his girlfriend's watery grave.

CHAPTER TWENTY-NINE

It promised to be a fine day at Waren: the forest dew was gone from the grassy runway, and there had been ham for breakfast, and even fresh eggs. A football match was about to begin, the pilots divided by drawn lots, although they were mindful of Oberst Fritsch's warning that they must not risk injury, even if such strictures were fast losing credibility, given it was now four days since their first, unsuccessful raid on Cambridge. Each night they prepared to fly again, but the meteorological gods were against them. The attractions of the country air had palled and the mood swung daily between morose boredom and sudden bouts of schoolboy hysteria. The night before in the mess an ugly brawl had broken out over a game of cards.

The football, once it began, was desultory. Several players were sick, testimony to the rank nature of the barrel of beer provided in the mess, which had fuelled the quarrel over poker matchsticks. Bartel alone played with a manic intensity despite his hangover in an attempt to block out thoughts of his family: there was still no news from Berlin, but renewed rumours of casualties and bomb damage. For a few moments the game degenerated into a scrum, the ball lost amidst flailing bodies.

Bartel emerged, bent double with a stitch. Straightening up, he saw that everyone else was rooted to the spot.

A civilian car – an Adler – had passed through the gates and was crawling slowly along the apron of the airfield towards them. Bartel would have recognised it anywhere – although the model was common – because he'd fitted the roof rack the previous summer so that they could take a tent to the Baltic coast, and the colour was striking – a milky pastel blue – which Bridget, his wife, had coveted from a distance when they'd picked it out on the garage forecourt at Tegel.

The car stopped fifty yards away and then nothing happened. The sun's reflection had turned the windscreen into a blazing shield and it was difficult to see the driver. The ball stood untouched in the centre circle.

Bartel felt dead inside, and at some level his brain had decided that it would be best if the world came to a stop right now, right here, with the football players set in stone.

One of the back doors opened and Bridget got out. He knew it was bad news then, but not how bad. The other back door opened and Helga appeared, clutching a book, and even at that distance he could see her face, and how uncertain she was, and how lost.

Bridget was in her best coat, and he could tell she'd just brushed her hair in the car before stepping out.

The driver got out, leaning on the door, and he recognised his brother-in-law, Johann, who lived close by in the southern suburbs, and who had been his sister's idol since childhood.

Bartel walked towards Bridget and when he was six feet away he stopped and saw that she had a wound on her face which she'd tried to disguise with powder. Her hands were tightly clasped but he could see the knuckles were red and bruised. She took three unsteady steps towards him.

He asked the question to which he already knew the answer. 'What's happened to Ellen?'

'It was a bomb,' she said. 'We were running to the shelter, she was in my arms, but I am here and she is not.'

CHAPTER THIRTY

Brooke had slept for an hour in the news editor's chair before going home for breakfast. He found Joy in her uniform, already up, getting Iris ready for a day with Mrs Mullins. Bright, even breezy, she was unrelentingly positive. The night before she'd written letters to the Red Cross and the US Embassy, and they stood ready for posting in the toast rack, with stamps affixed.

'Mum said I had to do something, not just sit and stew. I've got a telephone number for the family of one of the others captured with Ben, so I'll ring tonight and see if they've heard anything. There must be news; I just have to find it.'

Brooke suggested trying to ring Luke as well. The commandos were based at Achnacarry House, near Fort William, and he might be able to get a message through and plead for a call, explaining about Ben.

Joy gave him a hug. 'Thanks, Dad. That would be wonderful – you know, just to hear his voice. I couldn't bear to lose anyone else.'

Claire was asleep, and Brooke briefly contemplated taking one of the Veronal sleeping pills. He felt desperately tired still, but the fact that he'd kept one of the tablets in his pocket, for emergencies, made him feel unclean, as if he was already addicted. So instead he ate a slice of toast, drank a cup of tea steeped in tannin, changed into a fresh set of clothes and set out for the Spinning House, hoping the exhilaration of the hunt would keep him on his feet. He knew now that if he could find Leon Zeri, the possible survivor of the *Arandora Star*, he could find his runaway son.

At his desk, Brooke flicked through the Whitehall directory. A man in 'liaison' at the Ministry of Health was Delphic, insisting that all enquiries were now being handled directly by the Home Office. It was clear that the sinking of the *Arandora Star*, and the deaths of hundreds of Italian, German and Austrian internees, was a scandal. Nobody wanted to talk, let alone help. Brooke was passed from bureaucrat to pen-pusher until someone in the legal office informed him the issue was now *sub judice* pending an official enquiry led by Lord Snell, the leader of the Labour Party in the House of Lords – Brooke was certain this information was being read to him from a prepared statement – which meant that they couldn't help.

Brooke said he didn't care about who was to blame. He was just trying to find the survivor described in *The Times*. He was fobbed off again: all enquiries related to relatives of the dead and survivors were being coordinated by Scotland Yard. Brooke should ring Whitehall 1212.

Which is when, finally, he struck lucky. The inspector in charge of foreign aliens was Ronald 'Timber' Woods, who'd briefly been in the bed next to Brooke's at the sanatorium in Scarborough, having been shot through the neck standing on the edge of a trench across the Ypres Salient, trying to urge his men to clamber out into a hail of machine-gun fire.

'I can't believe it's you, Eden,' he said. The voice was certainly unsteady, rasping and punctuated by a frequent fluid glottal stop. The wound had clearly left an enduring mark.

Brooke explained that he thought he knew the identity of the survivor in a coma who had featured in the newspaper article. Where was the hospital? Both the Ministry of Health and the Home Office had been evasive.

'Not surprised, Eden. This'll end a few careers, I can tell you. The boat sailed without an escort – you know that? They didn't bother to put red crosses on the funnels. They'd got 1,700 men on board – as a liner in Civvy Street, it managed 500. It stinks.

'Everyone's desperate to wash their hands of it. It's a devil of a job trying to find out anything. The spokesman who helped *The Times* got carpeted. They want it forgotten – Home Office, Downing Street, they're all in a fug. But it won't go away – some of these Eyeties will be missed. One was head chef at The Ritz – another at the Café Royal. Half the West End's looking for names – are they dead, did they get out alive?

'I've got a number here you can try – in Bury, there's an internment camp there and they've got one of the Eyeties dealing with relatives cos he knows the lingo. Pathetic, really – one man, eight hundred dead.'

The camp was called Warth Mills – an old cotton factory

north of Manchester, and within easy reach of the quayside at Liverpool. Internees had been gathered there before being shipped out to Canada.

The phone rang and rang. Brooke was about to give up when a soft voice answered: 'Father Rossi.'

The accent was extraordinary, a subtle blend of Scots and Italian. Father Gaetano Rossi explained he'd been scheduled to go to Canada on the next ship after the *Arandora Star* but had been hauled out of the line on the dockside and told he had a job to do. They'd given him an old office, and packing cases of passports and documents. He was to compile lists of the dead, and survivors.

'There's a church outside the factory,' he said. 'They let me say Mass. But there's no one here now. I am alone. And I am sorry – the papers are not in order, and I am struggling to answer the letters. The task is too much.'

Brooke explained what he was after and read out the paragraph at the end of the story in *The Times*.

'Yes, yes. No one knows this man. But if anyone does they have been told to contact the hospital, at Newton Mearns, outside Glasgow. My old parish is in the city so I know it well. It is very beautiful. For children – yes? A quiet place, and out of the way of the world, so they let this man have peace. I do not have the number, *perdonami*.'

Brooke asked him to spell out the hospital name.

'Good luck with your task, Father,' said Brooke. 'You can only do what's in your power.' There was a pause, and a whispered *addio*, and then the line was dead.

Brooke walked through to the switchboard where one of the girls was painting her nails.

'Can you get me a line to Mearnskirk Hospital, Glasgow? Just put it through to my office.'

It took ten minutes, and then there was a whirring sound on the line, a moment of total depthless silence in which Brooke was certain they'd lost the connection, before a soft Scottish brogue was whispering in his ear: 'Mearnskirk Hospital, switchboard.'

'This is Detective Inspector Eden Brooke, Cambridge Borough Police. You have a patient, an Italian man rescued from the *Arandora Star*. Can I speak to the ward sister?'

'We call him Mr Eyetie – sorry. We had to call him something, and it's stuck. He's on Lewis Ward; I'll put you through to the night sister, it's the end of the shift. It may ring for a while, there's just a light, not a bell, so don't give up. I'll keep listening.'

The line hummed, and then began to buzz softly, rhythmically, and he imagined the ward, and the light winking, a nurse perhaps tending to one of the patients, her back turned.

'Sister Kershaw, Lewis Ward,' said a clear voice in an Edinburgh accent.

Brooke introduced himself and asked the nurse to sit down for a minute, if she could, so that he could ask a few questions. 'It is important. I won't take up too much time.'

'It's alright,' she said. 'They've had breakfast an hour ago. It's blissfully peaceful. It's an acute ward so most of the men are sick. But the doctor's been round so they're resting.'

'My wife's a nurse,' he said. 'She says that sometimes it's a joy to listen to the silence. This Mr Eyetie – can you see him now?'

'Yes. He's been in a coma but he's back with us now – although the periods of consciousness come and go.'

'Has he had any visitors?'

'Yes. His son. He's here now, asleep in a chair by the bed. He hitched a ride up from Cambridge. He's been sleeping here because the doctors said that when the old man comes round it's a big help having a friendly face by the bedside – it softens the shock. And of course he can talk his own language.'

'He's there right now?' Brooke stood up.

'Yes. He's called Bruno. I think he came as soon as he read the piece in the paper about his father. He showed us his ID card, and proof of address. Do you want to speak to him?'

'No – thank you. It's good to know he's there. He needs to come back to Cambridge, I'm afraid, and answer some questions. But for now let's leave him be. I'll talk to Glasgow and get a constable to attend.'

'I see.'

'I don't think he's done anything wrong but I don't want to frighten him. We've been looking for him, you see. We need his help.'

'Shall I tell him you phoned?'

'No. Please don't mention it, Sister. I'll send a constable and we'll go from there.'

'He's very nice,' she said. 'It's wonderful, isn't it? That he's here.'

CHAPTER THIRTY-ONE

The sergeants' room, behind the duty desk, smelt like a greengrocer's stall. The long, plain deal table was obscured by carrots, lettuce, radish, potatoes, green beans and a small white mountain of cauliflower, which resembled a large fluffy summer's cloud brought down to earth. Edison was sitting, brushing red fen dust from the vegetables, before allocating them to punnets laid out on the floor.

The sergeant spread his arms wide. 'What can we do? Now the kids have gone there's more than we can eat so I thought I'd distribute the largesse. A punnet's coming your way, sir.'

Edison's allotment was out at Stourbridge Common, beside the river, just where the main line to the coast vaulted the Cam via a metal girder bridge. One spring morning earlier that year Brooke had watched his sergeant skilfully harvesting lettuce for Claire. The Wasp had been in use for police business and Edison had offered to run him home – but via the allotment, so that he could garner a gift, rather than see it all go to waste. It was an idyllic spot: where Cambridge gave itself up to the countryside, and the Fens. Houseboats clung to the banks of the Cam, and wild horses roamed the water meadows, and the only sign of habitation lay ahead, where the river swung in a curve past the village of Fen Ditton, with its church tower and old wharf. Edison had patiently fetched a pair of secateurs from his shed. Brooke had watched the Fenman Express fly at speed over the bridge, en route from sunny seaside Hunstanton to smoky King's Cross in the capital.

Edison stood up stiffly now, rubbing dust from his hands.

Briskly, Brooke brought his sergeant up to date on the events of the night.

'You're sure he's an innocent man, sir?'

'Possibly. Even probably. He's given his name and address to the hospital authorities, shown them his ID card and made no attempt to "lie low" – hardly the actions of a man on the run having committed two murders, Edison. But there's still questions to answer. He was the last person to see Peggy Wylde alive: where had they gone, what had they said, what was their plan? Did Peggy know about the deaths on Earl Street? Did he own the Lucifer, and why's it in the river? We need to know the answers.'

Brooke shrugged. 'It's still possible he's the killer, but if he is he's either stupid or extraordinarily clever. Either way we need him here to answer questions. I've just rung Glasgow – they're pretty much stretched up there, so they can't run him down to us. They've offered to get him to the nick in Manchester.'

From his inside pocket, Brooke produced a sheaf of petrol coupons. 'That should get you there and back, care of the chief constable. He'll be at Piccadilly – the central police station – by three o'clock.'

'What if he doesn't want to leave the old man?' asked Edison.

'They'll arrest him for obstruction. I've authorised them to inform him of the deaths of Peggy Wylde and Nora Pollard – nothing more. He was the last person to see her alive. He needs to face up to that. The father's recovering, and he can go back to the bedside when we're satisfied we have the truth.'

Edison heaved himself up. 'And you, sir?'

'Start again, Sergeant. At least we're not back to square one. I'm certain the Earl Street killing led directly to Peggy's death. I'm equally certain it's linked to looting, and blackout crime. We've a lead there: Norwich have just been in touch. They've found some goods, fitting the description of the items pilfered from number 36, on a market stall in the city. They'll interview the trader later today, and they're sending the stuff by messenger. If we can find our thief, maybe we'll find our killer.'

CHAPTER THIRTY-TWO

Brooke had hoped the autopsy on Peggy Wylde would have been completed by the time he climbed the Galen's concrete switch-back steps to the sixth floor. Students came and went, clutching books, and as he passed a set of doors he glimpsed a hall within, a white-coated lecturer at a lectern, a large diagram of a dissected heart looming as a backdrop. When he pushed through the metal double doors of the morgue he knew he'd arrived at precisely the wrong moment; Dr Comfort, assisted by his loyal 'servants' – armed with saws and instruments of greater finesse – had opened up the body of the young woman, removed the vital organs and set them aside. The reassembly of the cadaver, in the interests of a formal identification, had not begun, and the liver, heart, brain and offal stood in jars of preserving fluid. Brooke's eyes, shielded by the ochre lenses, slid away from the splash of red where the corpse lay on its steel table, but then all too easily came to rest on the organs, illuminated by the sunlight which streamed in through the windows on three sides.

'Inspector, a few moments, please,' said Comfort, washing blood from his hands and arms at a stone sink. 'Then I can talk you through our findings.'

One of the servants brought Brooke a mug of tea and set it on the window ledge. Once he had Comfort's report he'd visit the Wylde family. He'd already despatched a uniformed sergeant with the bad news, but he needed to interview them all. The prospect of this grim duty was weighing him down.

Comfort, lighting a cigar, joined him to share the view over the rooftops.

It occurred to Brooke for the first time that the habitual cigar was in fact a device to shield the pathologist's nose from the smells of the laboratory: the blood, the preserving fluid, the unmistakable gravid edge of the butcher's shelf.

'I'm sorry, Brooke; hardly a complete surprise, but there is something you should see. She'll be sewn up in an hour, but if you've the stomach for it we can look now. I can cover the body – or most of it.'

A bloody sheet had been thrown over the corpse, leaving just the head and throat clear, the hair combed back brutally and parted along a line running forward from the crown to the forehead.

Vividly Brooke was back in Palestine, picking his way through the dead scattered on the road to the citadel at Tyre, trying not to see the faces in the hope that he could pass by without seeing a friend, or worse – one of his own men cut down in the final assault. The sense in which he wanted to look, but couldn't look, was disturbing.

'Here – do you see – the bruises again,' said Comfort, his face a few inches from the corpse. 'Strangled like her grandmother. The internal fractures are identical.'

'Not drowned?' asked Brooke, studying Comfort's face.

'No, no. The lungs are dry,' said the pathologist, indicating the jars, but Brooke moved closer to the exposed throat.

Comfort let the green smoke from the cigar linger around his head.

'One thought presents itself yet again, Brooke. The assailant in this case, as in that of Nora Pollard, would have faced his victim. Two hands, the arms extended – that's the key; the pressure is exerted forward, the thumbs pressed inwards. In such cases the victim might be able to use their hands to inflict an injury – usually to the assailant's face. In Mrs Pollard's case I suspect she was near death when attacked. But this girl was in the prime of life. She'd have fought. I'd keep that in mind. Look at this . . .'

He edged the sheet away from one of the arms and picked up the hand, turning it over to reveal scratches and some bruising.

'Maybe she landed a few blows?'

'Anything that might help us narrow the field?' asked Brooke, unable to keep a note of exasperation from his voice. The room, the disaggregated body, always made him unaccountably impatient, as if the physical evidence of death was a personal challenge to find those responsible.

'The backs of her heels are stained with grass – but not much,' said Comfort. 'It's a surmise, but I'd say she was killed at a spot nearby, then hauled to the hatchery and thrown into the water. That could have been immediately after she was killed, or much later; much later sounds more likely. Perhaps the killer put her body somewhere out of sight – a ditch, a barn, a copse of trees – then he came back after dark. With no air in her lungs she wouldn't float – that's how she got caught up in the bottom of the net.'

Brooke nodded, turning to go, but Comfort held up a hand.

'I'm sorry, Eden, there's more. You don't need to see the evidence, but I have to tell you it exists. And it provides a possible motive of sorts: she was two months pregnant, so she would have known there was a child on the way. I'm not sure but that seems to make it a more heinous crime.'

Brooke's eyes studied the distant view of the city's rooftops, desperate to avoid the specimen jars and the floating organs.

'Morally, it depends if the killer knew,' he said.

CHAPTER THIRTY-THREE

The Wylde family lived in a terraced house on Palmer Road, identical in its two-up two-down layout to the one destroyed by the bomb on Earl Street. The Kite imposed its own brand of uniformity. The district was dense and claustrophobic, with teeming back yards and narrow alleys, corner pubs and shops. The contrast with the city's splendid medieval heart was stark. The Wyldes' house was closer to the river by a quarter mile than Nora and Arthur Pollard's, but stood on lower ground, and so felt damper, despite the warm sunlight that brought out the smell of the place, dominated by the acrid stench of the nearby beet factory. The area had probably looked the same for half a century, and there were few signs a war was being fought, except that a greengrocer's on the corner had only a few potatoes and leeks on show, and a butcher's window was empty, despite a queue of housewives, clutching ration books, waiting patiently in line.

The Wyldes' front door was open, a woman constable on the step.

'PC Jenkins,' said Brooke, touching his hat. The Borough had six female constables, and Jenkins was the best. She carried out the duties women constables were expected to perform in efficient silence. But on several cases she had exhibited a detective's eye for detail, and a sergeant's initiative.

Briefly she told Brooke what to expect inside.

Alice, the mother, had been distraught when she was told that her daughter had been found dead, although she must have feared the worst. She'd been given a pill by the doctor and was up in bed. A neighbour was sitting with her. The two sisters, Elsie and Connie, were downstairs with Connie's boyfriend, Ollie.

'I've taken in a lot of food – gifts from neighbours,' said the constable. 'They seem popular as a family – that's how people respond, isn't it? A stew, an apple crumble, cakes. The woman opposite has been ferrying tea across the road on the half hour.'

'Spoken to the neighbours?' asked Brooke.

She nodded. 'Peggy is – was – a popular girl. Everyone says the same thing: so beautiful, elegant, a pretty face, a film star, but there's something almost unsaid, sir. Maybe she knew she was special, so a bit above herself. I'd say the sympathy was for the family – for the other girls, and the mum. Not sure there's really too much for the dead girl. Sorry to say that.'

Brooke took off his hat. 'It's your job, Constable. And you're doing it very well.'

The sisters were in the front room. Elsie, in her overalls, had her arm around Connie, while Ollie sat rather stiffly apart, on the same sofa, smoking with an ashtray beside him. The contrast between the girls was even more apparent than it had been when they'd come to the Spinning House to report Peggy's disappearance. Elsie looked tougher, a bit world-weary, while Connie appeared lost, her make-up streaked by tears.

Brooke touched his hat. 'I've some questions,' he said. 'But first I should see your mother. Indeed, I need to see her alone, so if you could all wait here with the constable.'

He climbed the stairs, the house revealing itself as battered and worn, the stair carpet threadbare, the wallpaper bubbled, the once-white ceilings yellow with nicotine and old age.

There were three bedrooms, one of them a box, but no bathroom, so he guessed there was a privy in the backyard. One door stood open to reveal two single beds set together under patchwork quilts. He was at eye level with the floor so he could see the chamber pot underneath one, and some slippers.

He knocked on the closed door to the front bedroom.

A woman's face appeared, her hair hidden under a bright scarf.

Brooke held his hat to his chest. 'Inspector Brooke. I do need to speak to Mrs Wylde alone, please, if she's up to it. Can you ask?'

There were whispers, and the clatter of a teacup and saucer, then the neighbour reappeared and fled, leaving the door open.

Alice Wylde was propped up on pillows, settling her hands and dabbing at her lips with a handkerchief which had been embroidered in one corner with the letters AW. The room was bleak. A neat WRVS uniform hung from a hanger on the wardrobe door.

'I'm sorry, Mrs Wylde. There is something I need to tell you.'

Brooke felt this woman was a pale shadow of the matriarch he'd seen on the morning after the Earl Street raid. The loss of her mother had made her bitter and sad, but Peggy's murder seemed to have put her on her own death bed: she was grey, bloodless, less substantial than the pillow supporting her fragile skull. Brooke had to remind himself that she was likely to be little more than fifty years old.

'I've just come from the pathologist. There seems little doubt Peggy was murdered, but that it would have been very swift, and painless. She would not have suffered.'

Brooke was thankful that this lie always seemed to have such a magical effect. The woman's eyes – which were grey – caught the light for the first time.

'Thank you. Can you tell her sisters? They keep imagining the worst.'

'But there is some bad news. Peggy was pregnant, Mrs Wylde, two months gone. So she would have known her condition. Did she talk about this with you?'

She shook her head by a fraction, studying the wall, where a rectangle of sunlight was edging across flowered wallpaper.

'No – we didn't talk about such things. Peggy lived her own life. She knew what I thought. That's why she spent so much time at Earl Street. My parents were more forgiving. More fun. And this is where it's led . . .'

She drew herself up on the pillows.

'It'll be the Eyetie boy,' she said.

'Will it?' asked Brooke. 'They'd been going out that long?'

She nodded. 'The girls will know for sure, and they keep secrets. Perhaps there were other boys, they may know their names; I only hope Peggy did.'

Again, it was a bitter thing to say, and once it was out of her mouth Brooke could see she desperately wanted to take it back, but all she managed was: 'Can you go now?'

He closed her door, and heard the crimp of pillows, and imagined her turning her face to the wall.

In the front room they were eating slices of cake a well-wisher had left on the step. The simple act of sharing food had transformed the atmosphere. Ollie sat on the floor, a plate balanced on his knees.

Elsie looked stoical, already the senior adult. 'Have you found the Eyetie? It's him, isn't it?'

He told them Zeri had been found and was being brought to Cambridge for interrogation. As the last person to see their sister alive, he was a vital witness. There was no doubt Peggy was murdered, he told them, and Zeri was a suspect: at this moment, nothing more than that.

'I've just told your mother the results of the autopsy. The pathologist asked me to tell you all that her death was swift and painless.'

Brooke left a beat, letting that news sink in.

'I'm afraid I have to tell you something else . . .'

The girls, breaking their habit, looked at each other.

'Peggy was two months pregnant.'

Connie covered her mouth, and reached out for Ollie, while Elsie looked down briefly at her hands, held together on her lap.

'How long had she been going out with Bruno Zeri?' asked Brooke.

'About two months,' said Elsie.

'Were there other boyfriends?'

'Plenty of them pushed their luck,' said Elsie. 'It's the war. All the boys think they've got the right. Who knows, eh? We could all be dead tomorrow. So why wait?' She dabbed at her mouth quickly with a handkerchief. 'There was Tim – the pilot. She dumped him about that time,' said Elsie.

'Tim who?'

'Tim Vale. He's just got his wings or whatever they call it. He'll

209

be flying soon. They went out for a bit before the Eyetie came on the scene. He came round here – even Mum liked him. And he had a few bob. He came round at Christmas with a pair of ice skates for Peggy – brand new. And we all went to the Cricketers one night with Grandma and Granddad and he had a five-pound note in his wallet – I saw it.'

'And there were other boys, but we didn't get the names, did we, Else? And there was a secret admirer,' said Connie.

They all managed a grin, even Ollie.

'She wouldn't tell us who he was – but he wanted to run away with her, and start a new life, and he was going to buy her everything she ever wanted. I think she made him up.'

Elsie was shaking her head. 'I think he was real, alright. She said she couldn't shake him off. That it had started off as a joke but she was scared now.'

'She said that, Elsie – that she was scared of him?' Brooke asked.

Elsie nodded. 'She said she couldn't tell us who he was because she didn't want to hurt anybody. So maybe he was married.'

'But we don't know for sure,' said Connie, as if her sister had gone too far.

'We're pretty sure whoever got into Nora's house knew what he was looking for – the rings, and the hidden cash,' said Brooke. 'Did Tim and Bruno go round to Earl Street to see your grandma?'

'Oh yeah,' said Elsie. 'We all went – well, not Mum. Peggy loved showing off the boys. They'd all go down the Cricketers with Granddad too. We had a good time.'

Connie nodded. 'I was gonna take Ollie, but it's too late now. It would have been fun.'

'And there's no one with anything against the family? No feuds?' asked Brooke.

'We're just an ordinary family,' said Elsie. 'The only feud we had was with each other. It was silly, really. Mum's chapel – cos Dad was – and she doesn't hold with the pub, or dancing, or courting. Nana liked to kick her heels up. So did Granddad. It wasn't as if they couldn't have rubbed along if they'd all tried. It just festered. Take the Eyetie – he wasn't really welcome here, but Nana thought he was a hoot, so he and Peggy went round loads.'

'Mum likes Ollie,' said Connie, proudly, playing with his hair.

'He's new. Give her time,' said Elsie.

CHAPTER THIRTY-FOUR

This time Marshall airfield, on the edge of the city, was on full alert. It took them several minutes to get past the barrier in the radio car, despite the fact the Spinning House had rung ahead. An invasion warning had been issued for Eastern England, and a machine-gun nest on the perimeter wire was fully manned. The guards at the gate checked their documents, unsmiling, and Brooke was asked to remove his glasses; gone were the days when the airfield workers came and went in a crowd. Once their paperwork was cleared they were told there had been three separate reports of parachutists landing in Norfolk and then melting away into the Fens. Roadblocks had been set up on all major roads. Raids were expected on coastal defences and airfields inland. The base was busy, or at least affected to look busy. Traffic circled the runway: petrol dowsers, staff cars, REME lorries and army jeeps sped past.

Pilot Officer Tim Vale had been assigned to the night flight and was out on standby at the eastern edge of the runway apron. The police driver set off over the grass, the car bouncing lazily. Brooke counted six Spitfires ahead, all surrounded by mechanics, working in the blinding sunlight.

It was only as they got closer that he realised each of the aircraft was smartly painted in jet black, ready for combat at night and intercepting incoming bombers. There was something un-British about the brutal livery, as if each wing might sport a swastika.

Beyond the aircraft there stood a line of barrack huts. They had been directed by the guardhouse to Mess Hut 8: a wooden pavilion, with a ramshackle veranda. Three pilots were slumped in deckchairs out on the grass listening to a radio broadcast of the Met Office forecast.

Tim Vale was inside on his bunk. A wooden locker sported several magazine pictures of half-naked women, mostly Hollywood starlets. Vale was reading a newspaper, the *Express*, while smoking, and when he saw Brooke there was a perceptible moment of absolute immobility, the hand holding the cigarette poised an inch from his slightly plump lips.

'Pilot Officer Vale?' said Brooke, surveying the dormitory, which was empty except for four men playing cards at a table by the door.

He held out his warrant card.

Vale flushed, fidgeting, stubbing out the cigarette then

promptly knocking out a fresh one from a packet, forgetting to offer one to Brooke, while producing a gold lighter.

It occurred to Brooke that the slightly awkward adolescent manners might be a cover. Vale was good-looking in a clean-cut fashion, lightly built, with fair hair and blue eyes. In an RAF flight jacket he would have just about passed as old enough to drink beer in a pub.

'Sorry,' he said, sitting up, finally proffering the packet. 'My first duty shift,' he added, perhaps feeling the need to explain the nervous energy. 'If the balloon goes up tonight so do I.' He smiled at his own joke. 'They reckon the invasion might be on.'

Another pilot appeared at the door, shutting out the light.

'So what's Tim been up to?' he asked, in a loud voice. 'Must be serious. Gentleman has his own police driver.'

One of the card players looked up. 'I reckon he's done a ton in the MG.'

'Told me he had one of the barmaids from The Plough the other night – took her out for a spin after closing time,' said another. 'It's not her dad, is it?'

Brooke suggested to Vale that they go outside. The incessant banter was another cover, of course, and one Brooke knew well. Fear, anxiety, loss – all these painful emotions were camouflaged by jokes and innuendo. But he noted that Vale looked pleased with the reference to the pub barmaid.

One table on the grass had been set apart, and they sat in folding chairs, while the loud-mouthed pilot brought them tea by way of making peace.

'I'm still the new boy,' said Vale. 'I get some stick.'

'It's about Peggy Wylde,' said Brooke.

'I heard. They reckon the Eyetie from the canteen did it. That right?'

Brooke ignored the question, suspicious at the speed with which Vale had sought to misdirect the conversation. 'You went out with Miss Wylde; that's right, isn't it? When did that end?'

'She dumped me good and proper at the start of the summer – day before my birthday, in fact, 28th June. I went round and tried to patch it up – you know – after she said it was all off. I said I might get posted up country but I'd got the car, I could get back. It'd be fun . . . Then I heard that I might get on the black Spitfires here. I'd be just up the road. It would have been perfect. But you know, she'd fallen for Rudolph Valentino and that was it, which was a shame.'

'You said you tried to talk to her. Where was this?'

For a moment Vale hesitated and Brooke knew he was calculating, weighing up the answer.

'Their house, on Palmer Road.'

'Ever go to the grandmother's – Nora's?'

'Yes. We all went down the Cricketers. It was a laugh. We had some fun, alright. You've got to have some fun . . .'

'Did Nora boast about her nest egg – the cash she kept hidden in the house?'

Vale shook his head. 'Can't have been much; the house was a bit tatty and Peggy's granddad drank for England.'

A lone Oxford was overhead, circling for a landing, and for a moment they tracked its flight, although Brooke took the chance to watch Vale. There was something about this moment in a life – the boundary between a child and a man – which was oddly disturbing. He thought Tim Vale was probably growing up very quickly, almost before his eyes.

'When was the last time you saw Peggy?'

'To talk to? Like I said, two months ago. I *saw* her most days

215

up here but she just cut me dead, as if we'd never met or anything, which was a bit rich because she dumped me.'

Brooke took off his hat despite the sunlight and ran a hand back through his hair. 'So she never told you that she was pregnant?'

Vale's cheeks reddened, and for the first time Brooke thought he looked afraid.

'How – you know – how far gone . . . ?'

'Two months, Tim. So it's you, or it's Bruno Zeri. Or someone we don't know about yet. Did you get lucky? What did you say? That once you started flying you might not come back. Better live life for the day. Why not give a hero something to live for . . . Have some fun while we can.'

Vale was shaking his head. 'I never did. We had a kiss and that down by the river but that was it. I walked her home, but that was it, honest to God. It isn't me – it's the Eyetie, bound to be.'

He took up his mug of tea and began to blow and sip.

'You didn't ask her to marry you, then?'

'No, I didn't,' he said, but he wouldn't meet Brooke's shielded eyes.

In the Great War he'd heard the story a hundred times. Men – boys – proposing to girls outside dance halls and pubs, girls they hardly knew, who'd taken pity on them and said yes, they'd wait, so that they'd have a sweetheart to write home to.

'Where were you the evening she died, Tim, the evening after the air raid on the Kite?'

'Out in the car for a spin.' He pointed across the grass to half a dozen neatly parked cars in the lee of a line of poplars.

The blue MG stood out. It looked brand new. Brooke imagined it hurtling down dappled lanes. And sky-blue, of course, Peggy's favourite colour.

'You don't own a bicycle then?'

'Nope,' he said, shaking his head.

'Where did you go in the car?'

'A pub out at Hornsea – the Golden Fleece – then back over the downs at Newmarket. I had the coupons so I thought I'd use 'em up.'

'Alone?'

'Yup. I've got a girl in town but she works shifts at the Exchange.' The city's telephone system was run from a grey Edwardian block directly opposite the Spinning House. Each evening, each morning, young women came and went, keeping the switchboards running.

'Then what?' prompted Brooke.

'I drove home, had tea, and we listened to Haw-Haw.'

'Who's "we"?'

'My mother. She's a widow; my father was RAF, a squadron leader, but he got shot up over Amiens in '18, never recovered. He died a few years back. It's just her at home so I keep her company.'

Brooke took a note. 'That where the money comes from, is it? I doubt a pilot officer's wages cover an MG. And the girls said you were generous with presents for Peggy.'

'Mum says I should have some laughs now, before it gets serious.'

Brooke stood. 'Let's hope someone at the Golden Fleece remembers you,' he said, standing, stretching in the sun. 'You a regular?'

Vale's easy smile was back. 'Used to be. But this lot uses The Plough – you know, at Fen Ditton. So we'll go there when we're stood down. It's all new to me.'

He gave Brooke a boyish grin – a cool pint with his fellow

pilots after an aerial gunfight was clearly an idyllic prospect.

'Right. We'll check with the Golden Fleece. If they don't remember you, they'll remember the car,' said Brooke. 'It's a good job it's so flashy. You'd never forget it.'

CHAPTER THIRTY-FIVE

Brooke sat in the great lobby of the Fitzwilliam Museum, alone, in the dark, listening to the distant siren at the Guildhall. The mechanical wail, trapped beneath the soaring dome, circled, dying out, only to be pursued by the next identical note. The dome's architect, a man whose name escaped him, but who'd met his grandfather, had fallen to his death at Ely Cathedral – stepping out unthinkingly across the belfry floor of the West Tower, over an open trapdoor. The idea of that interior fall inspired a sudden bout of vertigo now, so that Brooke had to sit down on the marble bench and take a deep breath.

He had returned to the Spinning House from Marshall in a state of despair. It was extremely unlikely that Bruno Zeri was their double killer. Young Tim Vale seemed equally incapable of such crimes, although Brooke had the strong sense, which had grown since he'd left the airfield, that he was telling lies about something.

But a single phone call had transformed his mood. A sergeant from Norwich police station rang at seven o'clock. The market trader who had spotted stolen goods from Earl Street had given detectives the name of his supplier, and one of the items in question had arrived by motorcycle messenger: a silver-plate salver, engraved to mark the retirement of Arthur Pollard. The market trader said the man was a regular in the trade, and there was an invoice of sorts, with a name, but no address, although he knew he was from Cambridge. The firm's name was AA Supply.

Footsteps echoed in the stairwell and a guard appeared. 'Sir. The major will see you in the south gallery – down the stairs but turn left, not right to the BCC.'

Brooke descended, the persistent wail of the siren almost imperceptible once he'd reached the basement. A corridor led away into a large shadowy gallery, where Kohler sat at desk in a pool of amber light. In the shadows Brooke discerned the shattered face of a god, and the torso of a lion.

'Eden. I thought we could talk here. Fewer flapping ears. There's a raid on but it looks like a false alarm. Apologies in advance if I have to skedaddle. When I want to get away I come here, although it's a bit draughty. I can offer warmth . . .'

He held up a bottle of whisky.

Pouring drinks into tin mugs in the half-light, Kohler's face was caught in profile. He looked like a pharaoh's scribe, working deep, perhaps, in the bowels of a pyramid. The papers on his desk were held down by a piece of ancient stone sculpture, a scarab beetle, exquisitely carved.

'I've got this,' said Brooke, producing a satchel, and from within, the silver salver. 'It's on the inventory of missing items from Earl Street. It was sold on to a market trader in Norwich. The name of the seller was Joe Miller. All we know is that he's from Cambridge and he operates under the name of AA Supply. I don't suppose you've made any progress on the lists I asked for, Edmund?'

Kohler had them to hand, in a leather document pouch, which Brooke recognised from the desert campaign. It was an item which seemed to sum up the quartermaster's careful stewardship.

'They're not complete, but they run to hundreds, Eden. It's a hell of a job. But I've got the bare bones – alphabetical lists of all the men drafted in to civil defence.'

There were ten in total, each one allocated to one of the services provided under central control, from auxiliary firemen to motorcycle and bicycle messengers.

They split the lists. Unless Miller was on the electoral roll they'd have to apply to the Home Office to track down his ID card, and given the common nature of his name that might produce dozens of results, and would take months. Brooke's hunch was still that their thief wore a uniform of some kind.

An hour later they were still scanning columns of typed names and addresses: there were nearly two hundred auxiliary firemen alone, and twice as many ARP wardens – and it was here, on one of the longest lists, that they found Joe Miller at last.

'Got him!' said Kohler, triumphant. 'Well, I'll be damned,' he added. 'Address on Earl Street, Eden. ARP warden since a week before the war. Exempt from military service due to a dodgy heart. Age given as thirty-six. Married. Occupation "trader" – whatever that means.'

Brooke could even recall his face, glimpsed that night as he staggered out of the Wellington Arms after the bomb had hit. Fresh-faced, middle-aged, with an oddly persistent smile. At the time he'd only been really interested in the tin hat marked *W*. He'd tried, subtly, to discourage Brooke from going into number 36. And the next day he'd sat on the kerb smoking, watching the clear-up operation, running a hand through fair hair.

Brooke consulted his watch. 'I'll make sure the local bobby checks the house tonight. We'll apply for a warrant and go in mob-handed in the morning.'

'You think he's the killer?' asked Kohler.

'Well, he's flogged Arthur Pollard's silver dish. So I reckon he's a thief – or more likely the fence. He fits in somewhere. What's more, he lives opposite the Pollards. He was in plain sight. Maybe Peggy suspected him, and that's why she's dead.'

'You said this Peggy Wylde girl was a looker?' said Kohler, raising an eyebrow.

'True. The sisters reckon she had a secret admirer. Miller might fit the bill. We'll have to have a quiet word with Mrs Miller.'

Kohler lit his pipe. 'It looks promising,' he said.

'Tell me about the wardens,' said Brooke. 'Duties, jurisdiction, the lot . . .'

'Not much you don't know. They were allocated their patches in '39, with about five hundred civilians in each. It's their job to know everyone, where they sleep, if they're at home or away, where they go if they head to a shelter, if they've got an Anderson in the yard, if they've got family staying. They'll know each family, each house, what they've got, where they keep it. They'll even have a note of where they'll go if they're bombed out – that's a government requirement, so we can keep track.'

Kohler sipped his whisky. 'Only thing with the wardens is they stand out a bit. The helmet, the bluette overalls. The badge. People respect a uniform. They can hardly skulk about. And of course they live in the area. If they were spotted lifting anything they'd be caught red-handed.'

Brooke reset his hat. 'I thought I saw other wardens in the street that night?'

'Yes – I think most wardens would head for the bomb site once they were sure the raid was over. They help each other out. It's a network, like so many others. You don't think this is organised, surely?'

Brooke smiled. 'Wouldn't be difficult, would it? And you could slip people in. The council gives out helmets and armbands willy-nilly. It's like Ruritania. We'll find out the truth tomorrow. He may be a bad apple, Edmund. Let's hope there isn't a barrelful.'

CHAPTER THIRTY-SIX

Brooke found Edison laid out on the Nile bed in his office on the third floor of the Spinning House, the slatted moonlight from the blinds defining his substantial figure, which suggested a slumbering medieval knight, except for the stockinged feet which stuck over the end and exhibited extensive darning. It may have been an illusion but his sergeant brought with him the thrill of the open road, the distinct aroma of warm tarmac, and petrol, and spark plugs. A pair of driving gauntlets lay crossed on his chest.

Brooke crept away, fetched tea from the canteen and came back to find his sergeant sitting up.

'I am sorry, sir. I drove all day and thought you'd be along so I just lay down for a minute.' He yawned widely until his jaw cracked.

After his tea he seemed to wake up a second time.

'I've got Zeri downstairs in Cell 5, sir. He's not happy, but he hasn't made a fuss, so I didn't need to arrest him. I think he understands the gravity of the situation. He's been told by Glasgow that the Wylde girl's dead. I have to say it seems to have affected him very badly.

'Two issues, sir. He had £160 in five-pound and ten-pound notes on him which he insists was his old man's savings from the safe at the restaurant. But as soon as I clapped eyes on him I saw the real problem, so I got Dr Comfort to check him out and he's made a report . . .'

Edison offered a manila file.

'What problem?' asked Brooke, hanging up his coat and hat.

'Best you see it first-hand, sir.'

They tramped down past the duty desk and into the narrow corkscrew stairwell which led to the old cells, which had been carved into the chalk bedrock and had once held felons and highwaymen.

Zeri heard them coming because when they unlocked the door, and light flooded the cell, he was on his feet, and Brooke saw his face, marked by wounds: a series of thin abrasions, which had drawn blood, and marked one of his cheekbones.

'Let's talk upstairs,' said Brooke, standing back. Watching his prisoner climb the corkscrew steps he recalled Dr Comfort's observations of Peggy Wylde's corpse. The bruising to the hands suggested she'd hit out at her assailant. Unlike her aged grandmother she was fit and well, and could have injured the killer.

They sat in the canteen, deserted now that the night shift was out on the streets. The cook, closing up, made Zeri a fried egg sandwich and left a pot of tea. Zeri turned down a cigarette, but took tea and ate the sandwich in half a dozen bites. He'd only said a few words but the Italian accent was pronounced, and Brooke recalled that while he'd been born in Cambridge he'd spent most of his life on a farm in Italy with his grandparents.

Brooke smoked, reminding himself that the guilty rarely exhibit a healthy appetite. Zeri was an Italian from central casting: black slicked hair, olive skin, and the eyes – which dominated – were the colour of the river in flood: a deep, limpid brown. Tall, willowy, but with bony fists, which must have impressed the boys at Ollie Fox's boxing club. Brooke could see now why he'd idolised the Italian: he was everything he wasn't – tall, good-looking, at ease. A father figure, perhaps, for the orphan boy.

They let him finish, and he finally accepted a cigarette.

'Bruno. Listen,' said Brooke. 'This is a very important interview, do you understand? You were the last person to see Peggy alive. She's been murdered, and we need to find her killer.'

Brooke leant back in his chair. 'The general view, at least initially, was that you killed her. Did you?'

He splayed his hand against his chest. 'No. No – never. I love Peggy very much. I see her this last time by the river . . . I never hurt her.' He was half on his feet, and so Edison leant over and gently applied some weight to his shoulder until he sat back.

Zeri's eyes flooded, but he went on speaking quite calmly, the tears running down his face freely. Edison fussed over pouring tea, while Brooke reminded himself that tears could tell many stories.

'I meet her outside the airfield that day, I have to tell her what has happened, that my father is in his hospital – yes? That I must go to him. But I did not say these things there, in the street. I tell her we must go to our place by the river; there is a field, very quiet, beyond the place where the rich boys dive.'

Edison took a note, while Brooke leant back, encouraging Zeri to tell his story in his own way.

'We go there before, it is very beautiful.' His eyes lit up. 'Romantic. I say then I must go . . .' He held out his hands, playing out the role. 'But that I will be back. Our plans do not change. We will marry, and I will be a father.'

'It was your child?'

'Yes. This is why the field is our special place.'

'And you didn't fight with Peggy? Isn't that how you got those cuts?'

'No, never. I never touch her if she does not want to be touched.'

Brooke lit a Black Russian while there were more tears. He decided he'd come back to the cuts and abrasions on Zeri's face later. For now he'd try to establish the facts.

'Let's go back to the start. Tell me about the night the bomb fell. You were at the Roma?'

He held up his hands. '*Certo*. The bomb woke me up, I went out into the street, and then I go out into the park and watch, and there are no more bombs, and I think I don't like the shelter, so I go back to bed.'

'You weren't worried about Peggy?'

'I see the fires, they are far away, on the other side of the Kite. I know she is safe. *Per favore* – again, please?' he said, pointing at the cigarette. He took it carefully, but with the same easy grace with which he'd sipped his tea, the same measured confidence.

'So next day – what happened?'

'I find in the paper the story, this reporter says a man is alive after the ship is sunk – yes?'

'The *Arandora Star*,' said Brooke.

'*Sì*. He is in coma. They do not know his name. But he has a medallion . . .'

He unbuttoned his overalls at the neck to reveal a gold chain, with a medal, identical to the description in *The Times*: a green tree, against a red sky, a crown above, and white zigzag mountains.

He took it off and laid it on the tabletop.

'So I think it must be my father, and that I must go to him because my mother cannot because she is held in the camp and I cannot talk to her. So I ring family – yes? In Manchester – an uncle, my cousins – and they have been told of this man and they give me the name of the hospital but it is a long way and I must start the journey. First, I must tell Peggy.'

'Did she know then about the Earl Street bomb – that her grandparents were dead?'

He shook his head. 'She hear gossip – she is worried – there are people killed, and there is looting. But there are no names, no street. She says she will cycle there now, to be double sure, but I say we must go to our place because I have something to tell her. Something very important. And so she comes with me . . .'

'Then what?'

'She cries that I am going, and says maybe I do not come back. I promise, I promise I come back to her. But I must hurry, so I leave to pack my bag. I leave her on the bench by the river. She needs time – yes? Time to mend her face. Then she will go to the Kite.'

'You cycled back to the Roma?'

'*Certo*.'

'And took money from the safe? It's a lot of money. Everyone says you were in debt, that times were hard, but this is a fortune.'

'This is my father's money. It is mine to keep safe. I think he may need it now, in Glasgow.'

'You didn't steal it from Nora's house on Earl Street? You knew she had savings hidden in the house – did Peggy tell you that?'

'Yes. I like Nora – she enjoy life. But I don't take her money.'

Zeri licked his lips and, sickeningly, Brooke knew then that he was lying.

He let the silence stretch out.

'Why hitch a ride when you had money for the train?' asked Edison. His normal calm voice held an edge, and Brooke wondered if he too had sensed they were being told less than the whole truth.

'The trains do not run because of the bombs. Only beyond Birmingham.'

'But you went to the station to check?'

'*Sì.*'

'On your bike?' asked Brooke.

'No. I cannot take it with me so I walk, then when I find it all closed down I walk out of the city until I get lift.'

'What was the model of the bike?' asked Brooke.

Zeri's eyes searched the room, as if the machine was with them, and perhaps sensing a trap.

'It is black. Very old. No value. It has a bell marked with a red star. Otherwise, I do not know this model.'

'And you left it in the yard at the restaurant?'

'*Certo, certo.*'

'It's not there now, Bruno. Why is that?'

He shrugged. 'It is stolen.'

'An old battered bike from a back yard which is of no value?'

Zeri stubbed out the cigarette and slid his hands out of sight.

Brooke cut to the issue. 'The injuries to your face, Bruno. Can you explain them?'

He nodded, his heavy, jet-black hair flopping down. His eyes rarely rested anywhere in the room, but flitted from Brooke to Edison, and then to the door, and the high barred window.

'I get a lift on the Great North Road – a lorry, with two men. They friendly, but when they hear my voice they throw me out, in a ditch, and this is how they say goodbye.' He used the back of his hand to wipe his lips.

'Did you report the incident?'

'*Si*. I walk on road at night and a police car, it stop. They see the blood and so I tell them the story. The lorry, it has a big name . . .'

He waved a hand to indicate the width of the branding.

'It say PEACOCK – like the bird.'

'Did they take you to the station?'

'No. I say I must go. They say I must report this but I say no. They take me to night garage – there are lights, and tea. They drive away.'

'Where was this?' asked Edison, making a note.

'The Great North Road – a place called Scottish Corner?'

'Scotch Corner,' said Edison, nodding.

Zeri smiled, grateful for the help, suddenly calm, and Brooke recalled the shy, inarticulate man who'd served his mother that night before the Great War. There was a fleeting likeness, a glimpse of a softer, generous nature.

Edison asked more routine questions about the men who'd attacked him on the open road. Brooke assessed the suspect: he'd fled to his father's bedside, had used his real name, and made no effort to avoid the police. Could it be an elaborate double bluff? Might he be their killer after all? Was the child really his, or had the news sparked a passionate argument?

Brooke poured more stewed tea from the pot.

'Did you know Tim Vale?' he asked.

'He is the hero, the brave pilot, but he is not gentleman. He takes Peggy out into the country, to a beauty spot, but he is no gentleman.'

'He tried to force himself on her?'

'He is too fast. He only wants this one thing. Peggy is afraid.'

'She said that?'

'*Sì*. And he spends too much money, which makes her feel cheap, like she is kept woman – they say this? He buys presents and he drives the sporting car. Driving miles, picking up packages – this is a mystery too.'

'What kind of packages?'

'Brown paper. She asks but he won't tell. And the miles he drives, where does he get the coupons? There is no answer to this. And always the wallet is full – five pounds, ten pounds, even she say a fifty-pound note. This I have never seen.'

'Where does he pick up these packages?'

'Hospitals.'

'Which hospitals?'

'Here – in Cambridge. And then out . . . to the north, to the west. I do not know the names.'

Edison's pencil scratched away.

Brooke changed tack. 'You visited Earl Street – Peggy's grandparents. Did you meet a man called Miller – he lives opposite, an ARP warden?'

'He buys and sells goods,' added Edison.

'*Sì*. He is the *trafficone* – the spiv. He drinks in the pub on the corner and they all like him to his face but then they say he is a cheat when he is not there. Then he buys a round of drinks and they all forget again,' he added, shaking his head.

'Did he buy Peggy a drink?'

Zeri nodded slowly. 'Many times. Nora says his wife run away, yes? So – what do they say? He sniffs around, yes. Like a dog. No one trusts this man once his back is turned.'

CHAPTER THIRTY-SEVEN

They locked Zeri up again in Cell 5, telling him that they had to check his statement, and that in particular they needed to track down the police officers who'd dropped him at Scotch Corner. Then Edison fled to his bed at home, and Brooke took to the Nile cot in his office, watching the slatted moonlight creep across the walls, in a state of exhaustion, but robbed of even the prospect of sleep. The light caught the Kilner jar on the top shelf, the killer's petrol-soaked glove within. Spectral figures seemed to wax and wane in the half-light: Alice Wylde turning her face to the wall, Tim Vale at the wheel of his sky-blue MG ferrying mysterious packages, and ARP warden Joe Miller, directing sightseers back behind the barricade on Earl Street the night the bomb dropped. In the morning they'd raid his house: was he the key to the case, the fence who'd slipped the Pollards' treasures into the wider black market?

The puzzle defied him, so he grabbed his hat and clattered down the stairs, acknowledging a brief salute from the duty sergeant before he was out in the empty street, striding south into town. Crossing the river at the Great Bridge, he climbed Castle Hill, pausing at the summit to look back over the sleeping city, the skyline punctuated by spires and barrage balloons. There'd been no siren, and so it looked as if Tim Vale's entry into battle would be delayed, if only for a few precious hours. Turning his back on the panorama, he set off down Huntingdon Road – a leafy boulevard of Edwardian villas, leading out into open hill country. After a half mile he turned down a rough track that led to a small Victorian chapel of ease, which stood guard over a crowded burial ground.

His father, Sir John Brooke, had stipulated in his will that he should be buried here, with a plain stone, stipulating his vital dates and the award of the Nobel Prize for medicine. The purpose of the graveyard was to offer a place of rest for those doubtful of the claims of any religion. Brooke was always surprised by the degree to which this lonely spot radiated a spiritual presence, despite the absence of angels, crosses and scripture.

The light here consisted of two lamp posts, set either side of the chapel, so that the graveyard was a cat's cradle of shadows thrown by headstones, and trees, and a few monuments to the once famous. Many of the inscriptions on the stones, weathered by the passing years, defied interpretation now, like hieroglyphs on an ancient hillside.

He walked to his father's grave and felt what he always felt, a sense of disconnection and lost time. He set a small blue stone, fished out of the Cam, on the top edge of the stone, touched his hat and walked on.

There was a bench by the far wall that gave a view over open fields. In the very first light of dawn he could see the landscape emerging, gentle hills and full-leafed trees, which looked like a woodcut in black and white. It was a favourite spot to sit, and it meant he could contemplate the headstone he had actually walked out of the city to visit.

DETECTIVE CHIEF INSPECTOR
FRANK D. EDWARDES
5th January 1880–12th February 1940
Loved by his family, respected by his fellow officers
We trust in the few

Brooke had always thought it typical of Edwardes, who had been his mentor at the Spinning House between the wars, to choose the motto of the Borough for his epitaph. It was, after all, one of the smallest police forces in the country, but under Edwardes' guidance it had built a reputation for honest and even inspired detection.

'A summer's night, Frank. It's cool and balmy. I don't know what the temperature is like where you are.'

Edwardes had never given any hint of belief in the presence of a God, still less the existence of the Devil. It was the kind of joke Brooke knew he'd appreciate, given the remote possibility his old friend was listening. A long, slow, final illness had marred his life, but in his prime he'd been a gifted detective because he knew his *manor*, the real city outside the college walls, and its everyday life. He'd seen in Brooke a fellow enthusiast for the dark streets and the crooked alleys.

'You'll have surmised by my presence that I'm stuck,' said Brooke, sitting.

He liked talking out loud, because it inspired logical thought. In the two decades after he'd joined the Borough he'd often turned to Edwardes when a puzzle defied solution. He had never needed his help more urgently.

'I have a series of events which seem to lack any coherent sense of cause and effect. An elderly woman is murdered during a burglary at her house which has just been bombed. The next evening – the next evening, Frank – her granddaughter is murdered cycling home from Marshall airfield, the body eventually found in the river. Both were strangled, the killer standing in front of the victim.'

Brooke lit a cigarette. It was disturbing the extent to which once he'd started one of these soliloquies he felt that Edwardes was listening, and that therefore he couldn't simply stop talking.

'So, Frank, who is my man?'

He laughed at the silence. 'I know, Frank. Claire will remind me that the killer might be a woman. And I am trying to keep that in mind. There is no shortage of women in this case, but they're all victims of one sort or another.'

Brooke stood and rummaged in his pocket. Edwardes had two passions: his bank of transmitters and receivers, which had sustained his double-life as a radio ham, especially in his last months; and his trees, planted around the house which looked over Fenner's, the university cricket ground. One of the finest was a great walnut, too big to embrace, and Brooke on his midnight walks had pocketed a small sample of this year's harvest for the kitchen at Newnham Croft. He set a single nut on the top of the stone, knowing it would blow away, and possibly roll into the fertile soil, and maybe one day provide more shade for the grave.

'Three suspects, Frank, all very different: the dashing pilot, the shifty spiv and – just possibly – the romantic Italian everyone was so keen to blame in the first place.'

He laughed out loud at the line-up.

'The Eyetie's in Cell 5. If his story pans out we'll have to let him go.

'Pilot Officer Vale enjoys a healthy private income, which I need to double-check too, because he's up to something illicit with his fast car. He plays the innocent boyfriend but my guess is he thinks the girls have a duty to make his life as much fun as possible. And he might have got the poor girl pregnant. The Eyetie was keen to claim fatherhood, but then that serves his purposes.

'The spiv has to be the prime suspect. He's an ARP warden, which means he can come and go and nobody notices. It's the perfect cover. And if I'm right, and he's a fence, he fits neatly into organised petty crime, including adulterated petrol. And, once his wife left him, he's been playing the field in Earl Street. Chatted Peggy up – bought her drinks. I've got a radio car watching the house. And the magistrates have issued a warrant so we'll knock on his door first thing. Back in Earl Street where it all began.'

Birdsong was beginning to herald dawn.

Sometimes he felt that he could hear Edwardes' voice.

They'd probably worked on ten murder cases together in the decades after the Great War – leaving aside domestic violence, and killings where the culprit was immediately to hand, like pub brawls.

The chief superintendent's mantra was always the same when the case seemed intractable.

'It's the passion of the moment, Eden. That's what you've got to nail. To kill someone, to snuff out a life, the motivation must be overwhelming. Identify that compelling emotion and the light floods in: is it greed, hate, love or fear? Try to share that moment with the killer, try to feel it too. Step into their shoes, Eden.'

Walking home along leafy streets, and later lying in bed alone, he thought about the victims, and the passions of killers; and when he imagined Nora's pale face and her butchered fingers he thought of greed, and when he saw Peggy's – robbed for ever of its beauty, the blood running freely – he thought of unrequited love. He saw the killer then, propelled from one violent emotion to another, and wondered what he was feeling now, at this moment, and if that too would lead to murder.

CHAPTER THIRTY-EIGHT

The trap in Earl Street was easy to set. Brooke stationed one constable at the end of the cul-de-sac, outside the Wellington Arms, and one in the back alley, cutting off the only other means of escape. A radio car was parked around the corner, its driver on lookout in the distance, in case they had to make a rapid pursuit.

Satisfied with his deployments, Brooke, noting a clapped-out van parked at the kerb, knocked smartly. It was not quite seven o'clock, and the neighbourhood was still quiet, so the triple tap echoed. Like most policemen Brooke had a sixth sense for an empty house; this wasn't one of them.

He heard a footfall on the stairs and Joe Miller, ARP warden, and spiv of the Kite, opened the door by two inches, revealing a spotless white vest and suit trousers, bare feet on bare boards, his face partly obscured by the suds of a shaving stick.

Brooke showed his warrant card. 'A minute of your time, Mr Miller.' The sizzle of bacon in a pan came from the direction of the kitchen.

'Just off to work,' he said, but Brooke simply pushed his way in.

'I have the necessary paperwork, Mr Miller. A serious crime has been committed. We can take a ride downtown if you wish.'

Brooke took off his hat and placed it carefully on the stand in the hallway, shifting a large brown paper parcel under his arm. 'That your vehicle outside?'

'Yeah. What of it?'

'You don't own a bicycle?'

'I buy and sell goods. I need to shift stuff. Bike's no good to me.'

'As I say, I have some questions . . .'

'I'm shaving,' said Miller. The muscles in his shoulders and arms were tightly flexed. At some point in his life he'd done heavy manual work, or lifted weights.

'Give me a second,' he said, jogging quickly up the stairs and out of sight. 'Make yourself at home,' he called down.

Brooke went into the front room, which had a radio and two armchairs, and a drying frame, mostly crowded with shirts and socks, although there was a pair of nylons too. Brooke parted the net curtains: the view opposite was dominated by the blackened ruin of the Pollards' house, the windows blind.

A couple walked past on the pavement, heads down, sleepy after a night in the shelter.

'I didn't get much shut-eye,' said Miller, appearing, tightening a tie at his throat, a newly ironed white shirt immaculately creaseless. 'I need my breakfast. What's this about?' he said.

The frying pan held three rashers and an egg. There was one chair at the kitchen table, and a single mug.

'I understand you live alone?' said Brooke, placing the brown paper parcel on the table.

'Missus ran off with a soldier. I'm not bothered. I don't go short . . .' He had an odd mannerism, a sharp sideways movement of the jaw, a tic certainly, which made him look shifty. He eyed the brown paper package as he slid the contents of the pan onto a plate and sat down, setting the cigarette in an ashtray beside a bottle of brown sauce.

'And your work is?' asked Brooke, lighting a cigarette to divert his senses from the crisp fatty rind of the bacon.

'Wholesale supply. Buying and selling. I've got a stall on Market Hill of a Friday. Electrics is the big thing, but you know, I can shift anything. Look. I don't want to be awkward, but what is this about?'

'What was wrong with the army?' asked Brooke, unkindly.

'The old ticker's faulty,' said Miller, egg yolk spilling over his bottom lip. He sipped his tea with a steady hand. The man was a curious contradiction. The heavy build, the smooth patter, jarred with the face, which was oddly weak. He reminded Brooke of a school friend who'd been bullied mercilessly and had responded with boxing lessons. It was a dangerous combination, weakness and the potential for violence.

Brooke noted the new kettle, a bottle of beer on the sideboard, a paper carton of cigarette packets.

'Business is good, then.'

Miller finished the bacon and set his knife and fork aside. As he smoked he bit small corners off a slice of fried bread.

'I've got to go, you know,' he said. 'Some of us have work to get on with . . .'

'Where today? Norwich – they've got a good market. We've been watching a few of the stalls, and the lock-up shops, because they've been flogging stolen stuff. Not just stolen. Looted.'

Miller blinked, slowly, as if he'd been expecting the accusation. 'I wouldn't touch that.'

'You touched this, though, didn't you?'

Brooke slid the silver salver from the package.

'Stallholder even had a receipt,' added Brooke. 'Your name – no address, so we had to track you down. You are AA Supply, I presume?'

Miller nodded. 'What of it?'

'It was Arthur Pollard's. It's on the list of items stolen after the bomb fell. The night Nora was murdered.'

Miller leant back in the chair, smoking.

'I think the man who killed Nora, and looted the house, passed the stolen goods on to a fence. I think that's you. Or are you the thief yourself? That's what you do for a living, surely – cut out the middleman.'

Miller shrugged. Brooke wondered if this was how he'd got through life, sliding past every tricky question by pretending it didn't apply to him.

'You said you got the receipt for the silver, have you?' asked Miller. 'I'd take a closer look if I was you.'

Brooke took it out of his wallet.

Silver salver, worn. £2 6s 8p.

'Date?' asked Miller.

Brooke took off his glasses but the vital data was smudged.

'Unclear,' he admitted.

'I've got me own records somewhere. I flogged that silver two weeks ago, more.'

Brooke hadn't asked when the market trader had bought the salver, which was a cardinal error: he'd simply assumed that because the salver wasn't in the house it must have been stolen on the night of the bomb. It was an amateur mistake, and he felt Frank Edwardes' often-repeated reprimand: *One step at a time, Eden.*

'I would have got more but the inscription cuts the value. They have to smooth it away – takes hours.'

'I can check with Norwich, Mr Miller.'

'Go ahead. Be my guest.'

'How'd you get it?' Brooke tried to keep his anger under control, but it was a losing battle, because he was angry with himself.

'Favour for Nora and Arthur.'

'That's convenient.'

'Money was short. All that talk about Nora's nest egg was just that – talk.

'Who needs a silver salver in the Kite? I think Arthur had spent too much in the Cricketers and they needed to pay off the pawnshop. It wasn't the first thing I shifted for them.' Miller lit a fresh cigarette. 'I didn't mind helping them out. They're virtually family anyway. I've got me feet under the table there.'

'How's that?'

Miller went over to the drying frame and, parting two shirts, picked up the pair of stockings and ran them through his hand.

'These are Elsie's. We don't make a big deal of it. Some people love a bit of malicious gossip. My wife's got her own life now, but I like to keep me head down. But Elsie's my girl.' He blew an elaborate smoke ring across the kitchen table.

'I see. How long has that relationship been going on?'

'Six months. She doesn't want the old girl to know – Alice. Sour-faced cow. Least Nora knew how to have a good time. So it's been hush-hush.'

'Peggy turn you down, did she?' said Brooke.

A muscle flexed in Miller's jaw and he tried to laugh, and Brooke thought it was an old trick, getting close to the plain sister when the real target was the pretty one: was that Joe Miller's game?

'Don't know what you mean,' he said.

'I heard you were keen. Make yourself a nuisance, did you?'

'Look, I've got blood in my veins. Every bloke was keen. Elsie's my girl – and she'll vouch for the silver salver.'

'I hope so. But the thief got away with a lot more than a bit of silver on the night of the bomb. I'm going to ask you to stand aside while we search the house for stolen goods, sir.'

'It's an Aladdin's cave upstairs,' he said. 'Help yourself. But you'll find nothing of Arthur and Nora's, I'll tell you that for nothing.'

CHAPTER THIRTY-NINE

The line of villas on Midsummer Lane had been designed with a touch of playful Gothic, the shutters painted gaily in green, mustard yellow and even white. The iron-work railings sported lance-heads and crouching griffins. A fretted lamp over the door looked Middle Eastern. More than a year of the war had left some of the houses looking tired, with overgrown gardens and peeling paintwork. But Gardenia House, the home of Dr Elizabeth Vale, was in a disreputable class of its own. One shutter was missing and another hung at an angle. A thicket of rose and bramble obscured the small front lawn. Curtains were drawn upstairs, while downstairs they stood open by an inch or two, revealing a dark, lifeless interior.

Brooke knocked smartly on the door, straightening his tie, brushing house dust off his suit. It had taken two hours to work through the goods in Miller's house, and he'd left Edison to supervise the final sortie into the attic. So far there had been no correlation with any items on the Spinning House register of stolen goods, but Brooke still had hopes. The upper bedrooms had been crammed with tea-crates loaded with canned food, bric-a-brac, pots and pans (used), and a quantity of lead piping. A radio car had picked Elsie Wylde up outside the furniture factory during her lunch hour. She'd confirmed Miller's story that Nora and Arthur Pollard had asked for his help in selling the silver salver a week before the fatal bombing raid. She'd removed her nylons from public view and, rolling them up, had stuffed them in her overalls pocket. Then she'd asked for a lift back to work.

Zeri's story that he'd been set upon by a lorry driver near Scotch Corner was still being checked out by police at Durham. Which left Brooke with his other suspect: Pilot Officer Tim Vale, and more precisely his ample private income.

Brooke knocked again, and this time the simple force of his knuckles opened the door, to reveal a cool marble floor and a set of fine mahogany stairs rising up into the gloom. A cat's bowl was in the shadows, and he could smell sour milk.

'Timothy?' The voice was certainly aged but not feeble, and carried a cut-glass edge.

Brooke pushed open a door into the front room.

A woman sat at a large table spread with documents. As his eyes accommodated the gloom, he saw that she was in a bath-chair.

'I'm sorry, I thought it was my son. I'd get up but . . . Tim's at the airfield on standby. He won't be back 'til the day after tomorrow. God willing.'

The room itself was as dilapidated as the exterior of the villa. A threadbare carpet revealed the floorboards beneath. A sofa and chairs sprouted clumps of horsehair. In one corner a bed had been set up, which was neatly made.

He saw now the remains of a breakfast on the table: toast, jam and a bottle of milk.

'I'm sorry. I'm Doctor Vale – and you are?' Her voice carried a brisk professional authority.

Brooke showed his warrant card and said he was investigating the murder of Peggy Wylde – her son's former girlfriend.

'Yes. Terrible,' she said, her hand extending to lie on an open newspaper. 'Tim's started getting the local rag every day so I've followed developments. Father always took *The Times*, but there we are. I can't offer you tea, I'm afraid. The kettle's in the kitchen and I can't get this thing down the hallway. I'm trapped. This is my entire world, Inspector. In private I crawl around like a baby.'

She offered him a chair and he moved a pile of books to sit down. 'Did you meet Peggy?'

'Yes. Pretty girl. Stunning, really. Tim was stricken. But she gave him the heave-ho. I don't want to speak ill of the dead but I felt she was a bit disappointed with all this . . .' She indicated the general squalor. 'I think she thought we might be a bit wealthier than we are. Fact is, we are on what my late husband used to call "our uppers". Neither of us got anything from our parents and I can't do much . . .'

She swept her hand over the desktop. 'I have a few loyal patients. And I do a little research for the Ministry of Health. And a little teaching for the university. But it's pennies.'

Brooke noted a locked glass cabinet stacked with pillboxes, and a sink, a set of scales and, attached to the ceiling, the guiderail for a set of curtains.

'We'd sell this place at the drop of a hat but no one's buying, you see. And it needs a lot of work. The roof's a colander. Tim earns his money, at least he will, and I don't want him wasting his life looking after me.

'Why do you want to speak to him, Inspector, if I may ask? He's up at Marshall's as I say, in fact he's rarely home now. He has to wait for one of the others to give him a lift home – so he often sleeps over.'

It was clear she knew nothing about the blue MG. Or, presumably, the lifestyle which went with it.

And then Brooke thought about the stairs.

'We're just trying to piece together Peggy's last movements on the night she died. I wanted to check some details with Tim. Also, we're missing a few items of hers which we can't find. Tim said he gave her presents and she gave some back but he can't recall which. We think she had a silver lipstick in her bag but we can't find it – would you mind if I checked Tim's room? He said it might be there in a sock drawer?'

It was a tissue of implausible lies but it was the best Brooke could muster at short notice. For a moment he thought she was going to tell him to get a warrant.

'If you must,' she said. 'His room's at the back and the socks used to be in the third drawer down. There's a tree which needs cutting back, I'm afraid, so it's very dark, although he never complains.'

The house upstairs was coated in dust, and there was a smell of something dead – possibly mice, or worse. Tim's room was like a museum of childhood, with models of planes, and books on flying, and what looked like a toy Morse code set, and a tiny single bed.

But it hadn't been slept in.

Down the hall he found the front main bedroom. It was clear young Tim had decided to upgrade his sleeping quarters. The sheets were a bit grubby and whirled in a nest-like circle. What could only be described as 'dirty' magazines lay open on the old carpet. An ashtray on the bedside table was full of butts. A bottle of whisky stood on the dressing table beside a tooth mug.

But it was the boxes which caught his eye. There were several sizes marked with coded numbers, but one set were identical and marked *BAYER VERONAL*, the small print in German.

It was a moment of discovery, but also disappointment. The seedy room seemed to encapsulate what the war might become: a slow descent into petty crime on the home front, with high ideals corrupted by greed and opportunism. To find its evidence here, in a house once dedicated to ministering to the sick, was particularly sad.

There were always victims, and in another life, he might have been one of them, desperate each night for the relief brought by a small white pill. Ripping open one of the boxes and making a rough calculation, he estimated there were nearly two hundred smaller pillboxes of sleeping tablets. He ripped another larger box and found more tablets, but he didn't recognise the brand names.

What had Claire said about Veronal? They'd been named after Italy's sleepiest city. And here they were, stacked high in a back bedroom, on a leafy street in Cambridge. There was one golden rule about the wartime black market: it traded in anything that was in short supply.

Tim Vale, dashing pilot and war hero, stood now in a very different light.

It wasn't difficult to see how he'd secured a supply of the lucrative drug. Dr Vale would have the right forms for ordering much-needed drugs. One day someone would have spotted the pattern, but by keeping the thefts piecemeal and random, he'd clearly been able to build up a store. How long had it taken? A year, maybe more. So it was a meticulous, unhurried crime.

And a cold-blooded one, preying on innocent victims. What was more, it was black-market crime. There would be associates, lines of supply, the splitting of profits. Did Vale's desperate need for cash to fund his lifestyle, and escape this tawdry middle-class poverty, extend further, to looting, and theft, to adulterated petrol, and ultimately murder?

CHAPTER FORTY

The plan had been in place for forty-eight hours but the moon had hidden on the first night; now it hung like a paper lantern over the Guildhall, and there was no siren, so Grandcourt presented himself at the Spinning House in his oiled jacket, old pumps and a knapsack. In the desert they'd specialised in 'reccies' behind enemy lines, gaining a reputation for daring and light-footed infiltration. The truth was that Brooke was a studier of maps, and an observer of the lie of the land during the hours of daylight, and so the midnight forays were hardly heroic: their adventures were meticulously planned, and they took no risks. Reckless bravery was a vice to be avoided at all costs. They would slip away into the dark, lie low and wait for the enemy to reveal itself by night fires, torches and cigarette ends. And they would listen to the crawling trucks, the skittering motorbikes, the shuffling of the horses tied to the rails, and return with vital intelligence.

Brooke met Grandcourt at the duty desk where he left instructions for the night shift. The thorough searching of Jack Miller's house had not produced a single stolen item, but the local constable had orders to watch the house in case of a moonlit flit. Miller was more than capable of loading up his merchandise, and driving off to another life. Or did he have a lock-up somewhere – a secret place for goods too hot to sell in the city? Pilot Officer Vale was still on standby at Marshall and the duty sergeant had spoken to the guardroom: the pilot was not authorised to leave the base before the following evening, and would be available for interview in the morning, unless the Spitfire flight became operational. A radio car had been posted to Gardenia House, and Edison had dealt with the paperwork to obtain a warrant from magistrates for the removal of the stolen drugs the next morning, and their safekeeping in the Spinning House lock-up.

Brooke checked his gear: knapsack, flask, torch, maps, cigarettes and lighter. Grandcourt, always lightly equipped, had on an army belt with pouches, and a jacket with webbing, in which would be stored anything they might need. Like Brooke, he was a gifted planner.

'Who's running the shelter if the siren sounds?' asked Brooke, mindful that he'd dragged his friend away from his nightly duties on Parker's Piece.

'Dobson from Shelter 5 – he can double up for once. Everyone knows the drill anyway; sometimes I think they'd run the show better without the wardens. It's a home from home now.'

One nod to the desk and they were out into St Andrew's Street and the waiting car, which sped them out into the fields beyond Barton, to the doorstep of the Blue Ball. They had time for a drink before the bailiff arrived – old Potter again with his stick – and took them down to the river and the boat, which was as ordered: a clinker canoe, for two men, with bench seats and wide paddles.

Brooke attached a torch to the prow with a length of leather shoelace and they pushed away from the damp bank. The bailiff's lantern swung in the darkness, revealing reeds and pollarded willows, as they slipped round a bend in the river. At Byron's Pool they disembarked and used the portage steps to lug the canoe to the upper river, where the wide water lay still in the moonlight, covered in its veil of weed and lilies. The water looked innocent enough, but it was difficult to push aside the thought that it had yielded up the lifeless body of Peggy Wylde only twenty-four hours ago.

Earlier, Brooke had managed to get home for tea, and to see Joy, and try to gauge her mood. She had taken on a hopeful role and was busy with the baby. Brooke had sat with the child for a few minutes to let his daughter write to the War Office, pressing for news. Brooke had read out loud a few pages from *The Wind in the Willows*. The baby knew nothing, of course, of the story, but a reading voice seemed to send her to sleep, and to be honest the childish escape was just what Brooke sought: an attempt to re-establish the river as a benign, soothing presence.

The story was a favourite of his, which he'd first encountered as a young father reading to Luke and Joy. His own childhood had come too early to catch its first decade of popularity, and perhaps its real magic came in this gift – that he'd been given a second chance to relive the thrills of the riverbank. The book's sense of gentle adventure, and the cool unifying thread of the river, had never left him.

Now, slipping away from Hauxton Junction in the canoe, he felt the story's magical spell anew.

The canoe caught in its wake the first light of the moon. Swiftly they were at the point where the river divided between its two senior upper branches, the Granta and the Rhee. A tree branch swung out here and Brooke used his hand to bring them to a stop, turning Grandcourt's torch to illuminate Aldiss's map.

'There ahead, you can see where the two streams meet. The oil was on the surface to the right, in the Rhee. So the source is upstream, but none of the villages betray any sign of the thieves. The local constables have drawn a blank. I thought we'd try and narrow it down, Grandcourt. How's the nose?'

Grandcourt's moustache twitched as he sniffed. The wide river was a mirror here, the air utterly still.

'It's the night, of course, it sharpens everything,' said Grandcourt, sniffing again. 'There's the river – fresh water's like wine. And there's the fields, and night flowers, and some cow dung. But no petrol, sir.'

'Not yet,' added Brooke.

Paddling onwards they took the Rhee south-west, and the country opened up under a starry sky, and the banks were low, so it felt as if they were travelling overland.

After fifteen minutes Grandcourt touched him on the shoulder and they drifted for a moment in silence.

'Sewage farm,' said Grandcourt. 'Don't need much of a nose for that.'

Brooke had missed it, which reminded him that Claire said he obsessed so much about his damaged eyes it had relegated his other senses to the second rank.

The village of Haslingfield appeared, a church tower stood against the sky, and some architectural trees, which might denote a big house.

They stopped by a small stream which ran in from the west.

'Where does it go?' asked Grandcourt.

'To the manor house,' said Brooke, recalling exactly the detail on the map. It was a feature of these hills that several of the manors were moated, small streams trained to provide defences, before being allowed to dribble on downhill into the Rhee.

Grandcourt opened his flask and they drank hot tea. The village betrayed itself by a barking dog, the sound of cows in a barn and a single passing motor car, which gave no trace of light. A thread of music, on a gramophone record, came to them, until a slamming door shut it out.

One mile further on they approached Harston. Here they skirted a mill, and an island. Again a small stream led off the main river to Harston Hall. Through the heavy trees and hedges they could just see its windows. Brooke made a note: there was growing anger at the inequities of the blackout, which seemed to require hundreds of ARP wardens to keep backstreets dark, while the rich were allowed to light up their manors like Chinese lanterns.

They used the torch to examine the narrowing river, but there was no trace of petrol on the water, no dead rats floating, and they were running out of navigable channel.

Half a mile further and the moon started to dodge behind clouds as they reached Barrington. There was a chalk quarry here and they thought they heard the gears of a lorry grinding. The village lay across half a mile of water meadows.

Grandcourt put his hand in the current, producing a distinctive 'cloop', which made Brooke turn round. His former batman sniffed at the water as it ran out of his cupped fingers.

'That's it, sir. I'm sure. And it's strong, sir.'

It must have been an illusion but in the failing light the water looked oily and Brooke imagined that if he took a step on the surface it would support his weight.

The river split here between the main channel and a final streamlet which ran east to Barrington Hall, through the village, which clustered around a large green, used for sheep and cattle.

'Which way do you think?' asked Grandcourt.

'Let her slip back,' said Brooke, and they waited as the sluggish current took them back downstream by twenty yards.

He took out his matches, struck one and flicked it into the water.

The blue flame caught, creeping away from them over the surface, as he knew it would. It drew a line across the river from bank to bank, edging away, until it reached the fork in the stream, where it flared vividly, a sudden yellow-red, and swept away up the ditch towards the village, before dying out.

Grandcourt clamped a fist tight shut in triumph.

'It's too narrow, even for us,' said Brooke. 'Tomorrow we'll take a closer look at sleepy Barrington.'

The sound of the distant air raid siren on the Guildhall came to them over the fields from Cambridge. To the west, immediately, they saw the dull diffuse flash of anti-aircraft fire in a bank of cloud, and heard within a minute the drone of an approaching engine.

CHAPTER FORTY-ONE

Bartel's Heinkel was still several miles short of the city, on a path over Newmarket Downs, embedded in that bank of midnight cloud. The radar masts on the coast had picked them up, and there was already intermittent ack-ack fire. There'd been strong winds over the sea and so they'd had to abandon the plan to fly further north, avoiding the fighters and the barrage balloons. Schmidt was down in the Perspex niche below the pilot's chair, his eye on the bombsight. Their target, Bridge 1505, was now less than five minutes away.

The first bomb to fall, the one that would shatter the iron girders, carried its new chalk message. This time it had fallen to

Bartel to inscribe it, and the crew had stood silently watching, a little ceremony of brotherhood on the grassy airfield at Waren.

It read simply: *Für Ellen.*

Two days earlier, standing by the Adler, Bridget had patiently told him what had happened to their child. His wife had stayed in Berlin, at their flat in Lichtenberg, on the night of the air raid. The authorities had been adamant that RAF raids were unlikely, and that the city's defences to the north were robust. When the siren had sounded they'd rushed out into the street with the rest, his mother (who'd come to stay because she wanted to go shopping the next day) dragging a pre-packed suitcase, while Bridget had taken Helga by the hand, holding the baby within her overcoat, heading for the U-Bahn station on the corner. Old man Todt, in the flat above, refused to leave the building at all, insisting it was a false alarm and that the British bombers didn't have the range to reach the capital.

One bomb had dropped on the street, hitting the red-brick church at the corner, so that the windows exploded outwards, as if a tidal wave had broken from within. (Later reports, gleaned by his mother, said the shell had fallen in the small cemetery yard, shredding the tombstones.) Glass, slates and shards of marble rained down on them all. His wife had been knocked to the ground, while Ellen had died as she fell – *starb wie sie fiel.*

Bartel had noted his wife's gift for a telling phrase.

Bridget had carried her to the underground station. A group of women from their apartment block had gone in search of a doctor, and taken the elder girl with them. Eventually, Dr Rilke came and examined the child with trembling hands. The shrapnel wound on the side of her head was ragged, and there had been surprisingly little blood, but there was no doubt she had died instantly. Rilke, waving his hand over the small head, had been unable to touch the child's skin.

Bartel had been given leave to attend the funeral, held swiftly at the crematorium. Getting in the staff car afterwards he'd noted the smoke dribbling from the pencil-thin chimney. Then he'd been driven to his old family house in the woods beyond Spandau. The tragedy had revitalised his mother, who had offered to keep the family safe from further bombing raids on the city. She ferried cold drinks to his wife while she sat in the garden, and Helga was to be persuaded to go to school on the bus. His mother fussed, the matriarch back in control, while his wife watched the shadows in the pine wood, and pressed his hand when he said he had to go back to Waren, because there was a mission – unfinished business – and the weather was improving.

Oberst Fritsch called him to the commandant's office and sat him down, offering him a cigar, but there was no question, said Bartel, despite the offer, of deserting his comrades at this moment. He required no more leave. The pre-flight briefing was at six-thirty and he would attend. The summer storm in the North Sea had blown itself out. The Heinkel was undergoing its final fuel and bomb checks out on the runway grass, rocking slightly in the breeze which thudded against the wooden huts. He must fly, he said. The war, after all, was at a critical stage. The invasion must go ahead.

At dusk he'd simply collected his gear with the rest and trudged out to climb in through the bathtub. Only fleetingly, but for the first time, did it feel like wriggling into a coffin.

Now they were almost over the sleeping city.

'There she is,' said Schmidt.

Bartel, looking down, saw the silver river.

The ack-ack fire exploded around them, white flashes on port and starboard, and below. Bartel had seen the women at Waren covering damaged aircraft with the thin fabric, the wooden struts within revealed, and the fragility of the aircraft made him laugh out loud now, because it was strangely comforting that there was so little to hit. There was the acrid stench of fusing wires, but the engines pounded on, and so Bartel took them down another 1,000 feet.

'One minute,' announced Schmidt.

The searchlights found them, a dazzling numinous blaze of light, and Bartel thought of angels, and realised that he felt no fear, and that this was because he had been released from the duty he had previously felt to return at any cost. The family had been shattered, and now his place was here in the sky, while his mother cared for his wife, in the safety of the forest.

He pushed forward the lever and the bomb bay opened, the night air rushed in, bringing with it the smell of fields and the harvest, intensely reminiscent of home.

The river below was insanely close, so that Bartel could see the pattern of ripples on the surface, and the houseboats on the bank. He experienced the odd sensation that he was skating on its surface, a child on ice, yelling with joy.

'*Für Ellen*,' said Schmidt, and released the first bomb.

CHAPTER FORTY-TWO

From the steps of the Blue Ball, Brooke could see fires in the city producing a red glow in the cloudy night sky. The constable at the wheel of the radio car said the all-clear had yet to sound and there were fears the bomber would return on a second run, so he ran them into town straight to Parker's Piece, and the iron doors of Grandcourt's shelter. The streets had been empty and lifeless, and even here, where the tented army encampment covered the grass, there were no lights, no signs of life, except a few guards on duty along the perimeter.

Dobson, Grandcourt's stand-in as warden, let them into Shelter

4, which held about a hundred civilians in one of seven concrete chambers half buried in the edge of the grass common. It was clear, after a few minutes, that 'shelter life' was well established. Most people sat in family huddles on blankets and rolled-up overcoats, with a central nest of thermos flasks, blankets and pillows. The whistle of kettles on Primus stoves – swiftly stifled – filled the air, along with whispers and the gentle crying of a single child. A few elderly people had brought deckchairs.

The chemical toilets were – according to a large sign – behind a wall at the far end, but the smell was ubiquitous, mingled with the steamy stench of people, who'd been quietly sweating in their own beds until the siren had transported them from one bad dream to another. A low stratum of cigarette smoke hung in the air, lit by the single lantern hung from a hook in the ceiling.

Brooke smoked, and then Grandcourt appeared, padding softly in his socks along the central aisle, holding a tin mug in a claw-like hand to his chest. He had a battered tin hat marked *SW* – shelter warden.

He sat beside Brooke on the concrete 'bench' which ran round the perimeter of the room, and assembled a pipe-full of tobacco but, checking a fob watch, turned away the offer of a light. 'It makes the children cough, so I'll wait. Best let them get off at least.'

He nodded towards a family in one corner. They'd brought a picture and set it up against the wall, a photographer's studio shot of grandparents and parents and a host of children, set in a heavy frame, but minus the glass. A man, snoring gently, suddenly snorted, prompting a general turning-over, and muffled complaints.

'We've made some more progress tonight, Grandcourt. I'll ring the constable at Barrington tomorrow and see what we can set up: we need to comb that village from top to bottom, without raising alarms.'

'What do you think's there, sir?'

'Your man Bannister said adulterating petrol is a messy business.' He outlined the scientist's description of a typical blackout gang operation: the petty thieves issued with cans, the mixing with kerosene, then on-selling into the black market.

Grandcourt sucked his pipe. 'Flimsies, you say?' he said, judging the moment was right to light his pipe at last. 'Remember them in the desert, sir? On a long haul we'd lose a quarter of the water – more – from those cans because it just all leaked away. Same for fuel. They reckon Jerry's got much better kit and we're trying to copy it. Another job for a clever engineer . . .'

Brooke smiled. He should have thought of that himself. If they were storing the fuel in the cans, then that could easily explain the leak. The petrol was just bleeding away. The flimsies were so poorly made that they fractured under pressure.

The strains of the all-clear slipped into the shelter through the air vents. The crowd half groaned, half cheered and slowly began to stir.

Outside, the sky had cleared to reveal the stars, and a column of smoke rising from the Kite. Brooke could smell the fire, or rather its damp depressing coda: wet ash, sodden wood, drenched bedding and upholstery. Gossip amongst the crowd on the grass was that a single bomber had made a run, dropping a bomb on Stourbridge Common near the allotments, then one in the Kite, and the rest on the railyards.

Brooke set out, keen to keep an eye out for looters or thieves.

Palmer Road, where the Wylde family lived, was untouched, but Salisbury Street, just five minutes away, was crowded with emergency services. Smoke was pouring from a house, billowing from the downstairs and upstairs window. An ARP warden told him that according to his lists everyone was accounted for, safe and sound. The fire brigade had a hose playing on the frontage, so that steam was mixing with the black smoke. Brooke stood watching, and lit a cigarette, realising that the smells on the air had transported him back to Bonfire Night, standing with his father in the garden, watching the Guy burn, the thrilling whiff of sulphur left behind by every screaming rocket.

'Brooke,' said a voice, and he turned to see Edmund Kohler marching up the street. His old friend always walked as if he had a swagger stick under one arm.

'Thought I'd get out and see how it all works on the ground,' he said. 'It struck me when I gave you my little lecture that I was good on the theory, but low on practice.'

A shout went up from the fire brigade, and then everyone was running towards them up the street. A police constable stopped, breathless, and pointed back at the burning house. Bricks began to tumble from the roofline, then the chimney fell in on itself, and with a sickening intuition Brooke knew what was going to happen next: very slowly the entire facade of the house began to peel away, in one piece, from the floors and ceilings. Tipping forward, it fractured, but was still substantially a single wall of bricks as it hit the cobbles.

When the dust and smoke cleared the interior rooms stood revealed, like a doll's house, the front swung open. The staircase was charred, but the wallpaper in the front room, gold stripes on velvet red, was untouched, while upstairs they could see a wardrobe, the door open to reveal shirts and jackets, and a mirror engraved with a flying swan. Brooke thought this was the final insult for the family who'd lost their home, that their private lives should be left on public view.

Kohler was directing operations. 'You men . . . This isn't a tea party.' He marched off towards the Civil Defence squad which had settled down on the kerb with thermos flasks to watch the disaster unfold. There were grumbles, and Brooke thought he heard a whispered 'darky', before they hauled themselves to their feet and set about forming a shoring-up squad, presumably to make safe the buildings next door to the ruined house. A lorry was on standby with wooden props and iron stays.

Brooke felt a light touch on his arm and turned to see a face he knew, but somehow distrusted the moment of recognition. It was Alice Wylde, Peggy's mother. He was shocked to see white clean lines on her cheeks where tears had cleared a path through smoke and ash.

'Everything that's happened,' she said. 'And then this . . .'

She nodded at the exposed house.

'That's the Foxes' house. You've met Ollie – Connie's boyfriend. Sid and Marjorie were in the shelters. So they're lucky, really. Just doesn't feel like it, does it? They've come round to ours for tonight.'

'And Ollie, is he safe?'

'He was with Connie at our house. When the siren goes off we all pile into the Anderson in the backyard and there's room for another. He's family now and it's a comfort for us all really, to have a boy there.

'Sid and Marjorie take 'em in for the money, the orphans, but Marjorie's alright – she tries. There's worse mothers in the street, I'll tell you that. But it's not a real family, if you know what I mean. Not loving.'

Brooke nodded. It explained a lot: the lost look, the cigarettes to feel grown up, the desperate hold on young Connie's hand.

'They're all round at ours safe and sound. I said I'd pop out and have a look for them – now I've got to go back and tell 'em the whole lot's come down.' She shook her head. 'I'll pray for them.'

Brooke thought it was touching that she'd find time for prayers for others given her own tragedy. She had a mother and a daughter to mourn. He took her arm and walked her back to Palmer Road.

The Wyldes' front door was open. Inside, the ceremonies of tea and toast were in full swing despite the hour. The girls – Elsie and Connie – were in the front room squeezed into the same armchair. Ollie sat on the floor again, his feet to the grate, with Connie's hand resting in his thick hair. His face was smoky grey with smuts.

Brooke was introduced to Sid and Marjorie, who'd been given the other two chairs. Sid was trying to eat what looked like toast and dripping while smoking a cigarette, while Marjorie was weeping silently into a large handkerchief.

Brooke felt Alice, still on his arm, waver slightly as if she might collapse, so he tightened his grip.

'Bad news,' he said, taking over. 'I think they've got the fire under control but the front's come down, I'm afraid. Is there anywhere you can go tonight – it'll be for a while?'

Marjorie looked stricken but Sid had clearly been thinking the situation through. 'We can go to Jean's in Newmarket,' he said, leaning over and patting his wife's hand. 'Her boys are away now.'

Connie leant forward and hung round Ollie's neck from behind. 'You can stay with us, can't he, Mum – if he doesn't mind the sofa.'

'He'll need to stay local because of Marshall's,' offered Sid. 'It's a good job and he needs to fend for himself. We can't afford to feed any more mouths.'

Ollie pushed Connie gently away and stood up. 'I should get our stuff before anyone nicks it.'

'There's a handcart out in the yard,' said Elsie. 'I'll show you.'

'There'll be a guard on the house now,' said Brooke, waving for the boy to sit down. 'I'll make sure they stay overnight,' he added, thinking that was the saddest thought of all – that now the enemy had gone, they had to live in fear of looters.

CHAPTER FORTY-THREE

Brooke walked briskly home and opened the door with as little noise as many years of practice allowed. Climbing up to the attic, into his mother's room, which held the clawed-foot bath, he poured himself a malt whisky – the bottle and glass were always to hand in a fine mirrored box on the dressing table. Then he ran the water as hot as the boiler could muster, and slid beneath the surface, the scum of ash and smoke leaving a black line on the worn enamel. Lying there, he saw in the shadows the doll's house they'd bought Joy and kept in the hope that it could be inherited by grandchildren. The door stood open, revealing the rooms within.

Immersed in the water, washing ash from his face, he recalled the first bath he'd had in Jerusalem after he'd been rescued from the desert. It had been in the Grand Hotel, which was a ruin, but still had a water system. The medics had requisitioned the lower floors as wards, and had sent him upstairs to bathe his wounds, especially the gunshots to the knee, inflicted by his captors in the hope he'd die of thirst where they'd abandoned him. The water had turned slightly red as the dried blood had washed off. He'd been sent up a tumbler of whisky, requisitioned by Edmund Kohler from the bombed-out bar, and he'd drifted off in a daze of deferred pain.

It was one of those moments in a life, superficially meaningless, which never fade away. He slept now, as the water cooled. When he woke, possibly catching the echo of his own voice crying out, he managed to hold on to the fading threads of a brief dream, in which a doll's house facade swung open to reveal miniature versions of Dr Comfort's mortuary tables, upon which were unseen bodies, covered in sheets. The detail which made him cry out was that there were three bodies.

Unsettled, he dried himself, and slipped into bed beside Claire, gathering her arm up to lie across his chest. He noted that the alarm clock was not set, indicating that his wife was on a two-day down shift, and had allowed herself a lie-in. Two or three more short bouts of sleep filled the hour until dawn, when he dressed quickly in some starchy clothes in the half-light. Claire, stirring, asked about the bombing raid and what had happened. Brooke gave her the short version: no casualties, but plenty of misery. She said she'd had a fitful dream too: she couldn't recall the narrative but it had been about Luke and Ben – son and son-in-law – and they were together, standing in a cemetery, both in their respective uniforms. Luke had been holding a green beret, and Ben was in his No. 1 dress, looking smart.

Brooke gave his wife a kiss and told her they were both haunted by dreams because of overactive imaginations, while real life was often dull and tiresome. 'But it must be endured,' he added.

The morning was starkly beautiful, with a clear sky, the sun yet to rise. He wanted to clear his head with a cup of strong tea, but a visit to Rose might prompt more attempts to see into the future with the aid of the mystical leaves, and after a night of such visions he felt he needed a dose of lucid, lofty common sense. He slipped down the alleyway opposite Trinity College's gates and climbed the metal ladders to Jo Ashmore's Observation Post.

'I thought I might have missed you,' he said, hauling himself up the final six feet, to find Ashmore making careful notes in a large book attached to the conical metal hut by a chain.

'Just making out the log. Kettle's on.'

From such a high vantage point he could see into the various courts – the grass squares set within the college grounds – where flocks of birds pecked for seed untroubled by scholars or porters. It was still an hour short of the earliest breakfast. On St John's Great Court, just visible, he could see a lone gardener, with a hose, who had created a mist of falling water droplets, which the first rays of the sun were converting into a rainbow. On Trinity's Great Court a lone student, in a chorister's gown, plodded dutifully around the grass on the cobbled path, which made Brooke think of Burghley's famous run.

The war seemed a distant echo. But to the west an RAF Oxford tipped its wings and began its shallow descent into Marshall, while over the Kite and the railyards a thin layer of smoke hung in the air, the only visible evidence of the raid.

'How's George?' he asked, taking a mug of tea and a Craven A. He thought Ashmore looked tired, exhausted even.

He looked away, giving her time, if she wanted, to duck the answer.

'Well, it has to be said it is pretty gruesome. There's been two ops already, and of course it just looks worse, if I can see him at all for the bandages, but they said it would be like that, that they'd have to move bones, and cartilage, and that the eye socket was damaged too. But the surgeon's delighted. They always are. I've worked out why, but it's obvious really. They aren't treating Flight Lieutenant George Wentworth, are they? They're treating his wounds. It's as if they've drawn a magic line between him and the burns. So they don't get involved – not emotionally.'

'But you have,' said Brooke.

'Yes. I have. It's pretty much an ordeal. I'll go again tomorrow but it'll have to be by train – I've run out of coupons for petrol. It'll take all day and probably half the night. My uncle's got a house in Kensington – so I'll doss there.'

'Slumming it, in Kensington?'

She just smiled and nodded. She was perfectly aware that she lived a gilded life, despite the war.

Somewhere nearby they could hear a choir singing.

'Good God,' said Brooke. 'Is that all part of the routine – you get your own celestial voices as a going-home present?'

Ashmore smiled, sipping the tea. 'Yes. That's the choir at St John's. Every day, it is. It's heavenly.'

For a minute they listened to the voices, weaving and soaring.

'Money's on another raid tonight,' she said, settling into a seat she'd fashioned out of sandbags.

'Tonight? Why's that?'

'Because they missed again. We've been thinking it's the yards they're after, or cutting the mainline, but last night it was obvious – at least that's the intel.'

She tapped an elegant finger against her nose.

'The target was the bridge out by Fen Ditton that carries the railway. They missed it, then dropped the rest on the Kite and the railyards. Last time we thought they'd panicked and dropped a bomb early on the run-in. But the brass think it's been the bridge they're after all the time, and it's a "top-level target", no less. If they've got decent reconnaissance pictures, or a handy fifth columnist in the city, they'll soon know they've failed again.

'So third time lucky, that's the analysis. The gossip is if they do come back it means the invasion's on and it'll be the East Coast, not the South. Makes sense when you think it through. It's three hundred miles of undefended coastline, and a lot of it just sand and marsh, no cliffs to climb. If you knock out that bridge, cut the line, you can't get anything up here quick enough to fight back.

'If Jerry gets tanks ashore they'd be here in twenty-four hours, Eden. All leave's cancelled up at Marshall's and Madingley, and the ack-ack boys are being resupplied as soon as. The plan is to put fighters up at dusk, and make sure we give 'em a bloody nose before they get here.'

Brooke looked out over the city, serene below.

'It's a sobering thought,' he said. 'Nazi tanks on King's Parade.'

CHAPTER FORTY-FOUR

Brooke, braced against the warm wind, strode out from the hanger for the 'flight line' – six black Spitfires on the far apron of the grassy runway. He held on to his hat, head down, until he reached the first, and then tried to spot Vale's number: F 544. It was the last in the row, and he could see the pilot in the cockpit, but Vale didn't look round because a bowser, pumping fuel aboard, was chugging, and the noise covered Brooke's approach, as did the gusting breeze which seemed to make the fragile skin of the aircraft flex and shudder. The radio cable, taut between the mast and the tail, was humming, vibrating in the wind.

Vale had the cockpit canopy back, and was sitting still, his eyes shut. Brooke was going to speak when he realised the young pilot was talking to himself, his lips moving, while his hands seemed to be caressing the controls, lightly touching switches and dials, running from side to side, in what looked like an elaborate mime. There was something strangely sensual about the way he was touching the machine.

Brooke stepped onto the box placed aside for the pilot to clamber aboard.

He knocked on the cockpit trim and Vale's eyes opened wide: there was a flash of genuine fear, before the smile was back, a childish grin, as if he'd been caught smoking behind the bicycle sheds.

The fuel tanker was being disconnected and taken to the next aircraft in the line. It was suddenly quiet, except for the wind.

'The balloon's gone up,' said Vale. 'Looks like they're going for a landing on the East Coast, so we'll cop it. We're transferring east over by the downs so we can get up early and intercept any incoming. Two days – then we're back.'

He ran his hand over the controls again. 'I need to know my way round with my eyes shut . . .'

The cowling had been fitted with blinkers, presumably to shield the pilot from the intermittent flash of flame from the exhaust, which would blaze at night. Brooke held on to one as the wind gusted.

Vale set his hands on the control column, adjusting wing flaps, rotating the rear rudder. They were still a boy's hands, with narrow fingers, bitten nails and an elastic band around one thumb.

'What's that for?' Brooke asked.

'I need the map to hand . . .' Vale shifted himself awkwardly to reveal a document slot in the left side of the fuselage. 'It's stashed

274

here and I need to be able to put my hand on it in a second. Thing is I don't know left from right in a fug.'

'Listen, Tim. I could have a word with the staff sergeant now and have you grounded. I have every right to do that. I visited the house last night, and talked to your mother. I had a look at your room. I had a look at the front room. I suffer from insomnia, although I don't take pills routinely – yet. I know that there's a market, and that it's not a legal one.'

Vale looked ahead, nodding, as if everything was understood. 'I can explain.'

'I doubt that. The real issue is do you explain now at the station, because black-market trading in barbiturates is a serious offence. And we have yet to find out how you obtained the pills, or sold them on. But what I need to be certain about, Tim, is your whereabouts on the night of the Earl Street bomb, and the night Peggy died. The landlord of the Golden Fleece doesn't recall you, or the MG.'

The first Spitfire was rolling forward, the ground crew waving it into position to taxi out for take-off.

'Everyone's on the make, so I thought I'd have some of what was going,' said Vale. He looked at Brooke. 'I'm not a common thief.'

Vale's hand crept to the ring handle at the top of the steering column, and a button, which Brooke took to be the machine-gun trigger.

'There's a porter at the hospital; he takes delivery from me and gets them out to family doctors. The price has gone sky high so most turn a blind eye and he knows who to trust. But we send other deliveries out of town – to Peterborough, and Coventry, Bury, Lynn. I do the run in the MG.

'The night Peggy died I was on the road – Lynn that time. The night of the raid it was further – Warwick. If I get stopped the uniform helps. I tell them I've been posted out at late notice for an op.'

'The porter's name?'

Vale bought some time, wriggling back into a comfy position in the cockpit, trying to haul his parachute round and get his knees tucked in either side of the joystick.

The sergeant running the ground crew had spotted Brooke and was approaching fast.

'The porter's name, Tim. Or this ends here.'

'Cheaver,' he said, looking Brooke in the eyes, trying to see past the green lenses. 'They call him Roly – big lad, runs the porters – all of them. He's the man.'

'Two days,' said Brooke. 'It's only a guess but that's going to be your war, Tim. Make the most of it.'

Brooke stepped down and dragged away the box, as Vale drew the cowling forward and over his head. The Spitfire trundled away, impossibly fragile, shaking as it rolled over the heavy grass.

Brooke told the radio car driver to park by the gates of the aerodrome so he could jump out to see the take-offs: six black Spitfires, at thirty-second intervals, with Vale last. He couldn't be sure but he thought he detected a modest wing-tip as he flew overhead. It was a blue sky, and ten minutes before the last dot faded away.

CHAPTER FORTY-FIVE

Brooke knew the hospital's routines, so he arrived at five minutes to the hour and set off down the long corridor to Rhodes Ward, which was on the ground floor because it was for geriatrics. A series of full-length glass doors gave on to the small garden at the rear of the building, letting sunshine flood across the lino. The blue sky had resulted in an exodus of those who were not confined to bed: chairs were out on the grass, and the breeze blew the screens and curtains about as if it was washing day.

Joy, as a junior nurse, was patiently filling out a log at the sister's desk before clocking off.

Brooke smiled but it didn't work, because he knew his body language was transmitting other less encouraging signals.

'Can we talk?' he asked. 'I've no news – it's police business.'

His daughter finished her brief report, checked her fob watch and led her father outside into the garden.

Two chairs were empty, under a tree, and so they settled down. A few feet away an elderly man in a dressing gown sat sleeping, his chin down on his chest. The sooty black bricks of the old building rose up five floors, but most of the windows were open in the heat. Somewhere they heard a bell ring and a trolley clatter.

'What's wrong?' said Joy. Brooke noted that her eyes were flitting over the patients. It was a habit she shared with Claire, and it gave them both a sense of calm watchfulness.

'Do you know the head porter here, a man called Cheaver?'

Joy brightened. 'Roly? Yes, of course, we all do. This place wouldn't run for a day without him. There's a dozen porters but Roly's the only one who knows who's doing what. He's one of nature's organisers. Everything's on paper with Roly. You have to put in a chitty if you need a porter – or ring on the internal phone – and even then you have to sign off when they turn up to move a patient, or bring us one in. Bureaucratic – but efficient. Roly never lets you down.'

'Where can I find him?'

'In the canteen, Dad. He's not called Roly for nothing. He has a table up the far end and he runs it all from there most days. Pot of tea, toast, cakes, the cooks keep it coming. I think Roly gives them cheap ciggies.'

'I see,' said Brooke.

'He hasn't done anything wrong, has he? Nothing *really* wrong?'

Brooke pressed the heels of his palms into his eye sockets.

'Oh dear,' said Joy.

'Indeed. I think he's dealing in drugs on the black market. I don't think he's a very nice person at all, Joy. Sorry.'

She produced a packet of cigarettes and they lit up together, from one match.

'So that's his office, is it – the canteen?' asked Brooke.

'No. The porters have a den down in the basement near the boilers. That's where they've got lockers and files and suchlike. One of them had an asthma attack and I had to go down to look him over. It's a bit of a dump, but it's handy because it's by the lift. Roly stays in the canteen. Lord of all he surveys. Happy as Larry.'

'And you? How happy are you?' said Brooke.

Joy shook her head. 'It's fine as long as I can maintain forward motion. Walking, working, talking: I can hold back the thought of the future. But as soon as I stop, and the brain engages, it's bleak, Dad.'

'We should talk it through, with your mother. All of us. Iris can listen, even if she doesn't understand.'

'But she *knows*, Dad. Iris knows. Not in the way we do, but this has happened to her, not just me, and you, and mum. She's going to have to live with this a lot longer than any of us.'

Ten minutes later they were on the steps of the hospital. Joy checked her bag, briskly, and gave Brooke a swift hug. 'I'm going to walk a bit, clear my head, and then pick up Iris. Let's talk later with Mum.'

Brooke watched her walk smartly off towards the river, then turned on his heels and went to the front desk, where he showed his warrant card to a man in charge and asked to use the phone.

A minute later he was running up the eight flights of stairs to the fourth floor and the canteen. Lunch was over and there were only a few people smoking, drinking tea and reading newspapers.

Cheaver, when he stood up, was the shape of a child's spinning top. He had merry eyes and a big grin, and he shook Brooke's hand and told him he should be proud of his wife and daughter. 'They're the best, they are,' he said. 'Salt of the earth.'

Brooke sat down. Across the table were spread rotas, and typed lists, and chitties – the kind of bumph that seemed to fuel the war effort. On the wall behind Cheaver there was an internal phone on a hook.

A plate, discarded, was smeared with jam and cake.

'I've been talking to Pilot Officer Tim Vale,' said Brooke.

'Never heard of 'im,' said Cheaver, the voice hardening a notch, as he pushed himself back from the table. The transformation was instantaneous, the good humour evaporating, his breathing suddenly audible.

'He's heard of you. I'm sorry, Roly, I know you do a great job here, but we're heading down to the Spinning House for a chat, and I suspect you won't be coming back.'

'What's this about?'

'Veronal sleeping pills,' said Brooke. 'That's where we'll start, but I'm guessing there will be other – what do you call them in the trade? Lines – that's it – other lines, like painkillers, and pure alcohol. I've just put a call in for a car to pick us up. I'm going to ask a constable to go down to the porters' den in the basement, so that's secure, and we can have a look through what's there later. I understand you like keeping records.'

Cheaver seemed to relax, as if he'd given up, but Brooke thought his brain was working at speed, because his breathing had become shallow, and when he moved his hand off the table it left a damp print.

'I buy and sell a bit,' he said.

'Do you, Roly?'

'Maybe I can sell you something. What do you need?'

'Not much, Roly. At the moment I'd like to know where my son is – he's in the commandos. And my son-in-law – he's a POW who might have been shot trying to escape. In fact he's probably dead. So you see I don't *need* anything that you can supply.'

Cheaver's fleshy face seemed to shudder. 'I meant . . .'

'I know what you meant, Roly. The only thing I need from you specifically, in the short term, is a list of the nights on which Tim Vale ran drugs for you to Lynn, and Warwick. Do you write it all down? Like the rotas? I think you do. Because you're organised, and you make things work. I hope you do, for Tim Vale's sake – he's relying on it to prove he isn't a thieving killer.'

Cheaver's eyes widened. Brooke turned to the doors and saw that a police constable had arrived.

'Shall we?' asked Brooke, standing up.

'What do you think I'll get?' Cheaver asked, struggling to his feet.

'I don't care, Roly. But if you're asking, I think they'll throw the key away. You're lucky this isn't on the list of capital offences. If the war goes badly it will be.'

CHAPTER FORTY-SIX

By dusk, the secret life of the village of Barrington had been revealed. The local constable, a stout officer who allowed a mongrel to accompany him on his beat, had done a fine job of carrying on as normal. Brooke could just see him now, in the last light of day, standing out on the village green supervising a game of football. The pitch formed a handkerchief square on what the locals claimed was the largest village green in England: a stretch of parkland, about which were set houses in most of the vernacular styles from a medieval range through Tudor beams to a Lutyens' 1930s manor. Barrington Hall, with its moat, was hidden in the trees. Poorer cottages crowded along a stream. From Brooke's vantage point – a narrow arrow-slit window in the tower of All Saints' church – the scene looked timeless, and certainly blameless.

The truth was very different. The ACE garage, on the through road at the northern edge of the village, was a fading remnant of twenties panache – whitewashed and sleek, with faded red trim. A roof covered the forecourt and the single fuel pump. The office and a small shop were in a white-washed 'cabin' to which a small bungalow had been attached for the owner: Mr Jack Fitt, his wife Joyce and their teenage son Bobbie. According to the village constable the boy was a 'wrong'un', a regular at juvenile court and – latterly – magistrates' court. However, he owned a motorbike and conducted most of his criminal activities – principally petty theft – in Cambridge. On home turf he kept his nose clean. Mr Fitt senior had provided petrol and garage services without much comment for twenty years, but sustained a running feud with his wife, taking time off to prop up the public bar at The Boot, an inn which catered for the village's working men.

Behind the garage, in a yard which ran up to the woods that climbed the chalk hills above the village, there were several outbuildings. One of these, the constable had noted, stood beside a ditch, which ran down to the stream and fed the River Rhee. From this precise point any liquid entering the ditch would reach Peter Aldiss's X on the map – the point at which he'd detected adulterated fuel. It was circumstantial evidence, but there was more.

Fitt kept the barn and sheds securely locked. The previous night, when he knew the owner was in The Boot, the constable had accidentally let his mongrel stray into the yard and had gone to fetch it, engaging Mrs Fitt in a good-natured conversation about the warm evening air. He'd been able to note that the yard was crisscrossed by tyre tracks – all indicating a heavy lorry – and that the barn smelt strongly of petrol fumes.

Brooke could see it now: a corrugated iron structure with a lagged roof. The village had a string of electric street lights, although they cast a dim beam, and ended just short of the garage. The landscape offered one advantage in terms of a police operation: the single through road. The vicar, a young man recently down from Cambridge, had been eager to help, and had let them use the phone in the spacious rectory. Roadblocks, comprising two of the Spinning House radio cars, could be called into place within minutes to the north and south. All they needed was the arrival of an unmarked lorry for the trap to be sprung. The publican at the Catherine Wheel, a cousin of the constable, said he had noticed one such vehicle passing just after closing time on at least three evenings in the past week. He felt – and these were his precise words – that the driver had made a considerable effort to 'slip in and slip out'. There had been no crunching gears, and no effort to pick up speed.

Edison arrived with a tin jug of beer.

'I think chummy is the only man in the village who doesn't know we're here,' he said, settling down on one of the cushioned benches.

'He's not in The Boot so he must be at home – or, more likely, in the barn,' said Brooke.

A set of ropes were slung over their heads and gathered up neatly by a metal circlet. They could just hear the high-tension vibration of the bells above.

'The radio cars?' asked Brooke.

Edison nodded, pouring the beer into mugs. 'I'll ring the Spinning House using the vicar's phone when the time comes. I reckon if we set them off when the lorry arrives there's no way he can slip through our hands.'

'The best-laid plans, Edison,' said Brooke.

The light finally began to bleed away entirely, so that all that was left was the pale shape of the lancet windows, letting in the lambent flicker of the street lights. Over the fields came the distant sound of the siren in the city: the wail seemed impossibly far away, as if it came from another world.

Closer to hand they heard a door open, and a sudden gust of laughter – probably from the Catherine Wheel – and then the rhythmic barking of the constable's dog, which was downstairs in the nave of the church, with ten other uniformed officers. They heard the distinct clatter of a tin water bowl on stone, and the dog fell silent.

At ten Edison slipped away to the toilet. Brooke was standing at the window, keeping watch, when he saw the slit-eyed headlights in the far distance, long before he heard the gentle purr of the engine. His stomach turned over, and he had a premonition that the night would end in violence. He'd got the chief constable to authorise the issue of guns: two pistols, one for Edison, one for himself. He picked up his and weighed it in his hand, and tried not to think of the desert, and the shot he'd taken pretty much at random one night in the Sinai when they thought they'd heard an Ottoman patrol; the result was a hail of bullets, a firestorm, which had left two of his men badly injured.

The lorry passed directly beneath the church and Brooke crossed the belfry to watch it 'slide' past the pub, and then – slowing – turn noiselessly into the yard at the rear of the ACE garage. The slick, practised manoeuvre added to the sense of threat, and he had to admit he might have underestimated the thieves. The idle label 'blackout gang' suggested slap-dash adventure. This operation

285

looked organised and stealthy. Brooke had also noted the striped black-and-white tarpaulin on the lorry – identical to descriptions of the vehicle used to collect pilfered petrol.

Edison was at his shoulder. 'Make the call, Sergeant,' said Brooke. 'I want both roadblocks in position and then we'll give them an extra ten minutes before we introduce ourselves.'

When they did break cover they marched through the village on the grass verge to muffle the sound of their boots. At the rear came the Borough dog handler with the Spinning House's sole bloodhound, in case the culprits took to the fields. A few curtains twitched, and the landlord of the Catherine Wheel stood outside the pub smoking, watching from the shadows. When they got to the ACE garage, Brooke told the men to hold back while he and Edison went into the yard.

By the gate, Brooke drew his pistol and was surprised to see that Edison had beaten him to it, the gun held expertly, barrel down, parallel with the cut of his heavy coat.

Brooke glanced sideways at the bungalow and saw Mrs Fitt standing in her nightdress at the back door with a hand over her mouth. He signalled her to stay silent with a finger across his lips, and she backed away into the house.

The barn door was the sliding type which ruled out any attempt at a stealthy entrance. The lorry stood empty at the back of the yard, at the top of the slope that led up towards the woods, its tail-back down, the cab dark. From inside the barn they could hear a radio playing. There was a pungent smell on the still air, and Brooke thought of the Kilner jar in his office, the killer's gloves within.

They took careful steps across the beaten earth of the yard, the noise partly masked by dance music. They came to a halt and an owl hooted from the woods which edged the hill.

Brooke braced himself, getting both hands on the cold metal handle, and slid it open in one move. In that first freeze-framed second he saw everything in startling detail. To one side several hundred flimsies had been stacked against the barn wall. A large metal open tank, its rim at about hip height, stood at the back, containing a livid blue liquid, which had produced a thin gas, which hovered above the surface like a sea mist.

Down the middle of the barn had been set a line of trestle tables – a makeshift production line – at which Bobbie Fitt and his father stood working, filling cans (which had presumably arrived carrying petrol) with the adulterated mixture of kerosene, using milk jugs. They both wore motorcyclist's gauntlets, which reached to their elbows, and both had contrived home-made masks of cloth to cover their mouths, tied behind their heads bandit-style.

Bobbie Fitt stared at his father, eyes bright with fear.

'Don't move,' said Brooke. Bobbie Fitt put down the flimsie he was filling, while his father raised his hands. Brooke had the distinct impression they were both waiting for something to happen.

Brooke heard a pistol being cocked and then several things happened in rapid succession: they heard the distinct sound of a handbrake being released, and then the crunch of tyres as the lorry rolled backwards across the yard, using the steep gradient of the ground.

Jack Fitt looked back at his son with a slight shake of the head.

The gunshot came from the lorry. In the desert Brooke had dodged bullets, by a yard, a foot, but never this close. He felt the air pushed aside by the trajectory of the shell, and heard the gnat-like high-pitched passage of the .25 by his ear, and only ducked when it was gone. The sound of the ricochet against the corrugated iron of the chemical tank was like a bullwhip. His legs folded and he hit the deck. He had his head on one side, facing left, and so he saw Edison follow suit, collapsing in a heap, expertly bringing both arms up as he did so to protect his head.

The driver of the lorry, judging the momentum of the vehicle perfectly, let it reach speed before turning the ignition key, the engine firing into life as he shifted into first gear and swung the vehicle round, picking up speed and scattering the cordon of officers in the road. The tyres screamed as he sped north, loosing off a Parthian shot, the tail-back slapping against the rear bumper.

Brooke, back on his feet, got an arm round Edison and hauled him up, dragging him out into the yard. Two constables had taken a glancing blow from the lorry and were laid out on the tarmac. Mrs Fitt was already kneeling by one of the injured. The house had a phone and Brooke commandeered it to call the Spinning House, ordering the duty sergeant to summon the radio car from the southern roadblock to the garage, and to warn the northern roadblock that the lorry was approaching, and that the driver was armed and had already fired twice.

The Fitts had fled through a door at the back of the barn into the woods. The bloodhound was already in pursuit, and they could hear its guttural barks within the trees. Brooke organised the remaining constables into search parties and they checked the house, the barn and a series of outbuildings, which is where they made their most significant discovery. Just beyond the first line of trees they found a dilapidated shed about thirty yards long, although the roof had been newly laid with felt and creosote, and the interior was bone dry. It was stacked with goods arranged in bays made with plywood. Clocks, linen, pieces of expensive small furniture (chairs, inlaid tables, hat racks), kitchen implements, cutlery (silver separate from EPS), pictures in frames, gilded frames, bicycles, mirrors, prams, cheap jewellery, trinkets, ornaments and much else. All the goods were in decent condition.

Edison, still brushing down his overcoat, surveyed the scene.

'It's a clearing house, Edison,' said Brooke, picking through a pile of cutlery. 'Bring the stuff in, sort it out, then off it goes for sale away in London, or another big city where we'll never find it. The petrol's just another scam. Come daylight, let's go through the lot and see if we can find anything from Earl Street.'

A constable reported that the radio car had arrived.

Brooke jumped in the front, Edison in the back, and they sped north, through the woods, along the narrow winding lane, heading for the roadblock. It was the first still moment Brooke had to contemplate the single shot which had come so close: one spark from its zigzag ricochets could have ignited the barn.

'There, sir,' said Edison, leaning forward and pointing ahead. The lane was narrow with ditches on both sides and the dispositions had been agreed in advance: warning lanterns were to be placed across the road, two constables were to stand aside, the third to the rear of the radio car.

They could see the lanterns scattered to either side, and the lorry, off to the left in a ditch, its wheels still turning. The radio car was still across the road.

A constable ran towards them, swinging his torch.

Breathless, he came to the open driver's window. 'He tried to go round us but tipped it over, sir. He's done a runner, up the hill. He fired a shot, so he got a head start, but they've gone after him anyway.'

The chalky ground rose sharply away from the road. After a brief climb they could see a constable silhouetted against the stars. At the crest of the rise they found themselves on the edge of a chalk quarry, the pale bowl beneath them oddly luminous in the starlight. A pair of torch beams crisscrossed in the shadows below like divers glimpsed in the ocean's depths.

'It's a scree-ride down,' said the constable.

Edison stood back, but Brooke didn't falter, stepping over the edge, his brogues sinking in the pebbles up to his ankles. Gravity took him down the long incline although he had to work hard to keep his momentum going and avoid boulders marooned in the chalky dust. As he descended, the light from the chalk waxed so that he could see the scene below clearly: a workman's hut in the centre of the quarry, a conveyor belt, a cluster of open trucks, a row of machine mixers.

Once or twice the scree held him fast, and he had to shake his feet free and begin a fresh descent.

At the foot the two constables had found the runaway driver. It was a man, and he'd clearly broken a leg and an arm, because they lay unnaturally at an angle to the rest of his body. He was whimpering with pain. The pistol was in his belt.

Brooke took the torch from one of the constables and shone it directly in his face.

It was Elsie Wylde's lover, Joe Miller.

CHAPTER FORTY-SEVEN

Brooke stood on the doorstep of the Wyldes' house on Palmer Road. It was still the early hours of the morning. The all-clear had sounded at midnight, there would be no bombers tonight, and so the streets were silent. A cat mewed close by, and something like a tin can rolled in a gutter, but that could have been a mile away. Above his head the two upstairs sash windows were slightly open. The house had a knocker representing a hound's head which he raised and tapped lightly three times. A dog barked in response close by, and then he heard a footfall on the stairs within.

'Who is it?' asked a voice, and he recognised Alice Wylde.

'Inspector Brooke. I need to talk to Elsie. Can you ask her to step outside, Mrs Wylde? Can you get her up?'

The door opened a crack, and light flooded out. Alice, a nightdress held at the throat, looked twenty years older.

'What is it?'

'I'll explain to Elsie. It's nothing to fear. But it is urgent.'

'Wait there,' she said, and closed the door.

Brooke lit a cigarette. Edison had driven the Wasp back to Cambridge, the head of a convoy comprising the two radio cars and an ambulance – carrying Miller, and the two injured policemen, one with a broken ankle, the other suffering from concussion. At Addenbrooke's they'd transferred Miller to a private room, and Edison had been left on guard. The hunt for the Fitts had ended within the hour. The bloodhound had led the chase and sniffed them out in the ruins of an old sawmill, and they'd been frog-marched back to a Black Maria at the ACE garage, and were now in the cells at the Spinning House.

The door opened to reveal Elsie, on the doorstep, in her working clothes.

She looked grey, her face puffy and lifeless.

Before she closed the door she whispered up the stairs, 'Bye, Mum, Connie. See you later. Don't worry.'

The windows above were left open and Brooke wanted some privacy. 'We could walk,' he offered.

They turned left, walking away from Parker's Piece, deeper into the Kite. The air was still tainted by the ash from the bombs which had fallen the night before.

'Sorry to wake you up,' said Brooke.

'You didn't. Mum's been crying so I was with her. Connie's in our room, she'll be sound asleep. Ollie's given up on the old sofa and moved into the Anderson. We were all in there earlier with the siren. It's a bloody tight fit, whatever Mum says,' she laughed, offering Brooke a cigarette as he ditched his own.

'So what's this about?' said Elsie.

'It's your man, Joe Miller. He's alright – but he's in Addenbrooke's. He's in a bad way, a broken leg and a broken arm, but he'll recover. That's not really the problem. The problem is he's been running stolen goods, Elsie. I'm sorry, there is absolutely no doubt.'

She blinked slowly, and Brooke wondered if she'd always known it would come to this: that she'd fooled herself, but that at some level she'd always known he was a crook.

'He's part of a blackout gang. They've been using a village garage out in the sticks. They're flogging stolen petrol and fencing stolen goods from looted homes. The war's been good for crime. My guess is he's got a lock-up somewhere where he keeps his lorry and any stolen goods that need storing overnight. The house is clean – but that's just a cover. Sorry, Elsie – it's best you know.'

She leant her back against the cold bricks of a terraced house. 'He told me he'd stopped. He's good at what he does – buying and selling. And he's good with people. They trust him. It's just been a temptation. The war's changed everything.'

Brooke took off his hat, running a hand back through the black hair.

'Elsie. We're not talking about a good honest thief here. He had a gun, and he made a run for it. He put a bullet through a metal shed in which they stored something like three hundred gallons of petrol – plus a few drums of kerosene. One spark, Elsie, and I wouldn't be here now. There were two men in the shed; they wouldn't have found their bodies beyond some charred bone.'

'Christ,' she said, looking away. 'What a mess.'

They'd reached the corner of Salisbury Street, and they could see Ollie Fox's bombed-out house, the facade now replaced by a tarpaulin. It was a depressing sight, and Elsie looked suddenly overwhelmed, her eyes flooding.

'You can see Joe, if you want to see him, later today,' said Brooke. 'He'll be fine, as I said. But you don't *have* to see him.'

'He'll go to gaol, won't he?' she said, and he wondered if she was thinking about standing by her lover.

'This is desperate stuff, Elsie. It's not my decision, but that gunshot could amount to attempted murder. Most judges would make an example of him.'

They walked on towards the railyards.

'And we have to consider other crimes,' said Brooke. He checked his watch. 'When Joe's better he's going to have to answer questions. About Nora's house. That was looting, Elsie, and the house is right opposite Joe's. He's got his ARP uniform – nobody sees him come and go, he's just doing his job. And then there's Peggy. You might not have guessed what he was up to, but maybe she did. If he could do what he did tonight, Elsie, he could have killed Peggy. Were they close?'

It was a careful question, but Elsie took it in her stride.

'You get used to it – being the plain Jane. Joe fancied Peggy like they all do – and maybe he took me out to see how close he could get. It happens: three sisters, one a looker. But Joe wasn't her type and Peggy didn't muck about. She told him straight—'

Brooke held up a hand to stop her talking: he'd heard the dull thud of a timber falling, a rattle of spilling bricks. The sound came from the next street. They walked to the corner and saw a police constable emerging from a house that had taken a hit in one of the first raids of the war.

Something of the night, a movement of the air, the

constable's agitated waving arms, made Brooke's skin creep.

The constable was twenty yards away, brushing dust off his uniform.

'Constable. It's Inspector Brooke,' he said, advancing into the light.

'SC 015, sir.' SC was the designation for special constable – a volunteer recruited to allow the Borough to at least give the impression that the law still patrolled the streets. He looked less than twenty years of age, and he was out of breath, or panicking.

'Yes. But your *name*, Constable . . .'

'Root, sir. There's something in the house.' He shone the torch beam wildly in the direction of the blackened building. 'I should go for help.'

'What is it?' asked Brooke.

He looked at Elsie. 'I don't think it's for the young lady, sir.'

'Don't worry about her. Show me,' he said. 'Stay here,' he said to Elsie. 'It'll be rats. We won't be long.'

Brooke stepped within a yard of the young constable. 'Remember, Root. Never exhibit signs of panic or confusion. What is it, man?'

SC Root held up his hand. Brooke could see it was covered in what looked like sticky black paint, until the constable used his other hand to turn the light onto his fingers. It was blood, partly congealed.

'There's a hole in the floor of the front room, sir. So you can see down,' he said.

'Go ahead,' said Brooke. 'Walk slowly, Constable.'

The front door was off its hinges, and the hallway beyond in ruins, so that they could see the whole ground floor, strewn with rubble, and bricks, and roof tiles and rafters.

The jagged hole was in the front room, and out of it rose a thin cloud of dust, as if the bomb had only recently plummeted down through the floorboards.

'The neighbours rang the station about an hour ago saying they'd heard something and thought it was looters. I reckon someone was chucking stuff down into the cellar. I was going to use the box on Parker's Piece to get help.'

'Because of the blood?' asked Brooke.

Root nodded. 'Best I show you, sir. Follow me. The cellar stairs are safe,' he said.

The constable forced the cellar door open but stood back at the last moment, letting Brooke go first, then following.

'Give me the torch,' said Brooke.

As he dropped down the brick steps he saw a basement, swept and clean, but for a pyramid of rubble under the jagged hole. A smashed toilet constituted a pinnacle to the ruins, which included a length of bannister and a hat stand, a water tank and some heavy beams. Dust rose up from the pile, and motes hung in the air, and clogged the beam of the torch. Brooke got out a handkerchief and held it to his mouth.

'It's moving,' said Root, pointing at the floor.

The brick floor was covered in an old lino. Efforts had been made to clear up after the bomb, which had fallen earlier that summer, and the floor had been swept clean, and in one corner bricks had been piled neatly. Across this floor lay a pool of black liquid, which had its source beneath the pile of masonry.

Brooke knelt down and touched his finger in the liquid and held it up to the light. The vivid, arterial red was unmistakable, but he held it to his nose nonetheless and caught the distinct metallic tang of blood.

Standing up, he edged his boot to within an inch of the boundary of the blood. It was moving, very slowly, and Brooke

296

imagined a heart, pounding, so that the spreading liquid had a pulse of its own, but he knew even then it was a faint hope.

'Let's move as quickly as we can,' he said.

'Shouldn't we get help? Preserve the scene?' offered Root.

'There's a chance we can preserve life, Constable. Let's make that effort.'

They heard footsteps and looking up saw Elsie had come into the front room and was peering down into the cellar.

'Stay back,' said Brooke. 'It's dangerous. Can you get help, Elsie? Go to a neighbour and tell them to request an ambulance.'

They took off their coats and started hauling the biggest items first: the water tank, and two roof beams. Then they ferried bricks. After ten minutes Brooke called a halt and asked for the torch.

There was a fissure in the rubble, and a few feet down the light caught a pale glimpse of skin. He reached down and pulled a brick to one side and saw what looked like an ankle. From the position of the foot Brooke calculated the location of the head. Kneeling, he lifted aside a shattered window frame, and a roll of carpet. The last item shielding the face was a broken mantelpiece clock.

'Christ,' he said, closing his eyes. The face, as such, had been destroyed by a series of blows, to such an extent that Brooke suspected a concerted attack, rather than the random wounds inflicted by the falling masonry.

Even in that chaos of blood and bone he saw the ghost of a likeness he recognised. He inveigled his hand around the skull and felt for a pulse in the neck, but there was nothing, although the skin was warm and yielding.

'She's dead,' he said, turning to SC Root.

'It can't be,' said a voice, and they looked up to see Elsie Wylde looking down.

'Elsie, go back. I've said it's dangerous,' said Brooke.

'It's Connie, isn't it?' she said. 'But it can't be. She's at home in bed in our room. I've asked for an ambulance like you said, but it's too late, isn't it?'

She swayed dangerously.

'There's nothing you can do,' said Brooke, nodding to Root, who ran for the cellar door and the stairs.

'What's happening to us?' Elsie asked, her hands rising to her face. 'Who's going to tell Mum?'

CHAPTER FORTY-EIGHT

Three hours later, an hour short of dawn, Brooke was still at the scene. A neighbour had taken it upon herself to cater for the growing band of constables, a photographer commandeered from the county force, and the pathologist, who was in the basement examining the body in situ. A large brown teapot was being constantly refreshed and passed around for top-ups. Lights were on in most of the houses, and several residents stood on doorsteps, watching silently.

Brooke had been back to Palmer Road to the Wyldes' house and pieced together the series of known events. The family had gone to the Anderson shelter at just after eight, when the siren sounded from the Guildhall. At midnight the all-clear had roused them, and Connie had gone back to bed alone in the girls' room, because Elsie wanted to keep her mother company. Alice had been crying over Peggy, and didn't want to be left alone. Elsie had made them all one last cup of tea. Ollie, fed up with the sofa, had stayed in the shelter. He told Brooke that Connie was tired, missed her sister, and wanted her nana.

It was a cruel question but he felt he had to ask. 'Do you think she might have had a secret admirer – just like Peggy? Is it possible, Ollie?'

The boy had shaken his head, his eyes flooding. 'We were engaged,' he said. 'She'd promised we'd get married after all this was forgotten. She'd never lied to me. Ever.' He'd cried then, his mouth hanging open, the lips wet, and Brooke thought that he'd lost another family and he was alone again.

Nobody had any idea how Connie had got out of the house, or why.

Brooke had walked back to the house where they'd found her body. Warmed by a mug of tea provided by the diligent neighbour, he spread out a map of the city on the bonnet of the Wasp. This point, the bombed-out house, was less than a quarter of a mile from the Wylde family home: two streets away in fact – less than a three-minute walk. Had she met someone on the street?

A sudden silence descended on the scene and Brooke looked up, expecting to see the ambulance orderlies removing the body, but instead Chief Inspector Carnegie-Brown was stepping out of her old Ford. It was such a rare outing into the real world that the effect was to halt all operations, as if they'd been blessed with a royal visit.

She adjusted her cap, straightened her uniform and examined

the burnt facade of the house. 'Carry on, everyone.'

Brooke briefed her quickly on the earlier events at Barrington, and the discovery of the body of Connie Wylde.

'How has this young woman ended up here?' she asked. 'Why is she out at dead of night when she should be asleep at home?'

Brooke shrugged. 'Nobody heard her leaving the house, which suggests she crept out. A clandestine meeting, then – but not here. Perhaps she met someone she wasn't expecting.'

'What next?' asked the chief inspector, removing black leather driving gloves. 'I can't shift the conclusion, Brooke, that the Borough is not in control of the situation. What is your plan of action?'

Brooke lit a cigarette. 'Priorities are house-to-house here on the street, ma'am,' he said. 'One of the neighbours phoned the Spinning House to say they'd heard something earlier which they thought was looters. We need to track them down and get a statement. What precisely did they hear – where and when? It looks like the killer tried to hide the body in the cellar in the hope that by the time she was found she'd be written off as a casualty of war.

'And we need to carry out house-to-house calls along the route she took. Maybe she was attacked on the way, or someone saw or heard something.'

'I see,' said Carnegie-Brown. 'So we're somewhat lost, Inspector? Three murders, in a matter of days, and we're back to square one, relying on the random chance that we can conjure up a passing witness.'

It appeared she was on the receiving end of a dressing-down. Three years in the British Army had taught him the golden rule in such situations – never answer back.

He studied the map in silence for a moment until he judged

the moment had passed. 'Sergeant Edison is at the bedside of the spiv – Miller,' he said.

'But you say the body of this poor girl was still warm. So Miller's not our killer, is he?'

Brooke studied his shoes.

'And Bruno Zeri is in a cell at the Spinning House. And there's this . . .' She handed him a typed sheet. 'A note from Durham. His alibi stands up, I'm afraid, at least to the extent that he was picked up walking beside the Great North Road and the constables noted his wounds.'

She slipped a tortoiseshell cigarette case out of her pocket. 'And the pilot?'

'On duty, ma'am. Spitfire flight stationed at Newmarket for forty-eight hours. We've radioed the tower at Marshall's and they confirm he is on duty.'

She lit the cigarette with a silver lighter. 'Not him either, then. As I say, Brooke. Lost. Two sisters dead – what of the third?'

'I've left a constable with the Wyldes. We'll take formal statements in the morning from the family. I'll draw up a rota so that an officer is always at hand. We don't want Elsie, the surviving sister, left alone – certainly not after dark.'

'You think she knows something?'

'Possibly. The real point is that the killer might think she knows something. That might be enough to get her killed. The family clearly poses some kind of unknown threat to the killer. If we knew its precise nature we'd know the murderer's identity.'

She checked her watch. 'We need to make progress, Brooke. Scotland Yard is unlikely to find the short distance to Cambridge a barrier if they think the Borough is incapable of catching a triple murderer. Two sisters, the grandmother first. It's a nest of vipers, Inspector. Or are they all innocent of the crimes?'

Brooke took the question to be rhetorical. An awkward silence established itself until Dr Comfort appeared from the ruined house. He had a cigar lit before he'd taken a step into the fresh air. The green cloud hung in the air as he packed his bag away into the boot of the black Rover.

He tilted his head back, and they heard a cartilage in his neck creak.

Comfort's preliminary findings were curt and angry.

'It's pretty clear from an external examination that an attempt – several attempts – have been made to make the girl unidentifiable. It's a bit desperate, and it's worth noting that he used a half-brick – there are fragments in the wounds – and so presumably that came from the cellar floor, which suggests a lack of planning. Although there's no sign of the half-brick – daylight will help there. Blood stains on red brick are not easy to see. All the injuries you can see are post-mortem. She died like the others, strangled from the front.'

'The same killer, then?' asked Carnegie-Brown.

'That's my preliminary judgement, but my final report will have to wait for a full autopsy tomorrow. I wouldn't rule out separate offenders, but it's extremely unlikely, don't you think?'

They all looked to the east but there was no sign of dawn. Several stars still fidgeted in the sky.

'Takes a certain type,' said Comfort, producing a small silver flask from his long wool coat's inside pocket. 'She was dead, as I say, but nonetheless. An assault such as this would inflict psychological damage on the assailant, if he had a shred of moral character, which I suppose we should doubt.

'He looked into their eyes, you see. In each case he choked the life out of these women while looking them in the face. A dangerous man, capable of extreme violence, but able, it seems, to get close to his victims. The idea that he might *stop* killing if threatened in any way is unlikely.'

He produced a final flourish of green smoke. 'We should all be aware of that compelling threat.'

CHAPTER FORTY-NINE

Brooke found Claire asleep in their bedroom at Newnham Croft, and he slipped in beside her under the single sheet, their mirrored bodies stirring only slightly until he awoke an hour later to see sunlight streaming through the old shutters. He slept again, for a handful of minutes, and a final third time for a few seconds, but on every occasion he dreamt of a face: Nora first, Peggy next, and lastly Connie. And each time he saw them alive, and laughing, smiling, despite the fact he'd never seen Nora before that moment in the wrecked house when he stumbled on her body. So her face had to be a feat of his imagination, a collage of her granddaughters, her own cold, still features animated by the lives of others.

He kissed Claire on the neck, below the ear, and said he'd see her later at the hospital: he had a prisoner there and he'd have to take a statement.

'How was Joy?' he asked.

'Stoical. She's prepared for the worst, I can tell. She said we should have a family powwow. Perhaps tonight?'

'Yes. I'll try – but this case in the Kite has taken a turn for the worse.' When he could he always tried not to bring the details of crime into the house. He felt Claire had enough to worry about with the ward, and now with Joy and Luke.

She opened her eyes. 'She didn't put Iris down for a single moment last night, Eden, and I think she'd thought twice about leaving her with Mrs Mullins during the day. But work's good for her, it makes her feel needed.'

Brooke said he'd get the number for the Red Cross and get a constable to drop by during the day.

'So you both know,' he added, 'the head porter – Roly Cheaver – we've got him in the cells at the station. He's been selling illegal drugs on the black market.'

Claire sat up. 'Roly?' She shook her head. 'I thought I was good at judging people. He was so kind to the patients, Eden. Always time for a chat and a joke – so it was all a front?'

'Bad people do good things, Claire. Good people do bad things. I'm not a believer in complete evil – are you?' It was what he always said, but the face he'd seen in the rubble the night before made him doubt his own wisdom.

Half an hour later he was at the Spinning House. The duty sergeant had a note from the pathologist: Alice Wylde had agreed to the identification of Connie Wylde's body at eight o'clock at the Galen Building. There was also a report from Edison: Miller had regained consciousness and made a brief statement. His sergeant had left a typewritten summary for Brooke, before going home to sleep.

Brooke took it to his office, with a canteen sandwich of beef dripping. He sat at his desk, took the phone off the hook, and read. Miller, it appeared, was what their Victorian predecessors at the Borough would have called a 'kidsman' – a criminal fence, who employed a wide range of juvenile thieves to supply him with goods stolen from houses during the blackout, from bombed-out homes, and petrol from parked cars and vans. Claire's young patient, Bert Smith, had probably represented the lower end of the age range. Miller described the majority as 'tearaways' – a word which rang a bell with Brooke, but one he could not pin down, a failure he would later regret. Miller was keen, according to Edison, to avoid prison at all costs and had offered to cooperate in closing down the blackout gang, as well as identifying his customers: a network of fences, and a list of garages on major arterial roads which filled passing traffic with adulterated petrol.

Miller had flatly denied being involved in the murder of his neighbour Nora Wylde or her granddaughter Peggy. His alibi for the murder of Connie Wylde was airtight. He also denied receiving any stolen goods from number 36. He had spent the night of the bombing carrying out his duties on Earl Street as ARP warden – several police officers had seen him at work, including Brooke.

The appointed hour for Connie's formal identification was at hand so Brooke reluctantly set the file aside. In the hallway of the Spinning House, just out of sight, was a full-length mirror left from the building's workhouse days. Brooke had always suspected the looking glass had assisted overseers in keeping an eye on the women working at their spinning wheels. It seemed to radiate a penitentiary light. He stopped in front of it now; he was not a vain man, but he felt that the identification of the dead was a formal duty. He straightened a black tie and made a note to remove his tinted glasses when the moment came.

The grim ceremony did not, by custom, take place on the fifth floor of the Galen Building, close to the morgue, but on the first. A lift connected the laboratory above, with its steel drawers, to the room marked *Relatives of the Deceased*. Brooke always felt that the amount of space allocated for this duty was inadequate. The door opened to reveal a box room about ten feet by twelve. A pair of lift doors stood at one end. There was nothing else in the room but a wooden bench and a wastepaper bin. A single window gave on to a light shaft, so that the view was restricted to pipes and bricks, and the metal rungs of a fire escape. A pigeon, wings flapping, rose out of sight as he entered.

It wasn't Alice Wylde sitting on the bench; it was her daughter Elsie Wylde, and she looked up with a start. She'd abandoned her regulation overalls and headscarf for a drab brown dress and a dark threadbare coat. He experienced a sudden insight: that she'd considered taking something smarter from Peggy's wardrobe, or even Connie's, but baulked at a sense of sacrilege.

'It's you,' she said.

'I can stay if it helps,' said Brooke. 'Or there's a woman constable at the Spinning House? I'm afraid there has to be a witness.'

She didn't answer, but he took silence as assent, and they sat together.

'I was expecting your mother,' he said.

'Yes. Sorry – she's taken to her bed. Ollie's sitting with her. I think that boy's adopted us. And there's the constable, of course. Is that necessary?'

'I doubt it,' admitted Brooke. 'But the facts speak for themselves, Elsie. Two sisters murdered. I'd be drummed out of the Borough if I didn't do the obvious and make sure you're safe.'

She shrugged. 'Ollie couldn't face it. He thinks it isn't her, but he can't face the truth, which he knows really. It is her. I know it is. I saw enough. Felt it, really. This is just a formality. It just has to be done.'

'Yes. I'm sorry.'

The clock on the wall ticked. Elsie looked round the room and found the NO SMOKING sign. The disappointment, the incremental blow to her burden of sadness, made her shake her head.

'We have to try and find the man who killed Connie quickly. Do you see, Elsie? It's possible – isn't it – that Peggy and Connie guessed the identity of the man we're after and that's why they died. And if they guessed, you might guess too. That's why we have to keep you safe.'

They heard the distant clatter of metal doors in the lift shaft. Elsie stiffened and unclipped her handbag, then closed it.

'I know this is a terrible time but will you think, Elsie? When this is over, when you can, think about the family, friends, neighbours, everyone.'

The lift motor began to whirr.

'Can I still see Joe?' she asked.

'If you want to, yes. He made a short statement last night. He admits he's a common thief, a criminal fence and a black-market trader. He's promised us a list of his suppliers – kids mostly. He says he isn't a killer and I'm inclined to believe him. Although he'll have to explain that warning shot. It was reckless, Elsie. People could have died.'

In the silence he thought he'd been too kind: Miller's parting shot hadn't been reckless; it had been designed to secure his escape, regardless of the possible loss of life.

The lift arrived, and they both stood up.

The doors scraped back and one of Dr Comfort's 'servants' – who provided the heavy labour when needed – wheeled out a trolley. Suddenly they all seemed crowded into too small a space. The presence of death stilled the air, but Brooke felt yet again that the appearance of the body provided a flat emotional note, in that it always failed to meet the hopes of loved ones, looking forward perhaps to some kind of farewell, or epiphany.

Brooke asked if Elsie was ready, and when she said she was, the servant quickly revealed just a part of the face: the forehead on one side, the eye and the hair. Elsie smiled, perhaps because Dr Comfort had somehow arranged these few features into a semblance of peace, although the bruising and swelling was still brutally apparent.

She nodded. 'Yes. That's Connie. Now I'll have to tell Ollie.'

'Do you want a moment alone?'

She shook her head. 'No. I'd like to go.'

The servants moved quickly to take the body away but they must have inadvertently knocked the gurney because one of Connie's arms dropped down, lifeless and stiff.

'Oh God,' said Elsie. 'I hadn't thought.'

There was an engagement ring on Connie's hand. A silver ring with a tiny red stone.

'Can I take it for Ollie?' she asked. 'It cost him five

shillings. I helped him pick it out of the window of a jeweller's on Petty Cury.'

The servant gently eased the ring from the finger and handed it to Elsie.

'She was so proud of it. I think Ollie thought she could do with some joy in her life after what's happened to us. He said he knew they were a bit young but he wasn't in a hurry.' She examined the ring in her hand. 'She was so happy.'

Outside on the pavement, the sunshine was fierce and they stood for a moment in the shade of a plane tree.

'I could come with you,' offered Brooke.

'No. It's alright. Tell us if you find anything, or if you have any more questions. Just walk in – everyone else does.'

They stood in silence for a few moments, dealing with the sense of inevitable dislocation brought on by moving from the presence of the dead into a busy street.

'And you'll think about what I said?' asked Brooke, eventually.

'Yes, I'll think.'

'And stay with the constable after dark. He can sleep downstairs and keep Ollie company. Don't go out alone, Elsie. It's just a precaution, but it's necessary.'

She slipped the ring into a small breast pocket in the overalls.

'It must be nice to be asked,' she said. 'Joe can't – couldn't – his wife won't have a divorce. It's a shame because every girl dreams of it – don't they? The handsome suitor down on one knee, the light catching the engagement ring. It's like a story in a book.'

She shook her head and walked away, and Brooke watched her diminish in the crowd, but the image she'd drawn remained vivid. That was what had been in plain sight all the time: *the rings*. He'd always suspected that the theft was at the heart of the mystery of Earl Street; he'd been stupid to overlook the possibility that it was the precise nature of the items stolen that night which had unleashed the violence to follow.

It was all about the rings.

CHAPTER FIFTY

Back at his office Brooke lay on the Nile bed and closed his eyes, so that he could see the scene that night – the last of Peggy's short life – as it unfolded on the riverbank. An idyllic spot, where she sat alone, watching Bruno Zeri cycle away, beginning his journey to Glasgow. But he'd be back, the father of her child, and they'd share a life together. She'd have been keen to cycle down to Earl Street to check her grandparents were safe, but she'd never left the spot alive. One of her other suitors had arrived – surely watching for his moment – and offered an alternative, a life with him. And to seal the moment with an engagement ring, a beautiful ring, offered perhaps, slightly childishly, on one knee.

Peggy had no doubt planned to soften the refusal. Instead, she was overcome by that moment of recognition, the ring which she'd loved as a child and put on her finger when she wanted to be a princess, being pressed upon her now. And then the knowledge, crushing and frightening in that lonely spot, that the boy offering her a love token must have stolen it from her grandmother. That he was a thief. And that there'd been looting on Earl Street, and casualties. Someone had stolen from the dead.

Brooke smiled, because he knew he was right. It was that simple. The real clue, the final key, was the killer's ignorance. This suitor knew Peggy, but *he'd never met Nora* before the night she died, or seen her trademark rings. He had no idea where the grandparents lived because he'd only known the family a few weeks. He could never have guessed Peggy would know the rings so well, that she'd played with them as a child. A coincidence at last, and one that had cost Peggy her life.

His desk in the Spinning House bore witness to six hours' investigation. He'd written the suspect's name up on the blackboard in his office in capital letters. Every time he looked at it he was more certain he was right. But gut instinct, even inspiration, very rarely stood up in court.

Juvenile court records revealed his suspect had committed thirteen offences between the ages of six and fourteen, with charges ranging from criminal damage, common assault, burglary and wounding. The punishments he'd received mirrored the attitude of the day: that children – and certainly those in care – should be treated with leniency and encouraged to reform.

A separate file listed offences brought before magistrates after the age of sixteen. There had been none recorded for the last six months, but the last appearance in the dock, for handling stolen goods, had clearly tested the patience of the authorities in a time of war. The accused had been given a suspended sentence as long as he agreed to attend the Upper Town Sports and Athletic Club – an institution set up to distract poor working-class boys from crime.

A report entered into the court records from the club noted that the accused had made some progress, but exhibited a pugnacious attitude, a stolid strength, and what the coach described vividly as a 'rat-like cunning'. He was sociable, but it was noted that he often failed to make friends. There was hope for the future: the boy had been placed with new foster parents, in a part of town where he might build a new life, and a fresh reputation.

The boxing club provided a photograph, taken in a club singlet and boxing shorts, gloves held up to the fleshy jaw. Brooke had taken it to Addenbrooke's Hospital and found Joe Miller in a room, on his own, his body in traction. One arm was held up at an acute angle but he'd nevertheless inveigled a nurse into lighting him a cigarette, which he held with the other.

Brooke held the picture in front of his nose.

Miller nodded. 'Yeah. Can't remember the name, but he always had stuff. I'd park the lorry by the football pitches and they knew to wander over. Jewellery, watches, silver cutlery – he was no fool. And he always filled up his can with petrol. Nasty bit of work, mind.'

A phone call to Edmund Kohler at the Fitzwilliam provided the final piece in the jigsaw. The suspect was on the list of official Civil Defence messengers. He'd been provided with a tin hat marked *M* and a second-hand bicycle – the make unspecified, but Brooke knew now it was the Lucifer. His duties included running documents and messages from the central fire station to the hospital and the BCC. His presence at any bombsite would have gone unchallenged.

Brooke marched to the sergeants' mess and found Edison with his feet up. 'I think we have our man, Sergeant. Let's put him in the bag before darkness falls.'

The Borough's five radio cars were parked at various points along the edge of the Kite, and uniformed officers in a Black Maria were stationed in the next street to the Wyldes' house. In the alleyway behind the house two constables were now in place, blocking the only escape route. This moment, the closing of the net, always seemed hurried, even brutal, and reminded Brooke of the unseemly haste of an execution.

The lingering anxiety was identical: did they have the right man?

Elsie opened the door, the hall light spilling out, nodding to Brooke and then seeing Edison, who was hanging back.

'I need to speak to Ollie,' said Brooke. 'Can you ask him to step outside for a moment?'

Brooke had kept his voice flat and she just shook her head.

'He's gone out. I told him all about Joe, the stolen goods and stuff, and he seemed upset. I think he's had enough of the house, and I don't blame him. He said Sid wanted him to pick up something else from the old house – a dartboard. He's been running stuff back and forth with a handcart. So he went. What is it, what's wrong?'

'What's the quickest way to the house?'

Elsie leant back, one hand on the newel post of the stairs, and forced her wide feet into a pair of cork shoes.

'Mum! I'm out for a bit – back soon.'

They heard the ghost of an answer and then Elsie slammed the door.

'I'll show you the way,' she said.

Brooke sent Edison to tell the radio car driver to direct all officers to the Foxes' derelict house on Salisbury Street.

Directly opposite there was a 'tunnel back' – an archway between two of the terraced houses, which marked the start of an alleyway which cut across the Kite. Three minutes later they were at the Foxes' house. The light, under a cloudy sky, had almost bled away, so that the scene was painted in grey and black.

The tarpaulin still obscured the front of the house, which they'd seen collapse two nights earlier after the bomber raid. Pulling it aside, Brooke found the ground-floor front window was boarded up, as was the door, but two of the planks had been removed and so he could squeeze through. Elsie followed.

The house smelt of wet coal.

Brooke walked down the hallway and into the kitchen. The house was so gloomy it was difficult to see anything so he switched on his torch. The floor above had collapsed, a few burnt timbers left, so that the bedroom was exposed. Because the stairs had burnt away there was no way of easily reaching the room above. A set of ladders had been brought in from the yard, but they were clearly too short to reach, and had been left against one wall.

By the sink was a plate, on which a Woodbine had been abandoned, half smoked.

'Ollie?' said Brooke. Why had he needed the ladder?

Edging the torch beam along the wall, he examined what was left of the back bedroom above: a mirror, uncracked; a line of coat hooks; a bed head attached to the wall; a picture hook above a rectangle of clean wallpaper. In one corner the floorboards had survived to the extent that they could support a narrow wardrobe. The door had swung out on a broken hinge to reveal a few coats within, a pair of black shoes, a set of boxing gloves and what looked like a gas-mask case, adorned with red tassels and a lurid line of silver sequins.

Wide-eyed, Elsie looked up, and Brooke actually saw the colour drain from her face as she raised a hand and covered her mouth.

'It's Peggy's,' she said.

There was a moment's silence and then they heard the air raid siren from the Guildhall, the sound penetrating the ruined house through the vacant windows and the gutted roof.

Brooke checked his watch. 'Where will Ollie go, Elsie? Is there a place he could hide?'

'There's nowhere,' she said, looking around, as if he might have taken refuge in the ruin of his home.

'Didn't he have a secret place with Connie?'

'Sid had an allotment. I think they went there to be alone. There's a hut and he had a key. She said it was romantic cos it had a stove. She said they just kissed.'

'Which allotments?' asked Brooke.

'The ones on Stourbridge Common, by the river, where the railway bridge takes the mainline north to the sea.'

CHAPTER FIFTY-ONE

Bartel's Heinkel was twenty minutes from the target: Bridge 1505. Schmidt was lying flat in the Plexiglas cone, his eye to the bombsight, taking pictures of the gun placements on the downs above Newmarket. The shells, in their twin rows, vibrated visibly as the engines laboured, the aircraft penetrating the cloudbank, the damp cold air filling the fuselage. It was less than forty-eight hours since their last sortie and the illusion that they were merely reliving a nightmare, swinging like a pendulum back and forth, had inspired a form of collective dread.

Morale was poor. The pre-flight briefing, delivered by Oberst

Fritsch, had been badly misjudged. The latest reconnaissance pictures made it clear that the box-girder railway bridge was still intact, and that every hour trains carrying munitions and troops ran through – north to positions on the coast in readiness for an attack in the east; south to the Channel ports, in case the long-awaited offensive began across the Straits of Dover.

'The repeated failure to destroy this bridge has been noted at the highest levels,' said Fritsch.

They were in the mess at Waren, on camp stools, drinking coffee, looking at the map on the wall that they had committed to memory twice already. A large photographic portrait of Reichsmarschall Göring was on the wall above the bar. Fritsch had no need to glance in its direction. Göring had promised Germany the Luftwaffe would clear the way for invasion.

Tonight their orders were modified. They would locate the river and fly south, dropping bombs at the bridge. They would then circle and return, *unter welchen Umständen auch immer* – whatever the circumstances – and attempt to verify its destruction, dropping the remainder of their payload for good measure, before heading back towards the coast, the sea and the lonely airfield at Waren.

The crew had conducted itself in a professional manner. They had studied their orders and made no comment. Even later, when Bartel had gone out to check the aircraft, he'd talked to Schmidt about the meteorological reports, and the hope that a simultaneous attack on the docks at Tilbury, in the Thames Estuary, would divert fighters south from their target.

This time there were no chalk marks on the bombs. Their meal, of sausages and potatoes, was uneaten. The cork had stayed in the bottle of schnapps.

Now, in the clawing icy damp of the fuselage, Bartel regretted the lost opportunity. It might have been his last drink.

'Let's do our job,' he said, breaking his silence as the engine note changed, the aircraft beginning its long descent through the layers of cloud. 'Then we can go home.'

Dropping out of the clouds, he saw the earth below. There were breaks in the cloud cover, and a flitting moon, and the river seemed to pulse, as if carrying a weak electric charge. The Heinkel bucked as he swung it in a wide semicircle so that he could begin to track its surface south to the target.

'Conditions excellent,' he said, the static obscuring almost every syllable.

The river flashed by beneath, and Bartel hauled back the lever to open the bomb doors.

Schmidt had memorised the pre-target waymarks, and now began to count them off for the crew.

'Clayhythe Bridge.'

Bartel saw the crossing, a narrow road bridge and boats on the river.

'Baits Bite.'

A lock, and a weir, where the water glowed white.

'Gasometers.'

A cluster of three, one larger than the rest.

'Fighters on our tail,' said the rear gunner. Immediately they saw the tracer fire, burning lines of amber, lacerating the dark.

They all felt the first bomb go, the second, and then the third. The Heinkel bounced, almost joyfully, light-headed perhaps now that the burden was discharged.

The way in which the screams of each falling shell blended into a single sound made Bartel think of his lost daughter.

They waited for the gunner in the bathtub, with his rear view, to report whether they'd hit the bridge. Instead there was a burst of tracer fire, which rocked the plane violently.

'Fighter closing,' said the rear gunner, at precisely the moment Bartel felt the impact of a bullet slam into his left shoulder, puncturing the pilot's seat from behind.

CHAPTER FIFTY-TWO

The first bomb fell short but the second hit the river with a sharp crack, followed by a second's silence before the high explosive detonated, sending a plume of white water vertically into the night sky.

Brooke, at the padlocked gate of the allotments, threw himself on the grass and felt the pitter-patter of the water as a cloud drifted overhead, the moment shattered by the third bomb, which fell on open ground.

This time earth fell, a cloud of atomised peat and grass, clods thudding down, the air now full of the night-time stench of the Fens.

Brooke brushed himself down, and saw by the flicker of ack-ack fire that Bridge 1505 still stood, although it was wreathed in the mist created by the bomb which had plunged into the Cam.

Beyond it a gasometer was alight, the flames so bright that Brooke had to shield his eyes.

The Heinkel, trailing smoke, was on its way home. Searchlights in the hills crisscrossed the sky with a manic energy, and caught the fleeting image of a pursuing Spitfire.

Beside the gate was a large black bicycle, with the saddle let down as far as it would go. He saw Ollie then, in his mind's eye, teetering on the machine, which was too big for him. He checked the bell but knew what he would find: it was silver, emblazoned with a red star.

Edison, who'd taken Elsie and Alice Wylde to the Parker's Piece shelters, had given Brooke the allotment key, explaining that the single gate had been locked since the start of the war to keep scavengers out; the oiled lock turned easily, and he slipped inside.

There were perhaps fifty huts, in ragged rows, but only a few had stovepipes. Brooke checked two and was within fifty yards of the third when he saw the light, a pale yellow glimmer in a single pane of glass. A line of dead rooks had been strung across the path like an omen.

The noise of the raid, or rather its aftermath, masked his final footsteps: an ambulance bell, the ack-ack fire, more fighters airborne from Marshall airfield, the roaring flames from the gasometer.

He'd taken Edison's cuffs, and he stopped now to slip one over his left wrist, clicked it shut and then – before inaction turned to fear – he kicked the door of the shed in with his boot.

Ollie Fox, eyes white with fear, fell back from a suitcase open on the wooden floor.

The boy was shaking, and Brooke was certain that this was not an instantaneous reaction to his arrival, but that he was petrified of the bombing, and desperate to escape. Greed had brought him here to retrieve his hoarded treasures. His round plump face was bathed in sweat. But he didn't look like a grown-up kid any more.

Brooke turned sideways to close the door. When he swung back Ollie was holding a pistol: a standard issue Browning from the Great War, which perfectly matched the description of Arthur Pollard's souvenir of the Somme, stolen during the Earl Street raid.

'I doubt that will fire,' said Brooke. 'It's more likely to take your hand off. I've seen it happen. You'll bleed to death before help comes. I'd put it down.'

'I'm leaving,' said Ollie. His voice seemed older, as if until now he'd successfully hidden behind a character he'd created – the slow bovine boy who won't grow up.

'Elsie and I found Peggy's gas mask. Connie saw it too, didn't she? And that's why you killed her.'

'Stupid cow followed me out of the house. I was gonna fetch it down, get rid of it, but I couldn't reach with a broom handle. I turned round and there she was. It was her fault.'

'You never loved her anyway, did you? It was just that you wanted to be close to Peggy. You were her secret admirer: a very persistent secret admirer. And she wouldn't tell, because she didn't want to hurt Connie.'

'If you say so,' said Ollie, closing the suitcase, clicking the locks. There was a set of seed trays to one side and the top one held a wad of white five-pound notes, which he stuffed into his jacket pockets.

'Thievery pays,' said Brooke.

Ollie cocked the pistol and Brooke thought then he'd

misjudged Oliver Fox. The eyes held something more than greed and violence. There was a hint of brutal revenge.

'I deserve a life like everyone else. Not a hand-me-down one for the orphan. I'm going to buy one.'

'And this life you're owed included a pretty wife, did it?'

Ollie's eyes glazed over, and he looked beyond Brooke to the door, judging his chances of escape.

'As soon as Peggy recognised the ring she had to die, didn't she?' said Brooke. 'It was sweet proposing, but it didn't go well, did it?'

Ollie shook his head. 'She laughed at me,' he said, his eyes full of sudden tears. 'Like it was a joke, that she'd ever go away with me – someone like me. She was going to tell, right then. She said she'd cycle to the Spinning House. I had to stop her. It was her fault too, all of it was her fault, because she laughed at me.'

Brooke settled his weight on his left foot, ready to spring to the right, trying to judge if he could get to the pistol before Ollie pulled the trigger.

'You hid the body near Byron's Pool,' he said. 'Then came back later to slip it into the river. One thing I never understood: why dump the bikes?'

'I panicked, I wanted to cover our tracks. I went to the Roma, I was gonna plant some of the stolen stuff there and make sure the Eyetie was well and truly fitted up. The neighbour poked his nose in so I left it – but I took Zeri's bike; it's been handy, it's just too big.'

He tried a smile then, and a half-hearted laugh, which seemed to precipitate some kind of crisis, because the blood drained from his face and he stood unsteadily. 'I ain't getting caught. Not now.'

He clutched the suitcase, levelled the gun and fired.

Had he meant to miss? Brooke couldn't be sure. The bullet punched through the door.

Ollie cocked the trigger again.

'I'm going, like I said. You're staying here. Put the other cuff round the stove handle and give me the key.'

Would he shoot again? It was certainly possible. Edison had orders to follow him to the allotment as soon as the women were safely in the shelter. Should Brooke play for time?

An image of Joy, holding the baby, coming down the stairs at Newnham Croft and handing the child to Claire, played out in his mind. And Luke, as a boy, running for the line on the school playing field.

He cuffed himself to the wrought-iron stove, and flipped Ollie the key, which he caught easily, waiting for it to drop into his open hand. He was still sweating, and a muscle twitched below one eye, and he kept swallowing saliva.

At the door he looked back, the suitcase under his arm.

Then they both heard the Heinkel, returning from the south this time, the hum of the twin engines suddenly close, so that the single pane of glass vibrated in its flimsy frame. They heard tracer fire too, and ack-ack away to the south.

Ollie licked his lips.

'I'll take my chances,' he said, and fled.

CHAPTER FIFTY-THREE

When Bartel saw the flames he knew he'd never see home again. The bullet which had punctured his shoulder had shattered his collarbone, but it wouldn't kill him, and the pain was diffuse, like a burn. But the smoke that had appeared first, thick and white, leaking through the gun ports on the starboard wing, made it impossible to imagine they could return to the coast, let alone span the German Ocean. The Spitfire which had delivered the coup de grace, in its distinctive black camouflage, had swept past as the Heinkel's speed had faltered, trailing its own smoke from a flickering flame on the tail.

The ack-ack fire had caught the bomber hard as they banked to make their second run on Bridge 1505. A fusillade had left a gash behind the bomb bay, and despite being still at his station, the navigator was almost certainly dead. But the explosion had blown out any fire, leaving the ragged, howling hole in the fuselage. No: it was the fire in the wing which would bring them down.

They were too low to use the parachutes, and Bartel told the radio operator to get a message back, that they were on fire, and that they'd make one last run at the target and then he'd try and flop the aircraft down in the fen beyond. They'd drop all the payload, and the bounce would get them over the river, and out into the country. They had pistols, and they'd even studied the maps, noting the position of the nearest ports at Lynn and Yarmouth. They'd move by night, evade escape, and do their best to get home. There was hope, but it was a fading light.

Bartel had found the river again, retracing their flight path in reverse.

One of the bombs they'd dropped on the first run had hit something – a gasometer, perhaps, or a fuel dump – and so there was a blazing yellow fire beyond the target. Its girders stood out in silhouette, like a skeleton against the sun.

It was still half a mile ahead, and the Heinkel was dropping fast. The fire on the port side had reached the engine and it was labouring, the propeller blades visible, churning through the smoke, which had now turned sooty black. The Spitfire had shot up the tailfins, which were now vertical, so that they were dragging the aircraft back and down.

Bartel could see details of the riverbank: boats moored, a line of boathouses, a road bridge with a single lorry crossing, and open country, with a startled horse running wild in the water meadows. With a jolt it brought a memory: Helga on his shoulders as they stood at a low picket fence, looking down on the miniature village at Kiel, with its Dutch windmills and ponds, dotted with ducks. Bartel wondered if his life was beginning to play itself out, as death drew closer.

'We're not going to reach the target,' he said, and he saw his friend nod. 'Let them all go, Walther.'

A single switch released a crossbar, simultaneously allowing all the remaining bombs to fall. The aircraft rose briefly, the river taking them on a long, slow meander to the west, so the shells flew on, to fall on farmland to the east, with a series of dull detonations like thunder.

'Fifty feet,' said Bartel.

The ground was appallingly close. The starboard engine was failing too, and the aircraft only just rose far enough to clear a footbridge and a set of smallholdings and huts, and then they could see the common, with its ditches and streams, willow and hawthorn.

Bartel thought he could just discern an open stretch of grass ahead, so he brought up the bomber's nose, engineered a stall and let the plane flop down with what was nonetheless a shattering impact. He felt his thighbone crack against hip, and his head struck the instrument panel.

The fuselage was still moving, surfing on the grass, and they seemed to dip – possibly into a small stream – and then they reared up again, the fuselage breaking in two in the middle, so that the cockpit came to rest pointing skywards.

Bartel regained consciousness within a few seconds. There was a sharp pain in his left arm, and a dull one across his chest, and his skull felt numb. The bullet wound was now the source of a spreading fire beneath his skin. The blades of the port propeller were still turning. There was no sound, just an echoing silence, as if he'd held his hands over his ears.

Schmidt was gone, the nosecone shattered.

The world of sound came suddenly back into focus: he heard a horse neigh, and just as distinctly, a bell ringing far away, but getting closer. He felt a sensation of movement creeping over his forehead and when he looked at his hand it was covered in blood, which was dripping down his face and into his lap.

He must have passed out again because when he regained consciousness he was standing up in the wreck of the plane. The gash in the fuselage was big enough to act as a door. Just beside it, still strapped in, was the dead navigator.

Outside, the common was deserted. Illogically, he had been hoping to see the horse. The lurid fire behind Bridge 1505 still blazed, and he could see the landscape very clearly. In the distance there was a church tower, and the smallholding he'd first spotted on Oberst Fritsch's stereoscope.

Had Schmidt been thrown clear through the cockpit glass? Could he be alive?

The impact appeared to have blown out the fire, but he could smell aircraft fuel, and it was only a matter of time before a spark caused an explosion.

He walked as quickly as he could fifty yards forward from the wreck. He'd considered retrieving the body of the navigator, and the gunner in the bathtub, but thought it was better to search for Schmidt, who might be alive.

It felt like a blessing to stand on firm ground. He had to stop himself falling to his knees and simply embracing the tufts of grass and wild summer flowers, the blooms of which flickered in sympathy with the fire beyond the bridge.

He tried to think coherently, but when he saw a figure ahead, kneeling in the grass, he shouted out even though it was clearly not his friend. This man was small, but solid, with a round pale face.

Bartel advanced, drawing his pistol from its holster.

The kneeling figure looked up and Bartel saw the whites of his eyes, and how scared he was, and that in one hand he had a wallet, and something which caught the light. Schmidt lay in the grass by his knees. As Bartel got closer he could see that the Plexiglas had torn at Schmidt's uniform, and so the glistening black substance which covered his face and left arm, and his left leg, was blood. His right leg was missing, and his torso was buckled, like a folded pillow.

The kneeling figure had a small suitcase by his side, and a pistol in his belt, but he seemed utterly unable to move. The wallet shook violently in his hand, and so the contents began to spill out, and Bartel saw a black and white photograph flutter down. In the yellow glow of the distant fire it was impossible to see the image itself but Bartel knew it well. He had the same photograph in his own flying suit: the two families together, on the beach at Wannsee.

He was holding something else in his hand, and Bartel recognised his friend's lighter, which was silver and emblazoned with the Luftwaffe insignia.

The juxtaposition of his friend's broken body and this casual act of sacrilege seemed to break something, finally, in Bartel's mind. The world he'd loved, and taken for granted, deserted him, leaving behind the smoking wreck of the Heinkel, and this kneeling boy.

'*Stehe auf*,' he said, gesturing with the gun for the thief to stand up.

CHAPTER FIFTY-FOUR

In the silence after the Heinkel's crash-landing, Brooke smashed the window of the shed and shouted out for help. Edison found him quickly, and set him free, and Brooke sent him back to get help: Fox was on the run, and he was armed, and capable of using his weapon. Brooke's guess would be that he'd head north, out of the city, along the river. With the unlocked cuff dangling from his wrist, he set out across the common towards the wreck of the Heinkel, which he could see dancing in the light of the flames from the gasometer.

The aircraft stood out starkly as he got close, the cockpit angled sharply up, the back-broken fuselage behind, one wing crumpled, the other torn away. The air was heavy with the acrid smoke, the stench of wiring and electrics, and seared steel. Small flames guttered in the dark, and Brooke could smell air fuel, and wondered how long he had before the tanks ignited.

When he saw the two bodies in the grass about fifty yards beyond the wreck, he presumed the crew had crawled out of the fuselage, or been thrown clear. One man was in a flight suit, but brutally broken and bloodied, a leg missing, a pistol still unused in its holder on his belt.

Then he turned to his comrade, who lay a few feet further on, but there was no flying suit here, just a shirt and trousers, and the round white face of Ollie Fox. A bullet hole pierced his skull just above his right eye: an entry wound, because the grass beyond was dashed with blood and brains. He thought Fox looked resigned, as if he'd expected retribution here, on the common, falling from the sky.

A litter of cards and money – Reichsmarks – lay around the body. Brooke stooped and plucked a note from the grass – a *hundert* bill – and saw that others had blown away towards the river. Fox's hand, open at the moment of death, was empty.

Brooke went back to the stricken airman, and felt for a pulse at the bloody neck, but there was nothing; he saw now that his face was lacerated with wounds, and that small shards of glass or plastic were embedded in each. A distorted memory of Peggy Wylde's skin, punctured by the razor-sharp teeth of the pike, flashed once before his eyes, and was gone.

The sound of fire, not from the stricken Heinkel but from the blaze beyond the bridge, subsided in a heartbeat, to be replaced by the hiss of steam. Arcs of water from fire hoses hung against the night sky, a white cloud rising. Standing still, he could feel the tiny cool droplets touching his skin.

The blackened hulk of the aircraft seemed to crouch, beast-like, awaiting the final explosion which would end its misery. Flames licked now at the gun ports, and around the cockpit. Brooke thought the fuel tanks were in the wings, two in each, but that if one ignited the sudden heat would trigger them all.

The port wing, which had partly detached, was on fire, but the flames were half-hearted.

Unless they'd been thrown clear there were still three men in the wreck.

Brooke circled to the west, calculating that if the wreck burst into flames he had time to make the safety of the river. After fifty yards the gash in the fuselage, ripped out by ack-ack fire, came into view, the lifeless form of the navigator hanging dead in his straps.

The rear gunner had got out of the bathtub undercarriage to avoid being crushed in the crash landing, but his body lay lifeless in the grass, his head at a sharp angle to his spine.

The sudden stench of the air fuel was almost hypnotic, and when he filled his lungs the scene spun before his eyes and he had to crouch down.

After a moment he stood up and saw the pilot, in what was left of the glass nose cone, and it looked, bizarrely, as if he was climbing *back* into his seat. In silhouette he appeared agile, the movements fluid and unhurried. He sat for a few seconds and then turned towards Brooke and held up a hand, and then there was the slight inclination of the head which any smoker would recognise, and the small blue-white flame of a lighter.

Brooke imagined the engines firing, the stricken Heinkel suddenly lurching back into the sky, heading home. An almost telepathic instinct told him the pilot had imagined this as well, and that as he smoked he saw himself back at home, perhaps, surrounded by family and friends.

There was a moment of hesitation, in which the air around Brooke seemed to thicken and coalesce, in which he had time to turn towards the river and note the gentle ripples on its surface.

Then the explosion knocked him down, the air torn from his lungs, a sudden heat at the back of his neck. When he came round he was looking up into the sky, the fuselage fabric raining down, each shred alight.

CHAPTER FIFTY-FIVE

Three months later

The vicar, leading Brooke out into the churchyard, said that the roses were a source of mild scandal in the parish and that he'd been forced to instruct the women who arranged the flowers on the altar, and for weddings, not to remove them to the compost heap behind the boiler, which is where he'd found them on several occasions. They were shop-bought, but there was never a card, and they were always placed squarely on the single stone that marked the grave of the crew of the Heinkel which had crashed on Stourbridge Common.

It had fallen to Fen Ditton, the nearest village to the site, to provide a final resting place for these four German airmen who had died so far from home. The vicar, a man in his sixties who was a veteran of the Great War, had stepped forward on behalf of St Mary the Virgin to offer a burial plot. The crewmen were interred together, their names inscribed on a simple stone with their ranks, the information obtained from identity tags found at the scene and verified by the Red Cross.

It had been hot on the day of the burial, a clear sky overhead, and the vicar had spoken a verse in German – explaining afterwards over tea that he'd studied at Heidelberg before the Great War and served at a medical station behind the lines at the Somme because he could speak to the enemy injured. The verse had been a fragment of Goethe, which he'd chosen solely for its calm poetic lyrical metre.

Now winter had reduced the graveyard to shadows and stone.

'Here they are,' said the vicar. At the graveyard lychgate a black shiny car had pulled up.

'They've got bolder,' he said. 'Which is rather wonderful in its way. I've told the ladies who still mutter that we can all respect the dead, whatever their homeland.'

The driver got out to open the back doors for two passengers: both women, the younger – holding the bunch of roses – supporting the older, so that by the time they were on the path one leant against the other.

'Inspector,' said the vicar. 'I'll leave you to this. The church is open,' he added, looking up at the sky, which was low and grey and beginning to bleed a light rain.

Brooke watched Elsie Wylde approaching, her mother Alice looking down, as if her feet might betray her.

Nora and Arthur Pollard had been cremated in line with their oft-quoted desire for no fuss and bother. But the funeral of Peggy and Connie had been a grand affair, with a glass hearse and black-plumed horses, at Mill Road Cemetery, on the far edge of the Kite.

Hundreds had stood around the grave after a private service at the Methodist Chapel near the girls' home. Alice had been too sick to leave her bed. Uniformed constables had stopped the traffic to allow the stately progress of the hearse as it ran beside Parker's Piece and the serried rows of white bell tents. The only scandal on that day had been a minor one: Ollie Fox's foster parents had sent a wreath from Newmarket, which made it clear they would never return, a vow they kept when the boy was laid in a pauper's grave out at Milton.

The two women arrived, and Brooke thought Alice was a bit more stooped and that Elsie looked taller, less downtrodden.

'I don't care what people say,' said Alice, leaning forward and placing the flowers on the stone. 'God brought us justice and this man was his instrument.' She leant even further forward, stretching out her gloved hand, to touch the etched name: *Leutnant Helmut Bartel.*

Brooke had described the final scene, the broken bodies amongst the wreck of the Heinkel, when he'd gone back to their home a few hours after the crash. His own clothes had reeked of air fuel and ash, and his face and hands had been stained with blood. Elsie had made him tea, with a shot of gin.

Alice straightened up. 'Far worse the enemy within. To repeat the sin – the robbing of the dead – is beyond forgiveness.'

Brooke touched his hat and turned to go.

'Did you come all this way just to solve this little mystery?' asked Elsie.

Brooke shook his head. 'A private visit. I need to find a grave. Goodbye.'

The east end of the church looked out from the small clay island on which the village stood towards a long, unfolding curve of the river as it ran towards the sea. Trees obscured the view, but Brooke knew that a chain ferry crossed the Cam at this spot, and that on the near bank a pub called The Plough was a mecca for pilots from Marshall airfield, their cars parked lazily on the grass of summer evenings.

Which is why they'd chosen St Mary the Virgin.

The stone was new, and cut with the RAF insignia, the name and a simple dedication:

Pilot Officer Timothy James Vale
1921–1940

Killed in action over the city of his birth,
in pursuit of a German bomber

And the hero shall never return

Roly Cleaver had been sent down for ten years, partly because his meticulous records revealed an impressive black-market empire. They also revealed that Tim Vale had indeed been delivering packages to hospitals on the day Peggy Wylde had died.

There were flowers here too, but they looked blown and dusty, and Brooke walked away as a Spitfire flew low overhead.

CHAPTER FIFTY-SIX

When it came to it, after all the soul-searching and the endless talk, they simply walked out of Stalag Luft I with a work party of Polish prisoners, heading out with axes over their shoulders, to chop firewood down by the river. Ben was nominally in command, especially as the other four had served with him on the *Swordfish*, so they trusted each other, and had come to a kind of solemn pact that the war might last ten years, or twenty, and that their real lives were back in England and if they waited and stuck it out behind the wire, in effect they'd have died that day they were picked up on an ash-grey sea, the scuttled submarine belching oil and debris to the surface all around them.

The final plan, cleared by the top brass the night before, had been to get close to the gate, overpower the guards and sprint to the apron of the forest, which lay just sixty yards to the north. But the harpoon man – Stone – had kept his wits about him and spotted the line of Polish prisoners dragging their feet across the compound, heading out to cut timber. Crucially, while they had a guard leading them, there was nobody at the rear. The work detail coming in were all Royal Navy, and so Stone had simply collected their picks, and then they'd all tagged on the end of the line of Poles going out. Ten minutes later they were in the woods. When he thought they were safe, Ben – leading – simply ducked into the shadows of the trees and they all melted away.

It wasn't a reckless thing to do. They'd got hold of a map, and they'd saved food, and they'd paid a woman in the canteen to make them reversible jackets, which would just about pass for a peasant's harvest coat. They'd all sat in the dark shadows of that wood, rubbing peat into their faces, but unable to stop grinning stupidly. Ben had been overcome by the idea that he might answer the question that had come to define his life: had his child been born, and what was its name? One desperate night, before they'd decided to make a break for it, he'd lain in the chipwood bunk and made a pact with God: that he'd die happy if he could just have the answers.

Now there was a chance he might hold the child.

He found out later that in those first few moments of freedom they'd all been thinking the same kind of crazy thoughts, which is why they hadn't heard the rear guard trudging along, stuffing his shirt into his trousers, because he'd had to run into the latrines to ease his bowels, stricken by the runs which were endemic in the camp.

Eddington, stepping back out onto the path to check the work detail had gone, walked straight into him.

He was so close, so quickly, he was able to get his arms round the guard so that he couldn't level his rifle, but it went off, and the rest of them ran deeper into the woods, blindly, in the kind of panic which Ben thought would probably end with a bullet in the back. Eddington must have held on, because they were able to run for twenty minutes, hearing a few more shots, then silence, until they finally found a shack, full of coiled wire for telegraph poles, which meant they were close to the edge of the forest, or a road. So they slept, exhausted, not even bothering to post a watch.

Two things saved their lives. Andersen, whose father was Danish, could speak the lingo like a native and knew where to go: north skirting Lubeck, missing Hamburg and Kiel, striking for the lonely west coast of Denmark, and the small fishing village of Tonning. Perhaps they could get aboard a boat and sail far enough across the North Sea to rendezvous with a sub, or a convoy.

It was eighty-five miles to Tonning and it was clear by the third day that they would not make the journey. They were close to the border, but Denmark was occupied, and the autumn was wet, the harvest over, so there was no food in the fields, and they couldn't risk getting close to the farmhouses they skirted at night. By day there were regular German patrols on the roads. The woods were interspersed with marsh. The nights were cold, and they were all soon soaked through and couldn't get dry.

The other thing that saved their lives was a moonlit meeting on that fourth night at a crossroads on a heath.

By the time they'd seen the man on the open road it was too late to hide, and anyway, there was nowhere to hide. It took three minutes for him to reach the crossroads and they'd decided that if he was Danish they'd plead for help, and if he was German they'd have to kill him, and bury the body, although Ben felt, looking back, that they were so demoralised that they might not have carried the plan through. They might have just given themselves up, for a warm fire and a plate of beans.

Luckily, the peasant was called Poul Melsing, and he was in the Danish resistance, out waiting for the RAF to drop a cache of arms, despite the rain. He must have seen them for what they were because at twenty yards he simply announced that they had nothing to fear.

'He says he can take us to a farm, and then organise a lift in a lorry, but we'll have to go one at a time,' said Andersen. 'I think we should trust him.'

'So we did,' said Ben, raising a glass of red wine. 'And that's why I'm here.'

The table was lit with candles and the first course – of figs and cheese – had disappeared from the plates. It was icy cold outside so the windows of the Roma were impenetrable with condensation.

Ben had been given the place of honour at the head of the table.

Brooke surveyed the rest of the guests, family and friends, all talking at once. Grandcourt was deep in conversation with Rose King, who'd dug out a summer dress of green and white, because she said she couldn't imagine eating Italian food in a jumper. Jo Ashmore was next to Brooke, and the only guest really struggling to share the celebratory mood. Her wounded pilot had discharged himself from hospital, heading to Canada to fly transport planes, leaving a note to explain that the failure of repeated surgery meant he felt he couldn't ask her to marry him.

'You could go in pursuit,' said Brooke, filling up her glass with Montepulciano.

'I might,' she said. 'But I don't think I will. It says a lot about what he thinks of me – doesn't it? That he fears I couldn't put it aside – the burns, and the surgery. I think he's happier running away from that than trying to make a go of things. It just shows you, Brooke, that there are all kinds of heroes.'

Brooke, listening, was watching Joy, sitting next to her husband, Iris on her lap. Claire was opposite, flushed and happy, but haunted – as was Brooke – by the empty chair at the other end of the table.

Bruno Zeri appeared, ferrying out plates of ragu and tagliatelle. The Roma was open for one night only. His father was on Joy's ward at Addenbrooke's, recovering slowly, while his mother was still in the camp on the Isle of Man. Zeri's sister had been dragooned into helping in the kitchen. The meal was a special occasion, but there were plans to reopen if the old man recovered enough to return as maître d'.

On Brooke's other side sat Edmund Kohler.

'When do you sail?' asked Brooke, transferring the bottle to his right.

'A week. It's via Gib, of course, so it'll be hell. But I'm looking forward to it, Eden. It's my home.'

Kohler had been appointed adjutant to the British commander in Alexandria. Egypt, an armed camp, was embroiled in the desert war on the Libyan border.

'What does Celia think?'

'She's coming. It's an adventure, and I've told her so many stories about Cairo, and the old house, she thinks it's terribly exciting. Let's hope the Germans don't feel the need to lend Mussolini a hand.' Kohler took a mouthful of the wine. 'And when it's over we might stay. Let's be honest, I'm a fish out of water here.'

He searched his pocket and produced the stone scarab beetle that he used as a paperweight at the Fitz. He set it down on the checked tablecloth. 'I'm taking him home too. Technically, that's theft of course, as he's part of the collection. So maybe you should clap me in irons.'

Later, Brooke found Zeri in the kitchen. 'Can you add two bottles of the Montepulciano to the bill, I'll take them with me.'

Doric had been unable to get away from his duties for the evening at Michaelhouse, while Peter Aldiss's experiments into circadian rhythms had reached a crucial stage in the laboratory. Brooke planned to deliver consolation bottles.

He counted out pound notes and added a tip.

The Italian gave him an envelope marked ELSIE WYLDE.

'What's this?'

'It's some money. I lied – I think you knew I lied, yes? The money I have in Glasgow is no from the safe, no from savings. Peggy, she ask her grandmother for help, help for me, for us, for the child. She likes me, she is happy to see Peggy happy, so I have the money. Peggy say it is now our nest egg. Give it to Elsie.'

Brooke was going to argue when there was a huge cheer from the dining room.

The occupant of the empty chair had arrived after all. Luke, his son, stood in the light, raindrops on his great coat, a kit bag slung to the floor, looking fit and a stone lighter.

He took off his green beret and kissed Claire. Joy burst into tears.

'I'm off to Portsmouth first thing, Dad,' he said, seeing Brooke. 'I hope the bar's not closed; I could do with a farewell drink.'

ACKNOWLEDGEMENTS

The Eden Brooke books would not be possible without two invaluable sources of reference: Jack Overhill's diary – the wartime section of which was published in 2010 by Peter Searby – and the digest of the Cambridge News compiled by the city's own local historian, Mike Petty. Both help flesh out day-to-day life between 1939–45. Anyone who wants to dig deeper should go to www.mikepetty.org.uk. *Bradley and Pevsner's The Buildings of England – Cambridgeshire* has also been an unbeatable guide. *The Night Raids* also draws heavily on *The Fitzwilliam Museum – a History*, by Lucilla Burn, and *First Light* – the wonderful memoir of Spitfire pilot Geoffrey Wellum. I am indebted to the expertise of all those at the Cambridge Museum of Technology, and the Conservators of the River Cam, in helping me understand the daily miracle that is fresh water. Anyone interested in the story of Britain's Italian community can do no better than start at www.ancoatslittleitaly.com.

I must thank my publisher Susie Dunlop and the team at A&B; particularly my editor Kelly Smith, Kirsten Munday in marketing, and my copy-editor Becca Allen: the success of these books reflects their high standards of professionalism. I am grateful to fellow crime writer Chris Simms for reading the draft of *The Night Raids* and providing valuable suggestions on the plot, despite being immersed in his own books. My agent, Faith Evans, represents a constant call to meet the highest standards in storytelling for which I am forever grateful. Lastly, my wife Midge Gillies inspired the whole idea of *The Night Raids*, and often cast a professional eye over the progress of the narrative.

JIM KELLY was born in 1957 and is the son of a Scotland Yard detective. He went to university in Sheffield, later training as a journalist and worked on the *Bedfordshire Times, Yorkshire Evening Press* and the *Financial Times*. His first book, *The Water Clock*, was shortlisted for the John Creasey Award and he has since won a CWA Dagger in the Library and the New Angle Prize for Literature. He lives in Ely, Cambridgeshire.

jim-kelly.co.uk
@thewaterclock